WHAT

'This book is full of magic, wonder and mystery. I'd really love to see this book turned into a film!"

— LAYLA EVERITT

"This book was enthralling and I couldn't put it down... a unique mix of mystery, history, and fantasy."

— LINDA GORE

"This book deserves to become a classic ... the 'Huckleberry Finn' for our times, a paean both to a forgotten America and its enduring values."

— RUTH SMITH

To: Isabella

KATIE WATSON AND THE
SERPENT STONE

MEZ BLUME

Meg Blum

"Wado!"

RIVER OTTER BOOKS

First published 2018 by River Otter Books

Cover Illustrations by Patrick Knowles

PB ISBN: 978-1-9999242-2-5
Ebook ISBN: 978-1-9999242-3-2

In memory of Leonard Columbus Dean, "Papa", who handed down his Cherokee roots and Southern love of a good ol' story

NOTE FROM THE AUTHOR

Researching for this book was an adventure *almost* as exciting as Katie's. The story of the Cherokee People is older than memory, many-layered and carries on to this very day.

The characters in this book are fictional, but many are based on real-life people. The places too are real along with the Cherokee legends that haunt them.

I hope that as you, the Reader, venture back in time with Katie, you will find the ancient and living world of the Cherokees as magically mysterious as I have.

To discover more of this book's "behind-the-scenes" story, visit mezblume.com and sign up for my newsletter!

DEAR SOPHIA

ctober 1st, 2018

Dear Sophia,

Can you believe it's been nearly four months since we first met at Otterly Manor? My first few weeks of middle school have honestly flown by. I'm glad too. It's not that I haven't made any friends, but there's nobody who can compare with you.

"REEK!"

I put down my pen with an exasperated look at the guinea pig hutch where two sets of eyes stared at me out of two fat blobs of hair. "Don't be jealous," I consoled Fergie and Francis. "You two are wonderful friends. It's just, sometimes a girl needs a *human* friend who's interested in more than just pellets and lettuce." The guinea pigs stared at me dumbly, twitching their noses and clearly not grasping the weight of my problem at all.

I shook my head. The truth was, there *was* nobody at school or in the whole modern world that I felt as close to as I had felt to Sophia. After all, we'd been through a lot together last summer, solving a murder, beating Baron Black Sheep at his own game—stuff like that bonded people for life. The only problem was, my life had returned back to normal, back to modern times. Sophia's was still, well, back then. I was certain I would never find another friend like her. So I'd taken to writing her letters in my journal. I know it sounds slightly insane, but I honestly felt like she could hear the words I was writing... like she was really out there somewhere, not just in a spirit way, but in a real-life flesh-and-blood way, and not ... in the past.

Of course, I didn't send the letters anywhere. I hadn't gone so mental as to think the postal service could deliver to the year 1606. But I kept them safe in my journal for her, and I never *ever* let myself dwell on what I knew, deep down, was the horrible truth: my best friend had already grown up without me. She'd probably got married and had kids. Maybe she'd even told them about our adventures together. I would never know. I didn't want to know. I preferred just to imagine my friend as I knew her: the brave, kind, golden-haired twelve-year-old Sophia who had become like the sister I never had.

"REEK!"

The guinea pigs brought me back to my room once again.

"Stop interrupting, would you? I'm trying to think." I

chewed the end of my pen, trying to think of what to write next. My eyes drifted over to the shelf of riding ribbons and trophies. Just last week, I'd had to make room for a shiny new silver cup. And I'd completely forgotten to tell Sophia about it!

I forgot to tell you, I'm coming along really well in my riding. I competed again last week and won second place overall! It feels amazing to be back in the riding ring, and of course it's all thanks to you and Vagabond.

Instinctively, I pried open the gold locket around my neck and smiled at the miniature paintings — one of Sophia and me, the other of a giant black stallion.

How is he, anyway? Hope he's behaving himself and has given up stomping pigeons for good.

There was a rap on the door. I rushed to shut my journal, then shoved it under my pillow. Grabbing a book off my night stand, I opened it to a random page and leaned back as if I'd been casually reading the whole time. "Come in!" I called out in my best lazy-bored voice.

Mum pushed open the door, folded her arms and leaned against the door frame, obviously wanting to talk about something.

"Oh, hey, Mum." I had the terrible feeling she knew I was hiding something.

"What are you getting up to in here?" she asked in an overly casual way. *Yep. She was definitely on to me.*

"Oh just... nothing." I turned the page of *The Pale Horse* and tried to look caught up in the story.

"Nothing is the one thing you never do, Miss Busy Body. And didn't you finish that book last weekend?"

"Yea, but..." I had to think fast. "You know how mysteries are. After you find out who's done it, you want to go back and find all the clues that you should've picked up on the first time around."

Mum gave me a sideways stare, then shrugged, much to my relief. The last thing I needed was for my family to discover I wrote letters to a pen-pal four centuries away. I'd never told a living soul what happened to me last summer. Sometimes I wanted to, but I was pretty sure they'd never believe it, and that would just make things worse. It's lonely enough keeping a secret like that without people thinking you're batty on top of it. That journal was a secret I intended to keep.

"So, what's up?" I asked, eager to keep Mum off the scent of what I'd really been doing.

"Oh, uh..." was it just me, or was Mum the one looking slightly guilty now? "I have some bad news."

"What?" I asked.

"Charlie emailed to say he's been invited to go back-packing with friends. He's really sorry to miss the camping trip."

I turned my attention back to the page I'd been pretending to read. The Fall Break camping trip was a family tradition. I'd never gone without my older brother. This *was* rubbish news, but, I had to admit, not *entirely* surprising. Charlie had kept his word and had written to me every week since he'd gone off to university in Scotland; but lately his letters had featured a certain "friend" called Moira more than anything else. I guess I had a hunch he wouldn't be in a hurry to come home for the two-week autumn holiday. "Oh well," I replied, knowing Mum was holding her breath to see how upset I'd be.

"There's some… other news," she said after a minute's pause.

I looked up, a little worried by the tone of her voice.

"I just got off the phone to Auntie Virginia." She paused, taking a sudden interest in tidying up the pile of riding clothes on my floor. I smelled a rat.

"And… what did Auntie Virginia say?"

"Well," Mum chimed as she placed the freshly folded stack of clothes on top of my dresser, "it's rather good news, actually. I told her about our camping trip and how unfortunate it was that Charlie couldn't make it, and how you'd be stuck with just Dad and me, and…"

"And?"

"And she decided then and there to send Imogen over from London in a couple of weeks to join us. It's her half-term break as well. Auntie Virginia thought she'd be good company for you, and it might be a good cultural experience for her."

The Pale Horse dropped into my lap at the same moment my mouth fell open. "You're not serious?" I asked, sure this *had* to be a bad joke. If Sophia was the sister I'd never had, Imogen was the sister I'd never wanted.

"Katie!" Mum scolded as if it were any surprise I was not ecstatic about the news that my snobby cousin was coming to spoil our camping trip. "You know, I really thought you'd matured beyond this. All I ask is that you *try* to get on with Imogen. Auntie Ginny and I are as different as two sisters can be, yet we were still each other's closest ally growing up. It only takes a little effort—"

"Mum, I *do* try, but it's *impossible* to get on with her. She's only a year older than I am, and she thinks she's the queen of the whole world!"

"Well just bear in mind, Kit-Kat, that maybe Imogen's had a rather harder time of it than you have."

"But … What?"

Mum held up a hand. "I get that she's not your ideal friend. *But* that doesn't change the fact that she's family. No matter your differences." Mum cast me a just-think-about-that kind of look and left the room, pulling the door shut behind her.

With a groan, I face planted into my pillow. I'd think about it, all right. What did she mean Imogen's had a harder time of it? A harder time of what? Of life? Yea, right. The Humphreys family lived in a huge mansion in London and jetted off on amazing holidays all the time. Imogen got everything she wanted and never wasted an opportunity to brag about it. *She* wouldn't have survived a day against Nurse Joan or the Baron. *She* had no idea what it was like to leave her best friend four hundred years in the past. I was sure Imogen didn't know the meaning of hardship. She had the perfect life, and I was going to have to spend two solid weeks hearing her rub it in.

There was only one place to go for consolation. I pulled my journal out from under my pillow and flicked open to the page I'd been scribbling on before.

Sophia, I so wish you were here right now.

I stopped writing and tried to imagine what Sophia would say in this situation. I knew the answer, and it made me wince with shame. Sophia would treat Imogen with the perfect manners and thoughtfulness with which she treated everyone, even Nurse Joan. Sophia would find a thousand reasons to be grateful rather than complain about her own difficulties.

I lay back on my pillow and watched the ceiling fan whirl round and round. "I'll do my best, Sophia." But as I spoke the words, a hollow ache filled the pit of my stomach. There was no escaping the dreadful truth. Sophia was not there. I would have to face two whole weeks of cousin Imogen on my own.

2

UNWANTED COMPANY

"So, Imogen, tell us about your new school. Is an all-girls boarding school as scary as it sounds?"

Dad had been peppering Imogen with friendly questions from the start of our eleven-hour car journey from Pennsylvania – where I live – to Tennessee, a journey which gave me the opportunity to observe the strange creature who sat beside me in the back. The old Imogen might have been loud and bossy, but at least she looked and smelled normal. But it'd been a whole day since Imogen had arrived from London, and I could still hardly recognise her behind the gobs of makeup, the dizzying smell of cherry lip balm and the *very* badly dyed hair. Also, the new Imogen had a nasty habit of rolling her eyes at absolutely everything.

In a lazy, bored sort of voice, the new Imogen finally answered. "Boarding school's amazing, actually. I get to hang out with my friends like all the time. I share a room with my best friend, Poppy. She's practicing to become a beautician some day. She did my hair herself." She gave her streaky blonde and black locks a toss.

"Is that so?" Mum asked, a little too enthusiastically.

"Yea. She's a real artist," Imogen answered.

I snorted. I wasn't sure the mess on Imogen's head could be called "art." It looked more like a practical joke to me.

"Katie's made some nice friends at her new school too." I caught Dad's eye in the rear-view mirror, clearly giving me the hint that I should take over the conversation with Imogen.

"Yes, Katie. Why don't you tell Imogen about your new school?" Mum chimed in cheerfully.

I shot a glare at my plotting parents in the mirror and shrugged. "Oh… there's really nothing much to tell."

Imogen smacked her cherry lip balm lips and gave me a pitying look as if I were the saddest person she'd ever seen in her life. "I'm not surprised. *Primary* school is *so* lame. It doesn't get interesting until you move up to secondary school."

"I'm not in primary school," I corrected. "It's called middle school in America."

"Whatever." She rolled her eyes, flicked her streaky hair and started swiping through pictures on her smart phone.

Carefully ignoring Mum and Dad's scolding looks in the mirror, I took my detective novel out of my bag and dived in. They might force me to share our camping trip with Imogen, but they couldn't force us to become friends. There was no getting around it. We might be cousins, but Imogen and I were as different as two cousins could be.

. . .

WE STIFFLY MADE our way back to the car after lunch at a roadside diner where Imogen had made a show of looking disgusted at everything on her plate, then pushing it away and claiming not to be hungry. Meantime, she had gone from bored to outright cranky. "Uncle Peter, why exactly are we driving *all* the way from Pennsylvania to Tennessee *just* to go camping? I mean, people *do* camp closer to where you live, right?"

"Well, that's my fault, I'm afraid," Dad said apologetically, as he rifled through his pockets for the car keys. "My family comes from that neck of the woods. I thought it'd be a good opportunity to trace my roots."

Imogen made her disgusted face again. "Wait, your family were like, hillbillies?"

Behind Dad's back, I smacked myself on the forehead. I knew just what was coming.

Dad chuckled. "You could say that. Some of my ancestors were Scottish. The others Cherokee Indian. I've been doing some research into the Cherokee side ...."

Once Dad got started talking about his Native American roots, there would be no stopping him, possibly for hours. Before Imogen knew what had hit her, Dad had opened the trunk, dug up his family archive from his duffle bag, and was flipping through the pages of yellowed old records, photographs and certificates, completely unaware of the glazed-over look on Imogen's face as he held up bits of scraps for her to examine.

Even I glazed over when Dad got going like this. I had

to do something. "Dad, don't you think we should get back on the road?"

The spell was broken. "Good point, Kit-Kat," he said, gingerly closing the dusty old scrapbook. "Tell you what. You girls can finish looking through this on the drive. It'll make those last six hours fly by."

I grimaced as Dad dumped the weight of his dusty, treasured scrapbook into my arms.

Imogen leaned away from it as if the thing might strike out at her with a tomahawk. "Uh, I get carsick. Maybe I can look at it another time."

"Don't worry about that, Immy." Dad patted her on the shoulder. "There will be plenty of time once we get to Tennessee."

IT WAS dinner time before Dad announced we'd arrived in the small town near our campsite. The scrapbook lay on the seat between Imogen and me, carefully untouched for the whole six hours. I pulled myself out of my mystery novel to take a look out the window. We'd been on country roads past farms and through dense forest for the past couple of hours at least. Now we'd pulled into what was almost a patch of civilisation… not exactly a town, but a street lined with diners, motels and shops advertising local crafts, baked goods and hiking gear. Dad stopped the car in front of a small country convenience store.

"Thought we'd stock up with some survival supplies before we head to the campsite," he said over his shoulder. "You know, things like Twizzlers and Twinkies."

Imogen groaned and rubbed her eyes. "Ow." She winced. "My foot is completely dead."

"Why don't you girls stretch your legs?" Mum suggested. "You can explore the Native American craft shop while we grab some supplies."

At that suggestion, Imogen, of course, rolled her eyes.

A BELL JINGLED as we entered the door of a dimly-lit shop that smelled strongly of incense. I turned on the spot, letting my eyes adjust and taking in the odd assortment of objects that covered the walls and shelves, everything from animal hides to beaded jewelry, toy bows and arrows and neon-dyed feather headdresses.

"This is *so* primitive," Imogen muttered into a basket full of cornhusk dolls.

"Can I help you?"

We whirled around in sync to face the man who had crept up behind us so silently. He wore a long ponytail and a very serious expression. Had he heard Imogen's remark? Maybe that's why he looked so surly.

"No thanks," I answered as brightly as I could. "We're just having a look around."

"You've been to Cherokee Country before?" he asked in a tone as serious as his expression.

I shook my head. "First time. My dad's family come from here. He's part Cherokee."

At that remark, the man raised an eyebrow. "A red-headed Cherokee. It happens in a blue moon." He sauntered over to a counter and picked up a thin booklet. "Here." I took the booklet and read the cover. *Cherokee*

Legends, it said. "You're part Cherokee. You should learn our stories. It helps you understand the people."

"I'll have to ask my dad for some money…"

"It's a gift," he said flatly. "To learn your Cherokee heritage."

I thanked the man for the gift and followed Imogen back out into the still-warm evening sunlight.

"Find anything interesting?" Dad called out over the brown paper bag in his arms. "Some Indian jewelry perhaps?"

"Not really my cup of tea," Imogen muttered under her breath.

"The shopkeeper gave me this thing." I held out the booklet and examined the cover again. In the light, I could make out the weird illustration of a vicious-looking snake with horns on its head encircling a Native American man with a stone raised high in one hand.

"Ah, *Cherokee Legends*, huh? That's great, Katie! You can read us some stories around the campfire tonight."

I didn't even need to look to know Imogen was rolling her eyes as she climbed back into the car. I stuffed the Cherokee booklet into my rucksack, pulled out my mystery novel instead and disappeared behind its cover. I still had two whole weeks of her rolling eyes to look forward to. I would just have to find ways of ignoring them.

3

THE CAVE

"Isn't this just what heaven must look like? How about those bright red sugar maples, eh, Katie?" Dad plopped down on a stump and put his hands behind his head with a satisfied sigh. I plopped down on a mossy patch of earth beside him feeling exhausted. Camp had gone up quickly enough, but with no help from Imogen. While Dad and I pitched the tent and Mum collected firewood, Imogen had walked around in circles trying to track down a satellite signal for her smart phone.

"I think you're more likely to pick up smoke signals out here than phone signals, Immy," Dad called to her as she desperately waved the phone towards the sky. "You know, I can just about hear the river in the distance. Why don't you girls go explore? You can bring back some water while you're at it." He handed me a bucket and the water purifier. "I'll chop these logs and get a fire going before you get back."

I threw my rucksack over my shoulder and scooped up the bucket and filter. "Ready?"

Imogen looked like she'd rather sit in poison ivy than go exploring, but she finally pulled herself up and moseyed after me.

We trudged down a pebbly, fern-lined path that wound its way down a slope through yellow poplars, feathery hemlocks and jungly rhododendron bushes, all the while following the course of a little brook. Eventually, where the slope levelled out, the brook tumbled into a river that ran through the wooded valley.

I looked up and down the river until I spotted a shoal that jetted out over the water. "This looks good," I said, stepping gingerly over the moss-covered rocks with the bucket in hand. I squatted down and lowered the water filter into the glassy, churning water, shuddering as the shock of coldness rose up my arm.

Imogen kept a good distance between herself and the water, swatting at gnats and jumping at every little noise, from crows cawing to squirrels scurrying up the trees. She could not have looked more out of place in the middle of a forest if she'd been a red telephone booth.

"Is this your family's idea of a relaxing holiday?" she asked, taking a few wobbly steps closer across the river rocks.

I let my eyes travel up and down the tranquil, sparkling river and took in a deep, earthy breath of mountain air. "Yup."

"Last year we went to Dubai. Mum and I did tons of shopping, and Dad went to meetings or did work by the pool." She paused to smack at the gnats attacking her legs. "It's so weird, isn't it?" *Smack.* "I mean, our parents are nothing alike. Your dad is so... rugged." *Smack.*

"Well," I shrugged, though inwardly expanding with pride, "he used to be a mountaineer, back when he met Mum. He pretty much lived in the woods back then." Now she pointed it out, it was strange Imogen's family and mine should be so different considering our mums were sisters. "Doesn't your dad ever take you camping?" I asked.

"Pfff. My dad?" *Smack.* "My dad's an investment banker. He never camps unless it's on the floor of his office."

There was another minute of buzzing and slapping before she asked, "So how did your dad get to be a mountain man, or whatever?"

"A mountaineer," I corrected. "He's always felt more at home in the outdoors. I guess it's his Cherokee blood."

"I can't believe your dad's like, an actual Indian. That's so … bizarre."

I didn't answer. Truth be told, as much as I love my dad, I didn't have that much of an opinion about our Cherokee heritage. Those shops of Indian knickknacks had nothing to do with me, and I certainly had no plan of digging through Dad's musty old family archives.

"This is seriously *not* fun," Imogen whined, contorting to smack herself on the shoulder blade. "At this rate, there's not gonna be anything left of me after two weeks."

"There will be if you use bug spray instead of hair spray," I said under my breath. Part of me almost enjoyed watching Imogen suffer. Swatting gnats, her face flushed and sticky, she certainly didn't look like the Queen of the World now. So what if she attended a posh school or could run circles around me on a hockey pitch? For once, she was the helpless one, and I was in charge, no longer the pathetic little cousin.

My bucket was full. I wrapped up the filter and stuffed it into my shorts pocket, then bent down and heaved the bucket. As I hoisted it, water sloshing out the side onto my legs, I had a sudden flashback to last summer and my brief but painful career as a water maid. The memory felt sharp as a bee sting, as if I'd suddenly been whisked back to Otterly Manor, and it was Sophia standing there with her radiant smile and golden curls instead of Imogen looking cross and flustered. With a twinge of shame, I thought of Sophia's motherly care when she first found me, hot, muddy and completely out of my depth in her world. She had reached out and been a true friend without even knowing me.

I took a deep breath and tried to sound upbeat. "I think I hear a waterfall upstream. Wanna see if we can find it?"

Imogen made a face of utter exasperation. "I don't care," she snapped. "Just get me away from these blood-sucking little monsters."

Leaving the bucket on the rock to collect on our way back, I led the way upstream, towards the faint rumbling sound. The path took us uphill, and soon the river's banks rose steeply up on either side so that we were walking along a deep ravine with the river winding, gurgling and tumbling down little falls below.

I have to hand it to Imogen, it was a tiring hike, but she stayed right on my heels. She's always been good at sports, though I think the swarm of pursuing gnats especially motivated her. The crashing sound grew louder with each step until it drowned out all other forest sounds. Just around the next bend, we were both stopped by a fine mist moistening our faces. I lifted my eyes up from the trail, and up and up and up. The cascade must have been as tall as a six- or seven-story building. It thundered down into a foamy cauldron of rocks and rainbow mist.

"Oh. My. Gosh."

"I know," I agreed, my eyes fixed on the falls.

"Oh my gosh. Oh my Gosh. OH MY GOSH!"

Imogen's uncharacteristic enthusiasm made me turn and look at her. That's when I realised she hadn't even noticed the waterfall. Her eyes were glued on some tree roots in the path. I tried to see what was so fascinating about them, then, quick as a wink, one of the roots moved. It coiled itself up into a cinnamon roll shape, and I knew exactly why Imogen had turned so white. She threw herself behind me, grabbed my arm and squeezed while peering over my shoulder. At the same time the snake drew its head back, making an S with its neck, and hissed.

Imogen's killer grip on my arm slackened. Before I could so much as take a step back away from the snake, she shot like a loose arrow up the trail, straight for the waterfall.

"Imogen, careful!" I shouted. Forgetting the snake, I took off after her. "It'll be super slippery up there!"

She didn't hear a word. With knees high, she sprinted, leaping over boulders and roots as if competing in a 100-meter hurdle race. She didn't stop until she reached the slippery wet rock face that the waterfall spilled over.

"Imogen, it's ok!" I called. "The snake is way back there!"

But she looked just like a trapped animal, eyes darting

in every direction in search of an escape. Then, as I watched, she vanished, right behind the thundering waterfall.

I caught up to the spot a few seconds later, sliding on stones covered in wet, green slime, and discovered, to my relief, the opening behind the waterfall. She had disappeared inside a cave. I found her just inside in a huddle, hugging her knees.

"I. Hate. Snakes. More. Than anything." The words came out in shaky bullets of breath.

"Well, I'm pretty sure you outran it." I decided best not to mention that there were very likely to be more snakes inside this damp, dark cave.

Imogen didn't seem to hear or see me. She just stared at her knees, eyes glazed over, rocking back and forth. This was taking over-reacting to a whole new level. I took my water bottle from my rucksack and offered it to her. She gave a jerk with her head, so I had a swig instead. As it appeared I might be waiting some time for Imogen to get a grip, I figured I might as well have a wander around the cave.

As my eyes adjusted to the dimness, I realised it was much bigger that I'd originally thought. Brushing the lichen-covered stone wall with my fingertips, I followed the curve of the cave deeper back, into a sort of alcove. A hole in the earth above allowed a shaft of hazy sunlight to spill onto the alcove floor. The earth looked worn smooth. Right in the middle was a pile of what looked like bits of singed charcoal and white dust. I crouched down to examine it and noticed, there in the shadows against the cave wall, a row of clay pots.

"That is *seriously* primitive."

Imogen's voice so unexpectedly close behind made me start and lose my balance. My hand flew out to catch my weight and knocked into one of the pots. It swivelled and crashed into the pot beside it, cracking it right down its middle. Some sort of reddish brown, swirling goo oozed out onto the dirt floor.

"Great. That was probably some kind of ancient arte-fact," I growled. Not that Imogen was listening.

Once again completely ignoring me, she was squinting at something on the cave wall.

Getting to my feet and brushing the dirt and goo off my knees, I had a look to see what she was on about. I couldn't believe I hadn't noticed it before. The entire back wall of the alcove was decorated with a mural unlike any painting I'd ever seen before. It was clearly extremely old and the paint had faded, yet I knew the yellow, brown and red objects in an instant. They were horses— dozens of them in mid-gallop, their manes and tails streaking behind them like streamers. Some lowered their heads; others held their necks high and proud. But every one of them seemed to be in full sprint ahead.

"What was that?" Imogen whispered.

"Don't know." I couldn't take my eyes off the horses. Wouldn't it be wonderful, I thought, to be riding one of them, the wind rushing past, galloping away from Imogen and her rolling eyes?

"Katie?"

Something about the wildness, the otherworldliness of those horses made my heart drum against my chest.

"Katie, do you hear that? I think it's thunder."

Maybe it wasn't my heart beating after all. *It does sound like thunder*, I thought vaguely. *No, not thunder. Hooves. Hundreds of thundering hooves.* The moment the thought formed in my mind, my eyes played a trick on me. The mane of the painted horse I was staring at waved as if blown by a real breeze. I gasped as the same horse reared its head and lowered it again.

"Katie, snap out of it!"

But I couldn't. My breath caught in my chest. I watched wide eyed as, in unison, the horses picked up their legs and broke into a stationary gallop, their hoof beats in perfect sync with the thundering rhythm pounding in my chest.

I was vaguely aware of Imogen's boa constrictor-tight grip on my arm. Almost at the exact moment she grabbed me, an invisible arm wrenched me forward, headfirst into the cave wall. But I never felt the cold stone against my head. I felt nothing but the weightlessness of free-falling and Imogen's frightened fingers clenching my wrist for dear life.

4

STAMPEDE

*I*t felt like a dream. Just as it had before. I closed my eyes, or at least I thought I had, yet a cyclone of colour whirled past, browns melting into greens of a hundred different shades. When at last the swirling came to a halt with a soft but sudden *thud*, I opened my eyes. It was not the roof of the cave that met them, but rather soft, silvery sunlight slipping through the lacy gaps in a canopy of tall, tall trees. The trickle of a gentle river harmonised with the high chirrups of a blackbird. I might have lain there in that tranquil setting for some time, my mind floating somewhere between sleeping and waking, were it not for the throbbing pain shooting up my right arm.

There was a reason for the pain, but my mind couldn't quite recall what it was. Had I broken it? No, that wasn't it. Drowsily, my head flopped to the right, my eyes travelled down the aching arm and landed on the petrified face of my cousin Imogen, her fingers still clutching my wrist so tightly my hand had lost all feeling. One look at

Imogen brought everything rushing back into full waking memory. I sat upright, trying with my other hand to gently pry Imogen's fingers loose. She wasn't moving. Just staring straight upward, mouth open.

"Imogen?"

Nothing. I checked. She was still breathing. Her chest rose and fell steadily. That was something.

"Immy? Do you think you could let go of my wrist now? I can't do much to help you with one hand."

She gasped in a gulp of air as if just surfacing from a long stint under water. "What. Just. Happened?"

Relieved as I was that she could speak, I found myself at a loss for an answer. I knew exactly what had happened. There was no doubt in my now less-muddled mind that we'd just been tripped into another magic painting. Those painted horses had carried us away to the past, and who knew how far? But instinct told me Imogen wasn't likely to respond well to this explanation. I would have to break the truth to her gently or she was likely to have a complete meltdown in the middle of the forest... the last thing we needed on top of being stranded and defenceless in an unknown place and time. I'd have to string her along with a half-truth... I wracked my brain for something convincing. Meanwhile Imogen's head flopped towards me, eyes boring into mine.

"Katie. Tell me. I got bit by that snake, didn't I?"

My mouth opened, but before I could answer, her head rolled away so she was gazing at the sky again. "This is it. I'm actually going to die in this God-forsaken wilderness of America." She looked at me again. "Katie, I can't die yet. I've... I've never even kissed a boy."

Seriously? That was all she could think about on the verge of life and death? I couldn't let her go on like this. "The snake didn't get you, Im. You ran into the cave, remember? Then you ... you kind of fell."

Imogen's eyebrows knitted together as she tried to think back. "Did I?"

I gulped. Why did I have to be such a terrible liar? "Yea, yea, you did. 'Cause, well, what happened was—"

I didn't have a clue what I was about to say. I guess I'll never know, because right at that moment, the ground began to quiver, faintly at first, then a little stronger until it became an audible rhythm— *boom BOOM. Boom BOOM.*

Imogen sat up, her eyes darting in every direction. "What's that?"

I scrambled to my feet, listening, feeling the rhythm in the earth beneath me. The beat was growing closer and harder at a manic speed. "It sounds like... horses," I said.

As soon as the words were out of my mouth, the ground began to rumble like an earthquake. Then they burst into view, dozens of frantic-looking horses. These were not painted, but steaming flesh and hot blood, and they were storming their way up the trail straight towards us like a runaway train. They would thunder down on us in less time than it would take to shout for help. There was no time to think. I threw my whole body headfirst into Imogen. The momentum of the tackle sent us both rolling off the trail into a tangle of underbrush. When we stopped rolling, I looked back at the torrent of hooves beating the ground where Imogen had been lying a second earlier, but had to turn away again from the smothering cloud of dust kicking up.

"WE NEED TO MOVE!" I half shouted, half choked.

Together we scrambled to our feet, staggering over the trembling ground, and scrambled up a hill of boulders until we were high enough to escape the dust. Still coughing and gasping for breath, we both sat down on a broad, flat surface of the boulder where we could look down and watch the stampede from safety. The horses just kept coming, three abreast down the trail.

Then, as the herd finally thinned out at the back, a horse came into view with a rider on its back. Then two others followed. The men looked rough and wore broad-brimmed hats and rugged clothes and boots. I noticed a gun holster strapped to the leader's belt. All three were shouting — "YA! YA! Gidyap!"— goading the stampede forward.

Beside me, Imogen seemed to have lost interest in what was going on below. She was brushing the dirt off her arms and looking incredibly put out, though at least no longer panicked. "Ok. We nearly just died. What is this, the wild West or something?"

"*Shhhhh.*" I put my finger over my mouth and listened. "Why is it suddenly so quiet?" I whispered.

She rolled her eyes, expressing how much she couldn't care less. I crept to the other side of the boulder. From my new vantage point, I could see the trail open up into a wide clearing. A small lean-to cabin stood against the trees to one side. The last of the horses were being driven past it by the men's shouts, onward down some new vein of the forest. But in the torrent of running horses, one stationary horse, tall and grey, stood out. His rider sat still as a statue watching the herd pass. He sat very upright and wore a smart navy uniform with gold buttons, some sort of officer's hat, and white gloves. Squinting, I could just make out his straight golden hair that brushed the tops of his shoulders and his matching beard. But I couldn't quite get a good look at his face.

As if he'd sensed me watching, his head suddenly tilted. He was looking right at me! I dropped down instantly, squatting behind a bunch of fern fronds. But then it hit me. *What if this is our only chance of getting help?* After all, we were lost in the middle of a wood. It didn't even look the same as it had when we'd gone to fetch the water. The trails were wider, the trees bigger; the whole place felt wilder and more dangerous. And here was some kind of soldier, someone respectable who would at least see that we got safely out of the woods.

As I squatted there, contemplating whether or not to give up our hiding place to the golden-haired rider, another pair of thundering hooves came racing down the trail, along with what sounded like someone shouting hysterically. I parted the fern frond and saw the new rider yank his horse to a halt in the clearing as the last of the herders shot away. A brown-skinned man with a long black ponytail leapt from the horse and ran panting to the gentleman rider's side.

"What's this one on about?" Imogen asked, shuffling up beside me on her elbows.

"Don't know yet," I whispered. "Just listen."

The man's words came in heaves and grunts. He had evidently been riding as fast as he could go to catch up with the others. "Lieutenant Lovegood. The Great Spirit sends you to help me." He clutched his heaving chest with one hand and pointed with the other. "Those men. Bandits. They steal my father's horses, all but one. They steal many horses from my village. They kill our pigs and steers. Our meat. I thank the Great Spirit he has sent you at our time of need."

The officer remained a statue during the man's plea for help. Now he nudged his horse forward and walked it in a circle around the man. "You are certain these men took your father's horses?"

"Yes. And many others from the village. I ride after them. I never lose sight until I find you, for I know you and your men can do more than just I can on my one slow mare."

The officer stopped circling and looked down at the man. "Leave it to me," he replied flatly. The man bowed his head to show his gratitude. While his eyes were lowered, the officer lifted his pistol and took aim.

Without a second thought, I sprang up from my hiding place and screamed, "STOP!"

Just as quickly, Imogen reached up with both arms and yanked me back down, and only just in time. At the sound of my scream, the golden-haired officer turned his aim towards me and sent a bullet zipping through the air above our heads.

With my heart in my throat, I separated the ferns in front of me and peeked through. The officer's horse had reared up at the sound of the gunfire. The man with the ponytail stumbled back, but not quickly enough. The horse's raised front hooves pummelled down against the man's scull. Imogen and I both clasped our hands over our mouths as he wilted to the ground. With a last searching,

27

piercing look in our direction, the officer turned the horse and galloped off, full speed down the trail.

Imogen and I turned stunned faces towards one other. She was white as ash, and from my clammy palms, I guessed I didn't look much better. I felt sick with the thought that I'd almost turned us over to that officer. To think that it might have been us left to die on the forest floor.

To die… Could the man really be dead? What was this horrible time we'd fallen into that we'd already had to dodge a bullet in the first ten minutes?

Whatever we'd got ourselves into, I couldn't just lie there hiding in the ferns forever. With a shaky breath, I pushed myself up onto my knees. "I'm going down," I announced.

"Katie, are you mad?" Imogen remained crouched in the ferns, looking at me wild-eyed. "You were just nearly shot! *And* there's a man covered in blood down there!"

"Exactly," I said, feeling my resolution rise. "So if we don't do something about it, who do you think will?" But I felt another tiny pinch of guilt when, as I started the climb down, Imogen muttered under her breath, "You're welcome for saving your life."

5

FRIENDS AND FOES

"*D*o you think he's dead? Or just comatose? Oh my days, that is a *lot* of blood."

While Imogen helpfully stood a few paces off stating the obvious, I tentatively knelt down beside the wounded man. With a wave of relief, I watched as his chest rose then fell ever so slightly. He wasn't dead after all. Knowing that gave me the courage to creep closer until I was peering down into his face.

My first thought on closer inspection was how young the man was. Probably not more than twenty years old, his brown skin smooth as deer hide. Then my eyes wandered from his face to the blood oozing from his shaved temple and matting up his long, black ponytail in a pool beneath his head. My stomach lurched, and I looked away. Just the sight of his wound made my own head throb, and my hand automatically flew up to the scar beneath my hair, a permanent reminder of my riding accident. *Come on, Katie. Get a grip,* I coached myself. I could hear Imogen making little moaning noises behind me. This was no time for squeamishness. I had to keep my head.

"What are you gonna do with him?" Imogen asked apprehensively.

I let a big breath of air I'd been holding escape through my lips. "Not sure. But we need to stop the blood. That much I know."

I pulled off the blue bandana I'd tied around my hair that morning and, gently as I could, wrapped it around the man's head, tying it off in a tight knot. The blood immediately stained the blue a dark purple, but it seemed to do the trick. His face looked so calm and dignified. He was actually very handsome, though I didn't say so out loud. "I think he might be a … a Cherokee," I said.

Imogen tiptoed a step closer and peered over my shoulder at the man. "What, like an actual Indian?"

"Yyyea."

"That explains why he's dressed like that."

I took stock of the man's clothes: a cotton, blousy shirt with an open collar, tied off at the waist with a beaded belt, trousers made of some kind of animal skin—looked like deer—and tan moccasins.

"I'd have thought he'd have more feathers on his head or something," Imogen added.

"He does have one feather." I pointed to the black crow feather strung into his ponytail.

"Oh yea." She sighed. "So what now?"

I clenched my teeth together. How could she just stand there pestering me with questions? How was I supposed to know what to do? With another deep breath, I said at last, "I should go find help."

She gave me a blank look. "You mean *we* should go find help, right?"

"Well one of us has to stay here … unless you want to go off into the woods on your own …?"

"Katie,"— she spoke in her most patronising tone — "that's a terrible idea. Hello? Haven't you ever heard of the buddy system?"

"Well what about *his* buddy?" I half shouted, my temper spiking again.

"Not to mention," Imogen continued without hearing me at all, "this guy is a total stranger and probably some kind of nutter. He could be dangerous."

"He's *unconscious*," I said through gritted teeth. "There's not a lot he can do to us lying in the dirt. Look, there's his horse. I'll just ride up the trail and… and …" I hesitated. The truth was, I had no idea where to begin to find help.

"No," Imogen barked, her old superiority breaking through the *kill-me-now-I'm-so-bored* act. "You are *not* leaving me here with this… this half-dead Indian, Katie." She whipped her smartphone out of her pocket like a cowboy in a duel. "Why don't we just call an ambulance? What's the emergency number here?"

"You mean 911?"

She started thumping away at the screen.

"Immy … it's not gonna work."

She held the phone to the side of her head for a second, then looked down at the screen with a frustrated growl. But she wasn't dissuaded from her plan. Not yet. "If we go where I can pick up a signal, we can phone the police or search where's the nearest hospital. I just need to get higher up..." She started scrambling up the boulder again one-handed while the other hand held the phone up in front of her, her eyes glancing hopefully at it every step or two.

"It's not going to work, Imogen," I repeated, a good deal testier this time. All these wasted seconds could cost the man his life.

After reaching the top of the boulder, a few waves and shakes of the phone later, Imogen finally let the phone drop to her side. She gave me a withering look like it was all my fault. "Why won't it work?" she called down.

"Because..." This really was not the time to explain things. The last thing I needed on top of a dying man was a hysterical Imogen. "Because there *are* no signals around here. People don't use phones in this... area."

Imogen scowled. "Very funny," she said, with a sarcastic little laugh. But a look of panic quickly replaced her scowl. "You *are* joking?"

I wanted to smack myself on the forehead. It looked like I would be landed with a hysterical Imogen whether I mentioned the little fact that we had got ourselves thrown back in time or not. To her, being without a phone in any case was as good as being stranded in the past.

"I'm going for help," I said again in a tone I hoped meant business, and I didn't wait for her reply before moving around the unconscious man to his mare. "It's ok, girl. We're gonna help him," I reassured her in my calmest voice as I held out my hand to let her get a whiff of me. She must have smelled the man's blood on my hand, because she seemed to understand there was no time to lose. With a snort, she stepped forward, presenting her side to me as if waiting for me to mount.

"Do you even know the way back to camp?" Imogen sounded desperate now. "This doesn't look anything like the trail we came from."

I had no answer, so I chose to ignore her question. Swinging myself into the saddle, I called over my shoulder, "I won't be gone long, I promise. Just keep an eye on him. If he wakes up, tell him not to move and that help is on the way." *Hopefully.* For all I knew, the only other human being within miles might be the vicious officer and his horse-bandit buddies who had left the poor man for dead to begin with. With a last look at him, I pushed the buzzing *what-if*'s out of my mind and nudged the mare into motion.

JUST AS THE Cherokee had said, the old mare wasn't one for galloping. But after about five minutes, I managed to get her into a pretty good stride. "'Atta girl," I said, patting her neck. Raising my gaze to the trail again, I nearly screamed. A rider on a horse came flying towards us like a loosed arrow. I pulled back on the reins and squeezed my eyes shut, waiting for the collision. With a *whoosh* the horse and rider passed us, so close I felt the sleeve of his billowy shirt brush against my arm.

"*Whooooa,*" a deep voice sounded from behind.

I settled the mare and finally managed to turn to face the stranger, just as the rider turned his chestnut stallion to face me.

The face looking back at me, to my enormous relief,

belonged to a boy, probably around fifteen or sixteen. He was dressed very smartly in what looked like the sort of clothes I'd seen in paintings of the American Revolutionary War... maybe later. But young and nicely dressed as he was, the intensely suspicious way he glared at me out from under heavy, furrowed black eyebrows made me gulp as if I'd just been caught at a crime.

He trotted forward, not saying anything, just giving me a good look-over with the same displeased air. He looked almost affronted at my hiking boots and blue jean shorts... or perhaps he was simply confused by them.

At last he stopped sizing me up and spoke. "How is it you've come to have my cousin's horse?"

I choked. "Your... your cousin? He's your... Oh thank goodness! I mean, it's not good. I mean," I took a deep breath and tried again. "Your cousin's been hurt. I only took his horse to go and find help, but now that you're here..."

"Hurt?" He gave me a suspicious sideways look again.

"He chased after some horse bandits and was knocked unconscious," I explained.

I could tell he believed me. His face, just tan compared to his cousin's, went pale. He looked me squarely in the eye and said in a shaken voice, "Take me to him."

6

NEW WORLD

*M*inutes later, we galloped into the clearing. The boy leapt from his horse and swept past me to kneel beside his cousin. I don't think he so much as noticed Imogen, who was sitting a safe distance from the injured man with her back against the boulder hugging her knees to her chest. She had *definitely* taken notice of the newcomer, though. Her mouth hung open as her eyes swept over him with a half-confused, half-dazzled look.

"You said horse thieves did this? Did they stop the chase and come to blows here?"

I turned my attention back to the boy. "Uh, not exactly," I began, trying to sound in control and trustworthy. "He was chasing after horse thieves, but it was a man in a blue uniform who struck him down. He had blond hair and a beard. Your cousin called him Lieutenant something-or-other." I looked to Imogen for help, but the boy got there first.

"Lieutenant Lovegood," he said in a tone of surprise.

"Yes, that was it!" I answered.

He shook his head. "Can't be. Lieutenant Lovegood works for the Governor. He's responsible for *stopping* horse thieves, not helping them do the job. You must be confused."

An offended little gasp came from the direction of Imogen. She'd awakened from her stupor and stalked over to where we stood, arms crossed over her chest. "Excuse me?" I winced, preparing for Imogen's temper to flare up the way it did when anyone dared to contradict her. "Do we look stupid to you?"

The boy seemed to realise she was there for the first time. There was an awkward moment's silence during which his eyes scanned Imogen's *very* short shorts, insect-mauled legs and badly dyed hair. He seemed to be genuinely considering her question.

Imogen didn't wait for a reply. "It was definitely the Lieutenant who knocked him out, ok? We both saw it with our own eyes. Just wait until your cousin wakes up, if you don't believe us."

"I beg your pardon, ma'am. I didn't mean to offend you, but if what you're saying *is* true —"

She shot him an *I-dare-you* kind of glare.

"And I'm sure there must be some truth to it, as you claim it... It's just a bit mystifying is all. I can't think why Lieutenant Lovegood would behave in such a way."

"The point is," I broke in before Imogen could fire back, "Your cousin just asked the Lieutenant for help, and this is what he got." The sound of a twig cracking made my heart jump. I spun around on my heels. "What was that?" I felt instantly humiliated for asking. After everything we'd experienced in the past half hour, I'd become as jumpy as Imogen.

"Grasshopper," the boy answered.

"Huh," Imogen scoffed. "I highly doubt a grasshopper could make a noise like that—" She broke off into a screech as something tumbled into the clearing clutching a bow with an arrow ready on the string.

"*This* is Grasshopper," the boy said, gripping the newcomer's shoulder. "My cousin, and Crow Feather's brother." The new boy who had just appeared as if out of thin air barely spared us a glance before returning his arrow to a quiver on his back and bending down beside the bleeding man. He leaned his head against the man's chest to listen for a heartbeat. He was younger and scrawnier than his brother with not a single hair on his bare chest, but he had the same dark skin and thick black hair, only his stuck up in a wild mess rather than flowing down his back.

"He lives," the boy breathed before turning his dark eyes to his cousin. "Wattie, who has done this?"

Grasshopper looked just as sceptical when the first boy, Wattie, repeated our story to him. Meanwhile, my bandana had completely soaked through with Crow Feather's blood, and no one else seemed to notice. "Don't you think we ought to get him some help?" I blurted. "Is there a doctor around here?"

Grasshopper took his brother's hand. "He needs home."

Wattie nodded. "Grandmother Whispering Water can mend him if anyone can."

It took all four of us using every last bit of strength to

lift Crow Feather and drape him over the tall stallion's back. When we'd finally settled him, Wattie climbed up behind him and picked up the reins, then stopped as if just remembering something and looked down at Imogen and me. "We're mighty obliged to you ... ladies," he said, clearly a little unsure whether that were the right word.

Grasshopper stepped forward. "*Wado*," he said first to me. As he turned to say the same to Imogen, thanking her, it suddenly struck me that the boys were on the verge of taking off and leaving us alone and lost in the forest. Panic bubbled up inside me like a boiling kettle and came out in a desperate plea, "Couldn't we come with you?" I knew the request sounded mad, but what was I to do? Wait and hope that by chance another source of help turned up? It was already getting dusky under the canopy of trees.

The boys exchanged a puzzled glance. Imogen positively exploded. "*What?*" I winced as she gripped my arm yet again and pulled me a few strides away from the boys. "Katie, what on earth has got into you? We were nearly just trampled by horses, then shot by some lunatic, and now you want to go off with some Indian boys we know nothing about?"

"Look, I know it sounds crazy, but—"

"It's insane!" She was shouting now. "You know what? You can do what you want. I'm going straight back to camp to tell your parents to put me on the next flight to London. I don't know why I ever agreed to come to this stupid, backwards country in the first place."

"Imogen, wait." It was no use. Before I could even try to explain, she stomped off, then broke into a run down the trail.

I stamped my foot in the dirt and turned to the boys who'd witnessed the whole scene. "I'm sorry," I muttered. "Just go. I hope Crow Feather will be all right."

I knew those boys might be our last hope of getting out of the forest alive, let alone finding our way home from this dangerous world of the past. But I had no choice. I turned my back on them and ran, sick with dread, after Imogen.

"I DON'T GET IT. This *has* to be the campsite." Her voice was strained, like she was on the verge of tears.

I leaned against the rock wall, panting for breath. Imogen had always excelled at sports. When she decided to move, she moved fast. I'd only just managed to catch up to her.

"I followed that little stream, just like before. And look." She pointed at the rock above my head. "There's the face in the stone. The one your dad pointed out."

I craned my head back. Sure enough, she was right. This *was* our campsite, but there were no tents, no clearing with a brick fire pit and latrine. Gnarled old trees shaded the whole space, their knotted roots snaking through the ground where our tents had stood this morning, nearly two hundred years from now. Imogen was bound to notice one or two of those changes.

"Katie—" Her voice sounded choked, panicked. "What's going on? Where are they?" She leaned against a tree and slid down it until she was sitting right on the leafy forest floor and hid her face in her hands. I was sure I heard the distinct sound of muffled sniffling.

Never in all my twelve years had I ever heard Imogen cry. She was tough, sporty, in charge. I stood there stunned for a few seconds, then swallowed and quietly made my way over to sit crosslegged beside her.

"There's something I need to tell you, Im."

"Tell me, then," came the muffled answer from behind her hands.

"About what's going on..." I paused and rubbed my forehead. Why was this so hard? I just had to spit it out. Simple. Only it wasn't simple to say something I knew would sound crazy. Something I knew would cause an Imogen-shaped bomb to go off. "The thing is... The reason everything's so different ... It's because we've ... we've just ... we're not ..."

"Katie, *what is it?*" Imogen snapped, uncovering her bright red face and fixing me with an impatient glare.

I closed my eyes and took a deep breath. "Back in the cave, the painted horses on the wall..."

"What about them?"

"Do you remember how I couldn't stop looking at them?"

"Yea." She sniffled. "It was weird."

"Well, the reason I was zoned out like that was because the horses started..."—I had to force the word out of my mouth— "moving. Running, in fact. The painting sort of ... came to life."

She made a little sarcastic sound in her throat.

"And then," I carried on quickly to prove my point before she could interrupt, "do you remember how it felt like we were falling? Remember the swirling colours?"

Her puffy eyes narrowed. "Wait, that happened to you

too? I thought that was an hallucination from the snake bite..."

I shook my head. "I told you. There was no snake bite. It was the cave painting. It sucked us in, and when we opened our eyes and the forest looked all different, that's because we landed, well, here." Very slowly I added, "In the past."

She kept squinting at me with her mouth hanging open like I'd just been speaking gobbledygook. Then — I could hardly believe it — she actually started laughing. But when she spoke, she sounded anything but amused. "Very funny, Katie." She wiped her eyes and got to her feet so she was looking down at me, her arms crossed over her chest. "I remember how much you always loved playing make believe. But seriously?" The old snotty, superior tone was back. "I thought you'd have grown out of it by now."

"This isn't make believe!" I shouted, jumping to my feet in a fury. What was it going to take to convince her? "Just look around. You said it yourself—everything's different. This is our camping spot, so where are the tents? Where'd all these enormous trees come from? You wanted to know why my parents aren't here? They're not here because ... because they don't exist yet."

She wasn't listening. She was stumbling aimlessly from tree to tree with a hand on her forehead as if checking for fever. "Either you've lost it or I have. Was it something I ate?" she asked herself. "I *must* have been bitten by that snake, and now I'm in a state of delirium."

"You haven't lost it," I said loudly, interrupting her ridiculous hunt for an explanation. "This is really happening." I knew what I had to do. I had vowed to myself and to Sophia in my unsent letters never to tell a soul what had happened last summer; now that I'd managed to slip through time again, taking Imogen with me, I had to tell her the whole story. It was my only chance of convincing her. I reached down the collar of my shirt and pulled out the locket. Then, cornering Imogen to force her to see, I gently opened it and held it out for her. "I've never shown this to anyone, or told anyone where I got it."

She frowned at the tiny pictures. "What's that got to do with—"

"I'll explain. Just sit down. It's a long story, and it's going to sound mad, but it's not. It's true."

With a huff, she slid down a tree trunk into a squatting seat. I nestled down between the roots of an old oak tree, squeezed the locket tight in my fist, and began. "It all started with a painting."

7

A CLOSE CALL

"*J*ust before I left, Tom Tippery gave me this locket so I could always remember Sophia and Vagabond. But it's also proof. Proof that it really happened. Just like this is really happening. And the sooner we accept it"—we both jumped as somewhere overhead an owl hooted. I blinked and refocused— "the better."

I wondered if Imogen even noticed how dark it had become. She had listened at first with a grumpy grimace fixed on her face, mindlessly fiddling all the while with her useless smart phone. But as she hadn't interrupted, not even once, and my story went on, the grumpiness had given way to a look of confusion, then fear. Now that I'd finished, she took a shaky breath and looked up pleadingly into my eyes as if hoping I would crack and confess it was all a joke after all. When I didn't, her glazed-over eyes wandered over the rock with the face on it and the gnarled old trees before dropping to the smart phone resting like a dead thing in her hand. All of a sudden, something seemed to click.

She gasped in a sharp breath. "If this really is happening,"—her voice sounded unusually small— "that means everyone I know … my mum, my dad, Poppy…" She froze, looking horror struck.

I nodded. "They haven't been born yet. It's just you and me."

"But we can get back, right?" Imogen asked between breaths that were getting faster by the second.

"I … don't know," I answered and felt a prickly chill go up my spine. "I don't know any more than you do."

"What do you mean you don't know? You said you got back last time, so there *has* to be a way." Her panic was mounting like a tidal wave.

"There might be a way," I spat out in a rush. "I don't know what it is or how to find it. But we will. We just … we have to stay calm."

That was easy to say, but though I didn't dare show it, the seriousness of our situation was starting to sink in for me too. The dark gathering fast around us certainly didn't help. I wiped the hair out of my eyes and noticed the reddish-brown paint on my fingers. *The cave.* That's where this whole thing had started. I cleared my throat and tried to sound confident. "The first thing we should do is try to find the cave. Maybe we can get back through the painting … or at least find some clue to help us figure out who did it."

Imogen closed her eyes and took a deep breath, then nodded. "Ok, then let's go before it gets any darker."

Though the paths we'd taken on our trip to gather

water didn't appear to exist in the past, luckily the little stream we'd followed did, and we were able to trace our steps down the river, then follow our ears to the waterfall.

Imogen didn't speak on the hike — I think she was still too much in shock – which gave me the chance to think, to try to make sense of things. Imogen was right—if there was a way back last time, there had to be one this time too. But last time, I hadn't fallen through that painting by accident. It had been Tom's doing, and it was Tom who got me home again. But how could Tom have anything to do with those painted horses? Tom belonged to another time, another country.

And yet … my heart jumped at the thought – *what if, just what if Tom was behind this? What if, somehow, he'd travelled here too and painted those horses knowing I would find them?*

"Slow down, Katie. I can't run anymore," Imogen whined.

My pace had quickened into a jog without my noticing. But the idea that had hatched inside my brain, the idea that I might find Tom at the cave, and if Tom, why not Sophia, had given me a rush of excitement that gave my feet wings. I'd just fallen through a magical painting for the second time, after all. Anything was possible.

By the time I'd reached the slippery rock path that led behind the waterfall, my head was spinning with excitement. I felt sure of it. I was going to see Sophia any second now!

"Katie, SLOW DOWN!" Imogen yelled over the roar of the falls. "You're going to slip!"

Had she slowed down that morning, running away

from that snake? And I had much better reason to be in a hurry. A fine, cold mist tickled my face as I sprang from the last wet rock into the cave behind the waterfall and saw...

Nothing.

The cave was almost completely dark and showed no signs of Tom or Sophia. I heard Imogen drawing in shivering breaths behind me. "Come on," I said, edging along the stone wall of the cave. "The horses were deeper in, right at the back."

A small hole in the rock above filled the deep alcove with grey, misty light. It was enough to show me what I dreaded: there was no one there. And what was even worse, there was not a single painted horse to be seen on the stone wall. "It hasn't been painted yet," I whispered, a lump of disappointment inching its way up my throat. I gritted my teeth, determined not to melt into a heap of tears. *How could I have been so foolish as to believe Sophia would be waiting for me in a cave in the middle of an American forest?*

"But ... what does this mean?" Imogen insisted, her voicing rising with panic again.

"It means," I rubbed my forehead, "I don't know."

There was a pause when we just looked at each other. In the grey light, I saw Imogen's nostrils flaring with every breath. "Katie" – she spoke in a low, dangerous voice – "you got us into this mess, and you had better get us out."

I couldn't believe my ears. "I got us into it? *You're* the one who ran into the cave in the first place, all because of a harmless little snake!"

"Yes, but you're the one who looked at the painting. You're the one who made it move. You're the one with the habit of time-travelling!" Her voice rose and rose until it echoed off the cave walls, sending a couple of bats over our heads into a flurry. We ducked and I spun around to watch their flight out into the night air. As I did, something else caught my eye: a beam of light bounced off the rock. It was coming from somewhere inside the cave.

"Imogen, get down!" I hissed. "Someone's coming."

We huddled together in the shadows of the alcove, our knees pulled in tight, both holding our breath, listening.

The beam of light grew, accompanied by soft, padded footsteps. Suddenly, two dark figures appeared as if stepping right out of the stone. The light cast their strange shadows up on the cave ceiling. One might have been a giant. He stood head and shoulders over the other and looked like an oak tree standing beside a scrawny sapling. The smaller man was speaking to him in a hushed voice. One hand rested on his back hip, probably close to his gun holster.

"Look here, Black Fox. You know you ain't s'posed to be sniffin' around in here. Not 'til the treaty's been signed."

"You show me. Then I go." The big man's voice was as deep as a bullfrog's and sent shivers down my spine.

"You know I can't," the little man answered, and his shadow moved back a step. "Governor's orders."

The big man took a step closer so that he towered over his companion. "You tell Governor I want what's mine."

The little man's voice was considerably higher as he

answered quickly, "J...just, take it easy, Black Fox. Governor Blunt's a man of his word. You'll get wh...what he agreed to, b...but it's like I told you: not 'til the treaty's signed... just a week's time."

And with that, the smaller shadow disappeared, leaving the giant shadow standing in the dark with us. He made a sound in his throat like a bear growling. Imogen fidgeted beside me, and the growling stopped. I looked at her, the whites of her eyes practically glowing in the dark.

The shadow moved into the darkness so we could no longer see it, but we could just hear his footsteps, soft and slow. Were they coming closer? Imogen clenched my hand with all her might, and I clenched hers back, praying the footsteps would go away.

Then, sudden as a firecracker explodes, a hideous, snarling face appeared right in front of us, his teeth bared, his eyes menacing. Imogen let out an ear-splitting scream as the man drew a shining object from his hip. The toma-hawk glinted in the dying light, and all I could do was pull Imogen closer and squeeze my eyes shut.

"Black Fox!"

My eyes opened at the sound of the familiar voice and were met with a flood of light. The hulking beast spun around. It was Wattie. At that moment, he looked like an angel standing in a puddle of light from the little lantern he held over his head. He stepped forward without the slightest hesitation and spoke to the man in what I figured must be Cherokee. I nearly wilted to the ground with relief when, to my amazement, the huge man turned without a second glance at Imogen and me and disappeared into the night.

Wattie set down his lantern and offered us a hand up.

"What did you say to him?" I asked, my throat so dry that my voice came out in croaks.

"I told him you were guests of mine, that you must have lost your way and I'd come to find you. And I thanked him for seeing you were safe until I got here."

"Safe?" Imogen croaked. "He was about to kill us!"

"Trust me," Wattie said, raising his thick black eyebrows, "It's best I didn't accuse him of that. Black Fox has the temper of a mother bear. I'm just glad I found you when I did." He took a little pouch slung over his shoulder off and held it out. "Here. Drink."

I took the pouch from Imogen and took a long, wonderful swig of cold water, then handed it back to Wattie. "I'm glad too," I breathed. "But how did you find us? And why *did* you come looking for us?"

He smiled. "I tracked you at first. Luckily, when darkness fell, I was able to follow the screaming. Impressive how loud it was, even over the sound of the waterfall."

Imogen sniffled.

"As to why I followed you," Wattie continued, "you appeared distressed before, and a gentleman could never leave two young ladies distressed and alone in the forest. Especially after the good turn you did my family by saving Crow Feather."

"Is he all right?" I asked, suddenly aware that if Wattie had come after us, that meant he hadn't seen his cousins back home.

"He is with Grasshopper," Wattie answered looking grave. "They will have reached Nickajack by now, and then we will see."

"Nickajack?" I asked.

"My village," Wattie answered.

To my astonishment, Imogen rushed forward and grabbed Wattie's arm in both hands. "Please, take us with you!" she pleaded.

Wattie leaned back and smiled nervously. "Ah... of course I'll take you. My mother would welcome two girls most heartily. But..." He gently drew his arm away from Imogen, "don't you girls have somewhere to be? I mean, don't you want to tell me how you came to be lost in Cherokee Country in the first place?"

"Cherokee Country?" Imogen whimpered.

"We were travelling to visit our uncle," I blurted and shot Imogen a sideways glance. "Our Uncle Tom Tippery."

She nodded, slowly catching on.

"And where is your uncle's house?" Wattie asked.

"It's … uh …" My mind went blank.

"We lost the address," Imogen said confidently, coming to the rescue. She had always been a much better liar than I am.

Wattie rumpled his thick mop of black hair, thinking. "I don't know of anyone by the name Tom Tippery in these parts, and I know just about everybody."

For half a second, I feared Wattie was on to us. Imogen and I exchanged a quick look. I was sure we were thinking the same thing. What if he decided to leave us in the woods after all?

He picked up his lantern as if getting ready to go. "That settles it, then."

"Settles what?" Imogen asked anxiously.

"You're coming to Nickajack. You can stay at my house until we track your uncle down."

I felt so relieved, I could've hugged Wattie. Imogen must have been even more relieved. She flew at the stunned boy and planted a kiss on his cheek before collapsing onto his shoulder in a waterfall of tears.

8

NICKAJACK

"*S*ee the cabins down in the valley?" Wattie waved his hand towards a sea of cornstalks below us set against a backdrop of deep blue hills. The valley was dotted with little timber cabins with smoking chimneys and lit-up windows. "That's the village. Not far to go now."

"Aren't Indians supposed to live in teepees?" Imogen asked drowsily down at Wattie from the old mare. We were taking turns riding her while Wattie led us on what felt like a never-ending journey to his village. At last we'd stepped out of the trees and stood on a precipice overlooking a moonlit valley dotted with cabins with flickering windows and smoking chimneys.

Wattie eyed her sideways. "Teepees?"

"You know. Those cone-shaped tents that Indians live in?" Imogen said as if explaining something completely obvious.

"I don't know about other Indians, but we Cherokees live in cabins mostly ... same as you settlers."

"*I* live in a Georgian town house in London," Imogen corrected him haughtily. Embarrassed as I was at her tone towards the person who had just saved our lives, it was a relief to hear a bit of the old Imogen coming back after the shock.

Wattie frowned. "I forgot. Well, I hope our home will be sufficiently comfortable for you, Miss... Ha!" Wattie stopped in his tracks and put his hands on his hips. "I never asked your names!"

"Imogen Humphreys," Imogen answered, still in her high-and-mighty way. "But you can just call me Im. I think it suits my image better."

Wattie looked at a loss for a response, so I took over. "And I'm Katie ... uh, Watson." I added the last bit under my breath, hoping Imogen wouldn't hear. It wasn't quite enough.

She snorted. "Watson? Since when is your surname Watson? Your surname is Wolf... I mean ..." She caught my glaring eyes and cleared her throat. "*Woof!*" She waved her hand in front of her nose. "Is something burning around here?"

While Wattie was busy sniffing the air for burning smells, I slapped my palm against my forehead. I didn't expect Imogen to understand, but Watson had been the name I'd chosen for myself last summer when I'd travelled back in time, and it had served me well. I wasn't the same Katie then. The name Watson reminded me of that other Katie, the brave, daring Katie who had helped to rescue Sophia. I needed to be that Katie now, so Watson it was.

"Well then, Miss Humphreys, Miss Watson, welcome to Nickajack."

. . .

AT THE BOTTOM of the hill, we skirted around a cornfield that glowed eerie blue in the moonlight. A chill breeze rustled through the rows of cornstalks, making a sound like whispering as we passed. Our path soon met up with a wide dirt road that ran like a ribbon through the middle of the village. The log cabins we passed looked homey and inviting with their tidy rows of squash and beans and porches hung with drying herbs and woven baskets. And yet the frightened faces that peered around doorways or sent darting glances out of windows told a different story: Nickajack was in trouble. On one porch, a wrinkled old Cherokee man sat outside the door with a rifle across his lap. He dipped his head when Wattie greeted him in Cherokee, but continued to watch Imogen and me with a suspicious eye.

"It wasn't like this before," Wattie said, kicking a pebble in the road. "It used to be on an evening like this all of Nickajack would be outdoors. Women weaving baskets on the porch, men telling stories, and children playing chunky in the roads. Now fear chases them all inside, making caged animals of us on our own land."

"You mean the horse thieves weren't the first to attack Nickajack?" I asked.

Wattie shook his head. "Lately there have been many attacks, not only on Nickajack but on our neighbouring villages as well."

"But who's behind the attacks?"

"Outlaws. Bandits. Greedy people who see our land

and our goods as theirs for the taking ... people like Lieutenant Lovegood."

"I don't get it," Imogen yawned. "Why don't you just call the authorities?"

Wattie scratched his head. "It's as I said before. Lovegood *is* the authorities."

"Oh yea." Imogen sounded ready to fall off the horse with exhaustion. I silently hoped we would get to Wattie's house before she did ... and before she said anything else that might raise Wattie's suspicions about us.

To my relief, just a few seconds later, we approached a house at the end of the road, and Wattie announced we'd arrived.

"Well this does beat sleeping in a cave," Imogen slurred. She was right about that. Wattie's house was the finest in the village. It was not a log cabin, but a two-story wooden house with a brick foundation and a porch with tall column posts. Two flickering lanterns on either side of the door glinted off a brass doorknocker.

Wattie helped Imogen down from the mare's back and hitched the horse to a stake in the ground, then opened a gate in the fence and led us up a brick walkway to the porch. Before Wattie could so much as touch the brass knocker, the door swung open, and a woman threw her arms around him. Wattie looked a little embarrassed when she didn't let go for a long minute. At last she held him by his forearms, and the two began firing away in Cherokee. Watching them both, face to face, I could see the woman was, beyond doubt, Wattie's mother. She was very pretty, with smooth brown skin and pink lips, and her dark eyes framed with long, thick lashes, just like Wattie's. Though obviously Cherokee, she dressed like an American lady in a chequered dress and her hair twisted up under a lacy cloth cap. I was still examining the likeness between mother and son when both suddenly turned towards Imogen and me.

"This is my mother, Ulma McKay," Wattie explained as the woman smiled at us and made tiny curtseys. "I've explained who you are and how we met, and she insists you lodge with us for as long as you need."

Imogen blew out a puff of air. "Well, that's a relief."

Still smiling warmly, Wattie's mother gestured us both into the house. She called to a dark-skinned girl dressed quite plainly—I assumed she must be a maid—and before we knew it, Imogen and I were ushered into a room with nothing in it but a great big hearth with a kettle over an open fire and a large copper tub, full of water. The young maid didn't speak any English, but she made gestures to explain that she wanted us to undress and get into the tub.

Imogen and I looked at each other. Then she shrugged. "I'll go first. I'm dying to get this grime off." She peeled off her dusty shorts, t-shirt and even her designer tennis shoes and climbed into the copper tub while the maid carefully lifted the piping kettle from the fire and added some steaming water to Imogen's bath. I wearily sat on a stool meanwhile and waited while Imogen soaked and exclaimed how good the hot water felt on her aching muscles. When the maid returned with a towel, Imogen reluctantly got out to make way for my turn in what was by then lukewarm bathwater. Thankfully, the maid topped up the tub with some more steaming water from the kettle, and I sank down feeling for the first time just how exhausted I was from the extraordinary day.

I was scrubbing with a piece of soap that looked like a blob of hard fat and Imogen was wrapped in her towel drying her hair in front of the fire when the maid returned with two cotton dresses and draped them over a drying rod.

Imogen held up one of the dresses and gave a long sigh. "We have *got* to be back home. Soon."

"It's not so bad," I said, taking a blue gingham dress from the maid and slipping it over my head. "Last time I travelled back in time, the clothes were much less comfortable than this."

"Well it's bad enough being made to dress like *Little House on the Prairie*," Imogen grumbled, putting on the other dress, a pink and red gingham. She looked down at herself with a look of despair. "You do think she'll give us our own clothes back, don't you? Once she's washed them?" she asked, eyeing the maid as she slipped out the door with her arms full of our old clothes and shoes.

"I wouldn't be so sure," I answered. "Anyway, it doesn't matter. We can't dress in modern clothes while we're here. The point is to blend in, not raise every eyebrow in town."

Imogen made a growling noise in the back of her throat and mumbled under her breath about how much she couldn't wait to leave this primitive time with its terrible sense of fashion.

My stomach lurched as I slid my foot into the soft slippers the maid had brought us, not because the shoe wasn't comfortable – it was miles nicer than the hard little shoes

I'd had to wear at Otterly Manor – but because I knew Imogen was right. We needed to get home. But unlike last summer at Otterly Manor, here we were on our own with no clues of a way back and no one in on our secret who could help us find one. I still hadn't even managed to work out what year we'd landed in, much less how we were to get out of it. Worst of all, I had the feeling that Imogen was expecting me to figure out this predicament in no time, just because I'd found my way back from the past before. But at that moment, I was feeling less confident than ever in my detective skills.

I reached my hand into the collar of my dress and pulled out my locket, clenching it tight in my fist. "I need your courage, Sophia," I whispered with my eyes squeezed shut. A knock at the door opened my eyes.

9

NEW NAMES

*W*attie's mother's smiling face appeared in the doorway. "You eat. Then you sleep," she said cheerfully in her simple English. A high-pitched giggle erupted from behind her. Then a round, chubby-cheeked face peeped curiously from behind her skirt and disappeared again with another giggle.

"My daughter," Ulma explained, still smiling. "Little Beaver."

As we followed Ulma down the hallway to the dining room, Little Beaver's big dark eyes stayed glued on Imogen and me, but she seemed especially fascinated by Imogen. When Ulma invited us to join Wattie at the dining table for pork, beans and hot corn cakes, Little Beaver slid into a seat beside Imogen and stared at her before plucking up the courage to reach up and touch her hair. Imogen froze as if a wasp had landed on her as Little Beaver began to stroke her hair as if it were a pet kitten. I grinned down into my plate of pork and beans, privately thinking that at least someone appreciated the terrible mess Imogen's friend had wreaked upon her hair.

"What is she doing exactly?" Imogen asked Wattie warily.

He spoke to his little sister in Cherokee through a mouthful of corn cake. When she answered him, Wattie snorted and nearly choked on his food.

"What did she say?" Imogen demanded.

"She said," Wattie began, trying and failing to maintain a straight face, "that she likes your hair."

"Oh." Imogen looked suspiciously at him. "I don't see what's so funny about that."

"She says she likes your hair," Wattie continued, "because it reminds her of ..."—he looked down, trying not to laugh—"of Dilli."

"Dilli! Dilli!" the little girl chanted happily, stroking Imogen's hair more rigorously still.

Imogen squinted at Wattie. "And what does *Dilli* mean exactly?"

"You're sure you want to know?" He had a twinkle in his eye that reminded me of Charlie in a mischievous mood.

"Just tell me," Imogen said impatiently.

"It's an animal." Wattie was working hard to maintain a straight face. "I don't think you have it in England, but the Americans have given it their own name: *skunk*."

Imogen's face fell, and Wattie and I both burst out laughing, which only encouraged Little Beaver to chant "Dilli! Dilli!" all the more enthusiastically. After a moment, Ulma came into the room and took the little girl by the hand to lead her off to bed.

"It would make a good Cherokee name for you," Wattie teased, offering me his handkerchief so I could wipe my eyes. "Dilli. Has a nice ring to it."

"I don't need a Cherokee name, thank you very much," Imogen snapped, her nose in the air as she tossed her hair over one shoulder. "You can call me Imogen... or Im. But I am *not* answering to *Skunk*."

Wattie grinned, then looked at me and tipped his head to one side before speaking. "And your Cherokee name can be ... Katie Fire-Hair."

I was about to say that I was all right with that when the sound of fast hoofbeats and a whinny outside made us all turn to the window. A second later, the front door, which was visible from the dining room, swung open, and a white man with a rifle slung over his shoulder stepped inside, scuffing his boots on the doormat. He looked tired and winded from riding fast, but he was quite handsome. As soon as I saw his curly auburn hair, I knew—this was Wattie's father. Something about him reminded me immediately of my own dad, and a little stab of homesickness made my breath catch in my chest.

The man walked heavily into the dining room and looked from Wattie to Imogen and me and back to Wattie again.

"So, William. Do you care to tell me how you went out hunting horse thieves and came back with two young lasses?" He spoke with a strong accent that I recognised straight away from my visits to Scotland. "Or don't tell me these *are* the horse thieves?" he added with a hint of a weary smile as he rested his rifle over the mantelpiece.

"No indeed, Father," Wattie answered, jumping to his

feet to help his father off with his gunpowder horn and coat. "This is Miss Katie Watson of Pennsylvania and her cousin Imogen from England. I discovered them travelling the Federal Road on their own."

Wattie's father's eyebrows jumped in surprise as he looked at us. "You did well to bring them here, William." He gave us both a fatherly, disapproving look as he joined us at the table. "Why would two young lasses be travelling the Federal Road without a chaperone in such troubled times as these? You know you might've been crossed by bandits or highwaymen?"

"We were on our way to stay with our Uncle Tom," I answered in a rush. "We thought he lived around here, but turns out he doesn't. Well, not any more anyway." I was mortified to hear myself follow the explanation with a stupid little laugh. Wattie's father was sure to smell a rat.

I held my breath as he peered at us with his sharp blue eyes, clearly trying to make sense of my rather patchy story and Imogen's bizarre hair. Even with Ulma's dresses on, Imogen's many earrings and streaky black and blonde hair clashed with our surroundings. *If only I could persuade her to wear a bonnet*, I thought on pins and needles, waiting for the man.

"I see," he said at last, nodding his head distractedly. "Well you're welcome here at the McKay household for the time being."

"Thank you, Mr. McKay," I said, Imogen nodding her agreement through a great big yawn.

He gave us another kind but tired smile. Then, to my huge relief, he resumed talking to Wattie about more pressing matters than two lost little girls from the woods.

"It looks like ours are the only two horses left in Nickajack. The thieves must be local men. They knew a white man lived here or they'd never have left ours alone."

I watched Wattie. His dark eyes glinted angrily as he pursed his lips together, but he waited silently for his father to continue.

"I've been all over the village to find out the extent of the damage," Mr. McKay was saying as he took a pipe and some flint from his vest pocket. "It's the worst raid we've suffered so far. And it's not just the horses they took."

"What do you mean?" Wattie pressed him warily.

"They killed Old Turkey's swine. Didn't even take the meat. Just slaughtered the beasts in cold blood."

I shuddered. Wattie's mouth was hanging open in disbelief. Even Imogen looked disgusted.

Mr. McKay hadn't finished. "They set Tipping Canoe's cornfield on fire, and when he came out to challenge them, one of the rascals threw the lit torch at his cabin. His wife had a ready bucket of well water, praise be to God, and put it out before the flames took hold. Their new baby lay sleeping inside."

I couldn't believe this quiet, humble little village had suffered such horrors just hours before we'd arrived. "But why would anyone want to attack Nickajack just for the sake of it?" I asked. As terrible as robbery was, I could understand why greedy people took things. But destroying families' homes for no reason or gain?

Mr. McKay leaned his elbows on the table, his pipe cupped in one hand. "It isn't just Nickajack," he answered, at the same time pulling a rolled-up newspaper out of his vest pocket and laying it open on the table.

"There are reports of raids and attacks all across Cherokee Country."

As Wattie slid the newspaper across the table, I leaned over to get a glimpse of the heading. There were some strange, curly letters across the top. Then printed beneath them in all caps CHEROKEE PHOENIX, AND INDIANS' ADVOCATE, and below that in slightly smaller print, NEW ECHOTA, THURSDAY OCTOBER 16, 1828.

I nudged Imogen and drew her eyes towards the year.

To my horror, she shrieked, "1828? That's impossible!"

I gave her a kick under the table, and she got the message that she should stop talking. But Mr. McKay and Wattie were both eyeing us with a mixture of suspicion and amusement. How was I going to smooth this one over?

"I know," I said, trying to sound enthusiastic. "Can you believe it's 1828 already? Seems like only yesterday it was 1827..." The nervous laugh escaped me again. I gulped and tried to evade Wattie's and Mr. McKay's eyes.

The awkward moment was interrupted by a knock at the door. Mr. McKay and Wattie were on their feet in a flash, but before they could take a step, the maid and Ulma were at the door.

Grasshopper walked in, accompanied by a very sombre-looking older Cherokee man. His long greying hair fell from beneath a turban wrapped around his head. His hard, brown face was etched with deep wrinkles and made me think of the wood carvings I'd seen at the Cherokee gift shop that morning.

The man did not smile as he greeted Ulma in their own language, then clasped hands with Mr. McKay and Wattie.

He seemed to be looking for someone else as he advanced into the dining room. I swallowed when his eyes fell on us and he made straight for us.

The man stood statue still except for his eyes, which flicked back and forth between the two of us. There was silence as everyone in the doorway waited to see what he would do. In a flash, the gangly Grasshopper appeared at the man's side.

"These are the girls from the forest, Father," Grasshopper told him, "the ones who saved Crow Feather."

Forgetting my nerves, I looked at Grasshopper, eager to know. "You mean Crow Feather's all right?" I asked.

The scrawny, brown boy grinned and nodded. "He sleeps still, but he will live." He gestured to the man. "My father, Terrapin Jo. He wishes to thank you."

The older man held out his hand. I glanced at Grasshopper, who was nodding encouragingly and placed my hand into the big, rough one. "*Wado*," the man said, bowing his head slightly. Then he did the exact same thing to Imogen, saying "*Wado*" once again.

"It was nothing, really," I said faintly. I felt limp with relief. Our first day in 1828 had been one long series of disasters. And yet, here we were, safe inside the McKay home, and we'd played a part in saving a man's life. What if – the idea flickered faintly, but stirred up a rush of hope – what if I had come here for a purpose, just like last time. What if falling into 1828 wasn't just an accident after all?

THE WOMAN AND THE SNAKE

*T*he crackling fire, the soft creak of Ulma's rocking chair where she sat darning socks, the men's lowered voices as they smoked their pipes and discussed the events of the day, everything about the McKay's sitting room was conspiring against me. They were talking about Lieutenant Lovegood and what was to be done.

I tried desperately to follow the conversation, but my eyelids felt as heavy as horseshoes. Imogen was already softly snoring beside me on the settee, her head slumped over against my shoulder. It had been such a long day, I felt I was not far behind her.

Terrapin Jo was speaking, his voice low like distant thunder, but bitter. "If these raids continue, there will be no food for the winter. Some in the Council believe we will have to leave this land." He was shaking his head. "Things have gone from bad to worse for us ever since Jim Weaver stole the Uktena Stone."

My ears perked up. *I'd heard of that stone before ... but*

where? I was alert now, my full attention on what the men were saying.

"Joe, Joe." Mr. McKay was shaking his head now. "I know you're still angry about Jim. We were all hurt by his betrayal. But you can't actually believe that stone has anything to do with all of this ... with Lieutenant Lovegood and Crow Feather?"

I sat up a little straighter and cleared my throat. "What stone is that?" I asked, trying to sound innocently curious.

An uncomfortable silence followed in which Wattie and Grasshopper both seemed suddenly interested in their hands resting in their laps and Terrapin Jo just glared with eyes as hard as steel into the fire.

I was just about to say it didn't matter after all when Mr. McKay answered. "It is a legendary stone, called the Uktena Stone, or Serpent's Stone."

Without opening her eyes, Imogen stirred beside me. "I hate snakes," she whimpered, and flopped over to lean against the settee, allowing me to sit up completely.

With another weary smile, Wattie's father continued. "About eight years ago, the stone went missing."

"It was *stolen*," Terrapin Jo thundered under his breath.

"It is *believed* that a man by the name of Jim Weaver stole the stone. He was a man we all trusted. We counted him as one of us."

I shot a glance at Terrapin Jo. He glowered more darkly than ever.

"At any rate," Mr. McKay continued, "after the stone went missing, the serious troubles started for us here in Nickajack. Many believe it's because the stone was no longer giving us its protection. But I reckon," he cast his eyes at Terrapin Jo, "things would've got worse, stone or no stone. These mountains are crawling with horse thieves and greedy prospectors who consider this land as theirs for the taking if they can only bully the Cherokee off of it."

I wanted to ask more about this Serpent's Stone and why it mattered so much to the Cherokee, but something told me it would be better to drop the topic. Instead I asked, "But isn't there anyone who can stop the bullies? I mean, what they're doing is against the law, isn't it?"

"Washington sent us Lieutenant Lovegood to stop them," Wattie answered with a flash of hot anger in his eyes. "But he proved to be the biggest scoundrel of them all."

"If Lovegood sets foot in Nickajack, he will pay," Grasshopper echoed, cracking his knobbly knuckles threateningly.

Mr. McKay held up his hands to silence the boys. "Making him pay is not our responsibility. This matter *must* go to the Governor. *He* is the United States' representative to the Cherokee people, and we *must* keep peace with the United States. If they see Cherokee Country as a lawless place, the president may very well withdraw all protection, and that would be the end of us."

Wattie perched on the edge of his chair, looking as excited as a kid at a theme park. "Grasshopper and I will go to Hiwassee Garrison to see the Governor. We'll tell him everything that happened today."

Grasshopper was nodding his head enthusiastically, but Mr. McKay was shaking his. "You'll do no such thing, William," he said sharply. It was strange how he kept calling Wattie *William* when the boy clearly preferred his

Cherokee name. "Your duty is to stay right here, continuing with your studies and helping me at the shop. People depend on our honest trade more than ever these days."

"But—"

Before Wattie could argue, his father stood up. "That's final, William."

Flush faced, Wattie clenched his jaw and looked away from his father.

"The Governor is due for his visit here in a month's time. The Council will take up the matter with him then. Meanwhile, we must all remain vigilant and carry on as before."

Ulma's calm voice interrupted her husband's speech. She said something to him in Cherokee, and he nodded. When he spoke, his voice had changed, sounding almost cheerful. "Ulma is right. We should all get a good night's sleep. Tomorrow is the Stomp Dance, and the good Lord knows it is more important than ever that we preserve our traditions and keep hope alive."

I thought I caught Wattie and Grasshopper exchange a meaningful look. Before I could be sure, Wattie stood up and stormed out of the room without saying goodnight.

I HAD NEVER BEEN MORE EXHAUSTED in my life, so why couldn't I just fall asleep? Every time I closed my eyes, the day would replay itself in my head: the stampede, the earsplitting sound of Lovegood's gun firing, the blood matted in Crow Feather's hair ... and the way everyone had gone quiet when I'd asked about the Uktena Stone. Mr. McKay had said the stone was a legend, but legends can't be stolen. Terrapin Jo really believed the stone possessed some sort of magic. What if he was right? After all, I'd seen magic paintings with my own eyes. Why not a magic stone? And Mr. McKay *did* admit that things had got worse for Nickajack ever since the stone disappeared. Could there really be a connection?

The more I thought about the Serpent's Stone, the more I wanted to know. *If I could just remember where I'd heard of it before.*

I gazed at the wooden slats of the ceiling and screwed up my face, trying to remember. Imogen gave a little snort in her sleep, and, just like that, it came to me!

Throwing the quilt off my legs, I crept out of bed so as not to disturb Imogen. I thrust my arm under the bed and felt around until my hand landed on my rucksack. I'd thrown it under the bed in hopes the maid wouldn't find it and carry it away with the rest of our modern apparel. I unzipped it, thrust my hand in and pulled out the two items I'd brought with me to 1828: my detective notebook and the little booklet I'd got that morning: *Cherokee Legends*. A beam of blue moonlight lit up the picture of the giant horned snake rearing its head back from the man with the stone held high over his head.

I peeled back the cover and ran my finger down the contents page until I found it: "The Legend of the Uktena." My heart did a little jump as I rifled to the page and read by the moonlight…

This is what the old men told me when I was a boy. The Uktena is the great serpent who haunts the dark passes of the Great

Smokey Mountains. He is mightier than the ancient oaks and recognisable by his horns, like the antlers of a buck, and by the diamond set like a blazing star in his forehead.

Uktena lies in wait for hunters and travellers in lonely places. No man, not even the strongest warrior, can look upon his shining eyes and rippling scales. He will live, but he will spend the rest of his days wandering the hills in madness. Even if the victim can avoid Uktena's eyes, Uktena can still crush with his mighty coils or spit venom from his arrow-like fangs.

Only one man has ever outwitted the great Uktena: the wise medicine man Agan-uni'tsi, or "The Groundhog's Mother." He shot the serpent with an arrow through the seventh diamond on its back, straight through the heart. After seven days, he returned to the spot where the beast's carcass lay, all but devoured by the ravens. There he found the stone from Uktena's head.

Agan-uni'tsi thereafter became the greatest medicine man who ever lived, and the stone prospered the Cherokee of his village so that they always found game and defeated all their enemies.

I CLOSED the booklet with a shiver. *It's just because my feet are cold*, I assured myself. *Obviously, I'm not afraid of a giant killer snake with antlers.* I scrambled quickly back into bed and pulled the quilt up under my chin, glad to hear Imogen's steady snoring beside me. I wanted to think, to make sense of this strange legend and all that I'd heard that night, but my thoughts were tumbling quickly into nonsense. In no time, sleep had me tight in its coils.

· · ·

I'M FALLING AGAIN *through swirling colours – purple like the mountains, green like the pine trees, red like fire. Then the colours form into a stampede of galloping horses, running circles around me so that I am inside a cyclone of colour. They get faster and faster until all the colours blur together. Then at last the swirling settles, and I am standing in a meadow, knee deep in tall grass.*

A beautiful Cherokee woman with long skirts and a curtain of black hair down her back is holding her arms out to a baby with thick, black hair. The baby teeters forward on fat little legs and falls into the woman's arms, giggling. The mother scoops up the child and swirls her around, then stops. She looks over her shoulder, right into my eyes. She smiles, as if beckoning me to come forward, so I do. Still holding the baby in one arm, she waves her free hand across the sky, and suddenly a forest appears, its trees covered in a whole rainbow of autumn leaves. Next, she moves her arm up and down in a wave-like motion, and a sparkling, turquoise river appears.

I walk to the water's edge and peer in, but as I look, the water grows dark and murky, then starts bubbling up like hot tar. Before I can back away, a pair of antlers rise up out of the water, followed by a set of blazing red eyes. The giant serpent grows taller and taller, towering over me like a mountain, ready to strike. I have to run, to warn the woman that she and her baby are in danger. But my feet are stuck in mud like concrete. I open my mouth to scream, but no sound comes out. A hiss like oil on a hot frying pan draws my eyes up, up to those vicious, glowing snake eyes. I raise my hands up as it spits black venom from its fangs. This is it. It rears its head back and strikes—

BULLSEYE

I sat up with a gasp. My hands flew automatically over my head to shield against the snake's steel fangs before I realised I was sitting in bed. The droplets running down my temples were not venom spit after all; it was my own sweat. With a shudder, I looked beside me. Imogen was still in a deep, peaceful sleep. I decided on the spot *never* to tell her about the nightmare I'd just had.

The sky was only just starting to glow outside, but I was wide awake now, and not keen to re-enter my dream world. I slid my feet into my pair of soft, deer moccasins — Ulma had set out a pair for both of us along with night-gowns — and borrowed a crocheted throw off the end of the bed to wrap around my shoulders.

A strange sound in the garden drew me to the window. It was a sort of dull thud. It happened again. I touched my nose to the cold glass pane and peered out into the early frosty October morning and saw. A little way off in a grove of birch trees stood Wattie with his back to the house and a bow in hand. He nocked an arrow, took aim and let it fly. Half a second later, the *thud* came again.

Well that was one mystery solved. But already, a dozen other questions had fogged up my head like cobwebs from the moment I'd snapped out of my nightmare. My inner detective was hungry for answers, so I decided to seize the moment and go out to speak to Wattie.

Pulling the shawl tight around my shoulders, I marched across the dewy lawn, sidestepping a pumpkin patch and a chicken coop. Wattie heard me snap a twig underfoot and spun around.

"I hope I didn't wake you, Katie Fire-Hair," he said when he'd spotted me. In his deerskin leggings and a tunic, he looked full Cherokee.

"Oh no, you didn't," I assured him. "I just felt like seeing the sun come up on my first morning in Nickajack."

He nodded and went back to his target practice. I sat on a stump just behind him and watched. He was an impressive shot, I thought, wondering how to start the conversation up again without sounding like I was conducting an interrogation. "It's great news about Crow Feather," I said brightly.

Wattie turned halfway around, his profile scowling. "I wonder who will be attacked next time," he mumbled, then shot another arrow.

"Do you think Terrapin Jo is right? About that stone having something to do with it? ... I mean, do you think it really was magic?"

He shrugged. "Don't know. But magic or not, that stone has caused more trouble than it's worth." He released another arrow, and it hit the target with a particularly hard ping.

I was worried that if I'd made him angry, that would be the end of our conversation about the Uktena stone, but then Wattie put down his bow and quiver and plopped right down on the wet grass, his deerskin-covered legs sprawled out in front of him. "They don't like to talk about the stone because ... well, it's a long story, and not a very happy one."

"You mean the story about the medicine man who shot the Uktena in the heart?"

He looked surprised. "No, no. That's the legend of the stone. I'm talking about the story that happened just a few years back. About Old Grizzly."

"Old Grizzly?" I asked, confused what a bear had to do with it.

"My father mentioned him. Jim Weaver's his Christian name, but he's always been known as Old Grizzly on account of the scar down his face. A grizzly gave it to him when he was trapping furs out West."

"Oh. So Old Grizzly's the man who stole the stone? The one everybody trusted?"

Wattie nodded, sticking a piece of long grass between his teeth. "That's the one."

"So, this Old Grizzly," I began, trying to piece the story together bit by bit, "he must've believed the stone was magic. Why else would he steal it?"

"That's just it," Wattie answered, his voice rising. "Besides being an honest man – he was like a brother to my father and Terrapin Jo – well, he's just not the type to believe in fanciful stories." He shook his head before adding, "Of course, they *say* he took it for his wife."

"What did his wife want it for?"

"It's all hogswallop," Wattie said, waving his hand dismissively. "They say she was some sort of sorceress and wanted the stone for her magic."

I pulled my legs up under me on the stump and leaned forward. "What kind of magic?" Wattie shrugged. "Don't know. I haven't seen her myself since I was just a runt, and folk don't mention it much around my family because … well, because of Ka-Ti."

"Ka-Ti?" I asked, puzzled by the word.

"Old Grizzly's baby daughter. That is, she's not a baby now; she's practically a woman." I could swear Wattie blushed as he said the last bit. He cleared his throat before going on. "When Old Grizzly was thrown in jail for his treachery, Ramona, his wife, brought Ka-Ti here to us and asked my parents to look after her until Jim got out."

"But why couldn't she look after the baby herself?"

"With all the nasty rumours folk were telling about her, she felt she had to leave Nickajack, but she wanted Ka-Ti raised among her people. Among the Cherokee."

"Wait a second." I held up my hands, needing to rewind. "Old Grizzly's wife – Ramona – she's a Cherokee?"

Wattie nodded, but he was looking at me curiously. "What of it?"

"Oh, nothing," I answered casually, but my head was stewing over all this information. The image from my dream flashed into memory of the Cherokee woman and the toddler … it had been a little girl. "So what happened to Ka-Ti?" I asked.

"We grew up together, she and I," he said with a happy, far-off look. "Then, three years later, Old Grizzly was let out of prison. My mother wanted to keep Ka-Ti with us, but my father remembered the promise they'd made to Ramona and gave her back to her father. He could never come back to Cherokee Country after what he'd been accused of, so he took Ka-Ti away to the mountains."

"Oh." I was beginning to understand why the story was so difficult for Wattie's family to recall. "Then, you never saw her again?"

To my surprise, Wattie grinned. "Well yes, I've seen her. And Old Grizzly too." He lowered his voice as if about to tell me a secret. "In fact, I go to visit Ka-Ti every couple of weeks and take a bundle of goods to them from the shop."

"But you just said—"

"I said Old Grizzly isn't allowed in Cherokee Country, but he didn't go far. After all, his wife wanted him to raise Ka-Ti near her people. He built a cabin up in Raccoon Mountain, just over yonder, across the Tennessee River. It's about halfway between here and Hiwassee Garrison."

The image of the Cherokee woman and the baby played across my mind again just as a crisp breeze rustled through the birch trees. I shivered. "Whatever happened to Ramona? Didn't she ever come back?"

Wattie pushed himself up and brushed the wet leaves off his backside. He shook his head. "Old Grizzly won't talk about her, but my mother reckons she travelled west to sell her trade. She was a painter, you see."

I thought I'd swallowed my tongue. Wattie rushed over and patted me on the back as I leaned over choking.

"Are you all right, Katie Fire-Hair?"

"Fine," I sputtered, wiping my watering eyes on the corner of my shawl, meanwhile trying to think of how to ask my next, burning question. "Exactly what *kind* of paintings did Ramona do... I mean, were they anything ... out of the ordinary?"

Wattie scratched his chin. "I can't say, really. She was gifted. I know that much."

I could see I wasn't going to get much more out of Wattie about Ramona. "When do you think you'll visit Ka-Ti again?"

He stepped away and gave me a hard stare, as if deciding whether I could be trusted or not. "Can you keep a secret, Katie Fire-Hair?"

I nodded. He looked very grave, and I wondered what he was about to tell me.

"Grasshopper and I are leaving on a journey tonight. Just after the stomp dance. We're going to Hiwassee Garrison to tell the Governor what Lieutenant Lovegood's been up to. We'll have to break the journey, and Raccoon Mountain is halfway to Hiwassee."

"But your father said—"

"My father wants me to grow up to be a white man, go off to a university in New England and forget who I am. Well I'm a Cherokee of Nickajack, and I intend to stand up to Lovegood and anyone else who thinks they can bully us off our land." In a fury, he picked up his bow, strung an arrow and let it loose.

"But," I hesitated, not wanting to sound cowardly, "are

you sure it's a good idea? Going off like that against your father's orders?"

He gave me a stern look, probably wondering if he'd made a mistake telling me his secret.

"I won't tell," I assured him.

He took a deep breath and blew it out. "You needn't worry, Katie Fire-Hair. I travel for my father's trade all the time. I know the route backward and forward. Besides, Grasshopper and I are nearly men. That makes us responsible for what happens to this village. The decision is made. We're going." With pursed lips, he turned back towards his target.

After a minute of feverish thought, I scrambled off the stump to stand beside him. I couldn't let this moment pass. There was something in this story about Old Grizzly that *had* to be important. Magic and paint in the same place could *not* be all a coincidence. "Couldn't we come with you, Imogen and I?"

He didn't even give the idea a thought before shaking his head. "No, Katie Fire-Hair. But I've been thinking about it, and I will ask in Hiwassee Garrison if anyone's heard of your uncle, Tom Tippery. It may be he has travelled through that way." He started to string another arrow.

"But that's all the more reason that we should come with you! If we *do* find our uncle, then we'll be on our way. And anyway, we should be with you when you see the Governor. We are, after all, the only two people who saw exactly what happened to Crow Feather. We can testify!"

I watched as he seemed to be chewing over my arguments.

"And," I added for good measure, "I'd really like to speak with Ka-Ti."

I was surprised to see the frown on his face. "You can't speak with her," he said flatly before nocking the next arrow.

"Why not?"

He sighed and dropped the bow. "Because Ka-Ti doesn't speak."

I looked at him dumbly. "You mean she's shy?"

"Well, there's that. She doesn't meet many strangers. But I mean she doesn't speak at all. She's mute. Has been since her mother left. Of course," a grin began to play at the corner of his lips again, "she has her own way of talking."

"How?" I asked.

"She speaks in pictures. Draws, paints. sometimes she used to scratch out her thoughts in the riverbank. It takes getting used to, but once you do, it's … well, it's like seeing things you never imagined before." His eyes were glowing, but with one glance in my direction, he went pink and began to fiddle with his arrow's fletching.

I sat silently for a minute feeling more strongly than ever that I *had* to meet Ka-Ti. There were answers wrapped up in this strange, sad story, I just knew it. "Wattie," I said, breaking the silence at last. "Please let us come with you. We can help, and I'd still like to meet Ka-Ti, even if she can't speak in words. *Please*."

He clenched and unclenched his jaw as he thought. I felt sure he was about to say yes. Then, to my frustration, he shook his head. "I'm sorry, Katie Fire-Hair. I admire your courage, but it's just too dangerous. You saw what the forest is like. Bandits, outlaws…" He shrugged apologetically before letting another arrow fly.

I was far from giving up that easily. "If it's all that dangerous, why don't you teach me to shoot a bow? That way I can defend myself."

Wattie looked sideways at me as if to see if I was joking. "Girls don't shoot bows."

"Sure they do. Plenty of girls shoot bows in the movies … I mean… uh…"

"Movies?" Wattie frowned.

I scrambled around for a cover-up. "What I meant was, if I *moved* to England, I'd be sure to learn how to shoot a bow. All the girls there do it."

Wattie took his aim. "I don't mean any disrespect, Katie Fire-Hair, but you're not in England. You're in Cherokee Country. And to the Cherokee, this is a warrior's weapon." He gave his bow a loving look. "The warrior doesn't just learn to shoot. He earns his bow by practicing, first with a blowgun." From a tall woven basket nearby, Wattie took a long piece of river cane and a small hide pouch. "If you wish to shoot, start with this."

I looked at the blowgun uncertainly. It was nearly as long as I was tall. "How do I shoot it?"

"Like this." Wattie took what I guessed was a dart from the pouch. One end was fletched with something feathery and soft, the other end was sharply pointed. He fed the dart into one end of the blowgun, held it up to his mouth, breathed in, and gave a mighty puff of air. I didn't even see the dart until it landed with a *thud* in the target.

"But that takes years of practice." He handed me the

cane and the pouch. "Just see how far you can get the dart."

I took them, a wild idea forming in my mind. "If I hit the bullseye, will you take Imogen and me with you to Hiwassee Garrison?"

Wattie smirked, then gave me an appraising look. "Ok," he said at last. "You hit the bullseye – *on your first shot* – and I'll take you along."

"And Imogen," I added.

"Of course. We wouldn't leave your cousin the Skunk behind."

"all right then." Pretending more confidence that I felt, I did exactly what I'd seen Wattie do, loading the little dart into the pipe, and holding the end up to my mouth with both hands. I took a deep, steadying breath, fixed my eyes on the bullseye, and blew the biggest burst of air I could muster.

I don't know who was more shocked, me or Wattie, when the very next second, my dart appeared smack dab inside the red circle. Both of our mouths fell open as we gawked at the bullseye. I'd actually done it! Before Wattie could find his voice, I pulled myself together, handed him back the blowgun, and said, as if hitting the bullseye was all in a day's work, "Well, I guess I'd better go tell Imogen we'll be off tonight."

LITTLE BEAVER'S HELP

*T*he sun was only just fully up and already I'd managed to find out a little more about the mysterious Uktena Stone *and* persuade Wattie to take us along on his journey. Now all I had to do was get Imogen on board. *How hard could that be?* I thought, trying to keep up my optimistic streak.

I found Imogen apparently just waking up, sitting crossedlegged in bed with her forehead in her hands. She peered blearily from under her hand at me and groaned. "I was sure it would all turn out to be just a terrible dream," she croaked.

"'Fraid not," I said, plopping down on the bed. "But I think I *may* have some good news."

She dropped her hands, leaving her hair in a wild mess. "*PLEASE* tell me you've found a way home."

"Well not exactly that," I began. But before I could say another word, the wild-looking Imogen growled and started rummaging in the folds of the quilt.

"Where is it? Oh my gosh, where is it?" she shrieked,

looking wilder still, now on all fours, scrambling up and down the bed.

"Where's what?"

She sat back on her heels and looked at me like I was as thick as a brick. "My phone! It was right here all night, right beside my head!"

"We've been over this, Imogen," I answered grumpily, but tossing the pillows aside to appease her. "Your phone is useless here."

"It doesn't matter!" she said in a high voice, her head popping up from the side of the bed where she'd been searching the floor. "Katie, don't you get it? That phone is the only thing I have from home. It's got my entire life on it. All my photos, all my texts from Poppy and ... and Mum and Dad." She sank back down onto the downy mattress. "I don't care if it works here. It's going to work when we go back, and I need to have it with me when we do."

I stared at Imogen. She looked much younger, hunched over like that, wearing an oversized nightgown. "I *do* get it," I said finally. The truth was, though I still thought Imogen's phone obsession was a bit pathetic, I really did know how she felt, desperate to cling to any little piece of home. I had felt that way last time about my little Sherlock Holmes book that Charlie had given me. It had been my lucky charm while I was stuck in the past ... a reminder of the people I loved back home ... a tiny little spark of hope that I would get back to them somehow.

I reached out my hand, feeling awkward, and touched Imogen's shoulder. "We'll find your phone. Don't worry."

She sniffed. "Well it's not here. Somebody must've taken it in the night."

Just at that moment, a little giggle from behind made us swivel around. Little Beaver's grinning face disappeared behind the door in a flash.

"Immy, do you think maybe Little Beaver...?"

Imogen had had the same thought. She was on her feet and out the door in a flash. I followed, thinking we'd have bigger fish to fry if any of the adults discovered the mobile phone before we did. Explaining it would require some *serious* creativity.

We chased Little Beaver down the hall where she dashed into the kitchen. Someone – probably Ulma or the maid – was busy inside.

"Wait," I said, gesturing to Imogen to be quiet. Next minute, Little Beaver reappeared in the hall carrying some strange contraption. She held it up proudly to show us. I could have laughed. It was Imogen's phone all right, but it was acting as a chair. The little girl had tied a cornhusk baby doll to it with a piece of twine. Imogen held out her hands to Little Beaver, but the little girl spun on her bare feet and ran for the door at the end of the hall, waving us to follow before she disappeared.

We tiptoed passed the kitchen, then broke into a run, just managing to avoid a collision with the maid who was coming through the door with a basket full of linens.

"Sorry!" I called over my shoulder as I followed the pursuit across the lawn. Imogen was gaining on Little Beaver, but as the little girl raced towards the trees, the ground became pebbly, and Imogen, who hadn't bothered to put on shoes, was forced to pick her way slowly and painfully across the rocks. "Ow!" She winced. "How does she do that?"

I had my moccasins on and was able to keep up a bit better, but Little Beaver seemed not even to notice the rocks beneath her little feet. She reached the edge of a stream, flashed a smiled at us, then squatted down beside the water. "Oh no," I muttered. So that was her game – Imogen's phone would be the doll's canoe. She was going to drop it into the water.

Imogen must have had the same realisation. "Stop! Little Beaver, NO!" she howled, pushing past me. Little Beaver recognised the word "no"; she stopped and looked around a little uncertainly. That gave Imogen just enough time to reach the bank and snatch the phone, doll and all, out of a surprised Little Beaver's hands. I caught up just in time to hear Imogen's exuberant "Yes!" But Little Beaver's face was quickly changing from shocked to traumatised. As Imogen hugged the phone, the little girl dropped into a squat and started to bawl.

Imogen froze. "Oh great. Now what do I do?"

"Give her the doll back," I urged her.

She quickly ripped the piece of twine off to free the doll from the phone and held it out in front of Little Beaver. She stopped crying long enough to look up at Imogen with terror in her eyes, then burst into a second wave of tears.

"She's going to wake up the whole village!" Imogen said, looking at me desperately. "Wait, I have an idea." She bent down beside Little Beaver and got the little girl's attention. Then, holding out a strand of her hair, she said slowly, "Little Beaver, would you like to play with my hair?" She mimed pulling a comb through her hair and nodded, smiling. Little Beaver seemed to understand. A wide smile broke out on her tear-stained face and she nodded enthusiastically. Next minute, she had Imogen by the hand, dragging her back across the river rocks towards the house.

Once Little Beaver had installed Imogen back in the bedroom, she ran off and came right back with a comb and a little clay pot and happily set to work on Imogen's hair. I didn't take any chances but dove straight into telling Imogen about my conversation with Wattie that morning.

"So the plan is," I said, finally getting to it, "we leave tonight, just after the Stomp Dance."

Imogen's head was bobbing up and down with each stroke of Little Beaver's comb. "So... you're saying you think we should follow the trail of this snake stone thing," she made a disgusted face, "because that's somehow going to lead us to a way home?"

"I think it could lead us to the answer. If we could get that stone back to Nickajack, maybe it would help the Cherokees."

Imogen grimaced as Little Beaver yanked. "And if we can't?"

"Well then we can at least testify to the Governor about what we saw. We're the only witnesses, after all. It might make all the difference."

"Who cares if we make a difference, Katie? We just need to get home."

"I just have a feeling—" I began, but Imogen cut me off.

"A feeling worth risking our lives for?"

"A feeling," I continued, "that helping this village may be the reason we're here."

Imogen rolled her eyes. "What do you mean, the *reason*? It's not like we're *supposed* to be here. It was an accident, *obviously*."

"Maybe it wasn't," I argued, wishing I could have a go at yanking Imogen's hair. "Last time, at Otterly Manor, I thought it was an accident, but Tom Tippery said I was there for a purpose … to help Sophia."

"Katie," Imogen paused. She looked thoughtful, like she was chewing over what I'd said. At last she said, "That's probably the dumbest thing I've ever heard. Stop trying to be the hero, would you? Tom Tipp-a-thingy probably told you that to make you feel better."

I clenched my fists at my side, forcing my voice to stay calm. "Well whether he did or didn't, if I hadn't tried to help, I'd never have found him, and I'd probably still be there now. So maybe," I drew a deep breath and let it out, "maybe if we try to help now, it will lead us to a way home."

"I'm still not convinced. I think we should stay here where it's safe until we have something *real* to go by."

"Wattie's going," I said, quickly changing tactics. "You said you thought he was cute."

"Not cute enough to risk my life for."

"Fine," I said, giving up. "You can stay here and play with—" I stopped. I had just noticed Little Beaver dipping her hand into the pot and rubbing some kind of white paste in Imogen's hair. "What's that she's putting in your hair?"

Imogen reached up and touched her head, then pulled

her hand away and looked at a glob of goo on her fingers. She gagged. "Little Beaver," her voice quavered. She twisted around to look the little girl in the eye and pointed to the clay pot. "What. Is. This?" she asked, emphasising every word.

I was surprised when Little Beaver answered in a perfect imitation of Imogen, emphasising each of her words with a nod of her head. "Bear. Fat."

Imogen froze. I was afraid for a second that she was going to explode at the poor little girl again. Thankfully, she just turned back with her lips pursed tight together as if she were trying not to be sick. After a second, she took a deep breath. "Fine," she said in a defeated voice. "I'll go with you." Then, with her usual feistiness, added, "But Katie, don't you dare get us killed."

13

STOMP DANCE

*T*he sun was setting with a spectacular show of colours as we set off with Wattie's family for the stomp dance. Mr. McKay had gone off hours earlier along with Terrapin Jo to meet with the Chief and other council members, but Grasshopper and his mother, Ulma's sister, had come to help carry the baskets of food Ulma had spent the day preparing.

As Wattie hitched the horses to an old wooden wagon and helped his mother and aunt onto the driver's bench, Grasshopper sneaked up behind Imogen and me with his usual knack for not making any noise. We both jumped.

"Gosh. Could you give some kind of warning before you just appear?" Imogen said in a huff.

Grasshopper, who seemed in a very good mood, grinned and replied, "You mean like this?" He cupped his hands over his mouth and made a loud, high-pitched bird call.

Imogen covered her ears and moved away, scowling at him. "Just 'hello' or 'excuse me' would work just fine."

Grasshopper sidled over to her and leaned in so the women in the wagon couldn't hear. "What's wrong, Dilli? You are not looking forward to our journey together?"

"*Don't* call me that," Imogen snapped. Her scowl turned on Wattie who was offering his hand to help her into the wagon. Ignoring his hand, she muttered over her shoulder to me, "I can still change my mind, you know," then hoisted herself up onto the bench beside Little Beaver. I climbed up beside her, balancing a basket of hot *selu* cakes – the corn cakes we'd had the night before – and a clay dish of dumpling-like bean fry bread, fresh from the skillet and still steaming. Little Beaver reached across Imogen and snatched a sticky dumpling in her chubby little hand.

"Please don't put that in my hair," Imogen said, watching the little girl out the corner of her eye as she happily nibbled on the doughy lump. "It took me half the day with my head under the ice cold water pump to get that bear grease out."

I could see Imogen was in a mood. I would have to be careful or she really *might* change her mind. "You know the boys were just having a laugh," I said lightly. "It's probably because they secretly really like you."

She rolled her eyes, but I thought I detected just a hint of a smile on the corner of her mouth. I'd just have to keep her smiling a little longer. The plan was that we would break away from the stomp dance about midnight, while the others were still in the thick of the festivities. Just a few hours to go. In the meantime, I wanted to take in every aspect of life in Cherokee Country.

As we rumbled down the dirt road in the wagon, I

became fascinated by the sights and smells of Nickajack. Families were coming out of their cabins, weighed down with baskets and pots of their own, joining the procession winding its way down the road. Excited children whooped at their friends and ran ahead of their mothers, who walked nimbly and gracefully in their long, beaded skirts. But it was the men who stood out, dressed for the special occasion in their colourful tunics and wampum belts. Some of them wore turbans like Terrapin Jo, but others' heads were shaved except for a long braid or painted feathers on the crest of their scalps. Many had painted their faces with red and black war paint and wore all kinds of silver jewelry, nose rings and earrings. If I'd met men looking like that in the forest, I'd have run for my life. But here in friendly Nickajack, I thought they were simply fascinating.

Many people waved to Ulma and her sister as we rode past, then craned to get a good look at Imogen and me in the back seat, clearly as fascinated by two strange white girls as I was by them.

We arrived at a great open meadow at the end of the village, between a sea of cornstalks on one side and bluish mountains lined in gold from the sunset on the other, and followed Ulma to drop off our bundles on some trestle tables already piled with food.

"Let's see if we can find Wattie and Grasshopper," I said into Imogen's ear, then fell in among the jostling and happy chatter.

A large group of people were gathered together, evidently watching something. "Ooh, this must be the stickball game!" I said, pushing forward to the front of the crowd. "Wattie said he and Grasshopper were playing."

We finally wormed our way to the front of the crowd, then quickly stumbled back again as a stampede of shouting men and boys came hurtling towards us like a runaway train. Wattie was in front, sweaty and shirtless and holding up what looked like a wooden lacrosse stick. He had the ball!

He dodged his attackers with the agility of a jackrabbit, then spotted Grasshopper, who was waving his arms wildly halfway down the field, open for the pass. Wattie cocked back with the stick and let the ball fly, and not a second too soon. A millisecond later, Wattie was pig piled by a herd of some very large, very fierce looking men. But the tactic had worked! Grasshopper caught the ball in his own basket and shot off down the field unopposed as the other team were still scrambling to get up from the pile. His gangly legs moved in a blur right to the end of the field where he slowed, drew his stick back behind his head, then catapulted the ball through the air where it pinged off of a wooden fish at the top of a pole. The crowd went wild.

The excitement was catching, and I found myself jumping up and down.

Imogen, who, I'd heard, was something of a star on her school lacrosse team, was having none of it. With her arms crossed over her chest and a superior look on her face, she leaned over. "They must be joking if they think they're playing lacrosse. They've just completely ignored about six different rules of the game. They should just leave it to the English to do it properly."

"Actually," I said, feeling a little indignant, "my dad told me the Native Americans invented it. The English just nicked it and changed the name."

Imogen looked cross and grumbled, "Well, they're certainly not playing it *right*. I could give them a few pointers. For example—"

But before she got the chance to give any examples, the game was over, and we were being swept along with the moving crowd.

"Where is everyone going?" Imogen shouted over the excited murmur.

I stood on my tiptoes to get a better look ahead. "I see Wattie's family! Come on."

Mr. McKay spotted us and waved us over. "Ah, there you are, lasses. I've saved you seats with our clan." He escorted us over to a wooden structure covering several rows of benches where Ulma, her sister and Little Beaver welcomed us. The rest of the crowd too were finding seats in structures like ours all along the outside of a big square of smooth, red dirt. "This is the Stomp Ground," Mr. McKay explained. "And that there," he pointed to a smoking mound in the middle of the dirt square, "is the sacred fire."

Imogen raised an eyebrow. "What's so sacred about it?"

"Don't you know?" Mr. McKay looked excited by the opportunity to impart some cultural knowledge. "The Cherokee are the People of the Fire. The Sacred Fire must never be allowed to go out. As long as it burns, there's hope for the Cherokee."

"Which is why Katie Fire-Hair is a welcome visitor!"

Wattie added as he and Grasshopper slid onto the bench in front of me. They were still red faced and sweaty, but at least they'd put on their tunics and belts. "Come along, Katie Fire-Hair. You can be my partner for the quail dance."

"And Dilli can be mine," Grasshopper offered, wiggling his eyebrows at Imogen as if to tempt her.

Imogen leaned away and made a sarcastic sound. "Um, thanks, but I don't *do* quail dancing." But Ulma was already bent over and lifting the hem of Imogen's skirt, strapping a pair of turtle shells to her shins.

"No, really, I don't…" Imogen tried to protest, but an eager Little Beaver already had her by the hand and was tugging her up on her feet and off towards the Stomp Ground.

Imogen gave me a pleading look over her shoulder. I smiled and waved as Ulma fitted turtle shells to my shins.

She nodded. "Now you dance, Katie Fire-Hair."

With every step towards the dance ground, the beans in the turtle shells under my skirt made a rattling sound. The sound echoed around the square as more girls and women fell in line to dance. Then a man standing in the middle beside the fire mound raised a hide drum in one hand and started to beat it with a stick in the other. Keeping a steady beat, he raised his mouth and started to sing: "Wo hi ye hi ye, Wo hi ye hi." Someone in the men's line gave an ear-splitting shout which was echoed by everyone on the dance floor, and the quail dance began.

As I joined in, shuffling my feet backward and forward and waving my arms like chicken wings, I thought of the prim, graceful dances I'd learned last summer for the

King's Banquet at Otterly Manor. *If only the French dance master could see me now,"* I thought with a laugh. Cherokee dancing was certainly *not* graceful. It was wild and wonderful. All the dancers whooped and laughed and looked to be having the time of their lives. I glanced over at Imogen and could hardly believe my eyes. Her smile was nearly as big as Little Beaver's as they flapped their wings together, laughing.

After the quail dance came the bear dance, then the buffalo dance and the corn dance, where the men circled outside of the women and tossed corn cobs into our aprons. It was such great fun, no one seemed to notice the sun go down and the great, yellow full moon rise up.

Nobody even noticed the three men on horseback until they rode right into the middle of the Stomp Ground. Then the music stopped. Everyone moved back, clear of the panting, stomping horses, and several women screamed and ran to find their children. I grabbed Little Beaver's hand and Imogen took the other as we pressed against the frightened people, every one of them gazing up at the proud figure sitting high on a grey steed.

14

FLIGHT TO THE RIVER

*T*he spell was broken. For a little while, I, like everyone else at the Stomp Dance, had forgotten Nickajack's troubles. Now here they were, standing right in front of us in the shape of Lieutenant Lovegood and a couple of backup officers.

"I've come with an announcement from Governor Blunt," Lovegood shouted out in a voice that suggested he had better things to do.

Somebody pushed me from behind, and I looked up to see Wattie with a look that could curdle milk on his face. He was pushing his way towards Lovegood.

"No, Wattie, don't," I whispered and grabbed his arm. I'd seen just how reckless that cold-hearted man could be.

He yanked his arm out of my grip without a word, but the next second another hand reached over my shoulder and caught Wattie's arm in a much tighter hold. Mr. McKay shook his head at his son, then walked calmly into the clearing to face Lovegood. I could hear Wattie breathe as he stewed beside me.

"Lieutenant," Mr. McKay's voice was casual and welcoming. "So good of you to stop by for our little gathering. To what do we owe the honour?"

Lovegood looked annoyed to have to repeat himself. "As I said, I have an announcement from Hiwassee Garrison."

Mr. McKay, still smiling good-naturedly, replied in an almost apologetic tone, "I'm sure you're merely acting out of misinformation, but I should tell you this is not really the time or place. You see, you're trampling on sacred ground here. Unintentionally, I'm sure," he added.

Lovegood just smirked. "What better time and place could there be? The Governor wants the whole village to hear this."

Mr. McKay tried again. "Why don't we go to the Council House? We can discuss the Governor's message there. After all, it's customary for the Chief and the Council to hear it first."

"No time, McKay," was the flat answer. He moved his horse forward, forcing Mr. McKay to step out of the way. "Listen," Lovegood shouted to the crowd once again. "The Governor has heard of your troubles here in Nickajack. He wants to help."

Wattie and I exchanged a look as a hopeful-sounding murmur went through the crowd. But he and I were both thinking the same thing. What on earth was Lovegood playing at?

"Governor Blunt has applied to the President," the lieutenant continued, "and can guarantee that the United States will grant five acres of land in a settlement on the

Western Frontier to any man who wishes to sell his property here and move."

The murmur rose and became anxious.

"This land is our home!" someone called out.

"Why should we move?" asked another person.

"Yes. Why should we?" This time it was Terrapin Jo who spoke. He stepped into the firelight to face Lovegood beside Mr. McKay. "You were sent by Washington to keep lawbreakers out of Cherokee Country. Why should we leave our homes because you have not done your job?"

Lovegood just stared at Terrapin Jo a moment, then his mouth curled into the same sneering smirk. How I wanted to smack that stupid smile off his face. To my surprise, Imogen made a snarling sound to my other side. Apparently, she felt the same urge.

"And you think none of that lawbreaking is done by the Cherokee?" Lovegood leaned over his knee and lowered his voice so only those close enough could hear. "As long as you people are here, there will always be trouble."

Terrapin Jo's expression remained hard as a rock. "No, Lieutenant. As long as *you* are here, we will have trouble."

Lovegood leaned back in the saddle, smiling as if he'd just heard a joke. "I'd like to see you prove that," he said, almost chuckling.

"My son Crow Feather is proof enough."

For the first time, Lovegood's arrogant smile faltered and a shadow of fear crossed his face as he mouthed the name *Crow Feather*. Then, inexplicably, his narrowed eyes shifted about and landed on me. My heart leapt, but I forced myself *not* to look away. His cold blue eyes bored into mine — he looked as though he was trying to recall a memory – then, as if the moment had never happened, he snapped out of the staring contest as his smile returned. Taking the reins of his horse, he called out once more over the crowd. "You have three days to consider the Governor's gracious offer. If you choose not to accept it, you'll have to live with the consequences." He raised his white-gloved hands up by his face. "My hands are clean." And with that, he gave his giant steed a nudge and, with his two cronies behind him, galloped off into the night.

"We should have told the village," Wattie said angrily as his father turned back to our huddle amidst the now jostling crowd. "Then we might have taken him on, right here and now. We could've ended it tonight."

"No, son." Mr. McKay's friendly manner had vanished. He looked dangerously angry as he raised his finger in Wattie's face. "That is *not* how we do things. We will act according to the law. Do you understand?"

Wattie looked away, fuming, and gave one short nod.

"I have to speak to the Chief," Mr. McKay said, and scooping up Little Beaver, he disappeared into the crowd.

Wattie watched him go, then turned back to Imogen, Grasshopper and me. "We leave now," he said.

Grasshopper nodded, then disappeared.

"Where's *he* going?" Imogen asked.

"To ready the canoe. We'll meet him at the river. First, we need to get some supplies from my father's store."

"Are you sure about this?" I asked. As much as I wanted to go, I was beginning to worry our plans could cause a real rift between Wattie and his father.

Wattie looked at me with his eyebrows furrowed in

an intense glare. "You heard Lovegood. Who knows what he's planning in three days' time? We won't stop him by waiting around while the Council has more meetings."

I nodded. "In that case, lead on."

The chaos caused by Lovegood's unwelcome announcement made it easy to wind our way through the crowd and slip off unnoticed across the meadow, that is, once Imogen and I shed our turtle shell rattles. Wattie stayed low and ran almost silently down the dirt road while Imogen and I did our best to imitate.

The sight of the Lieutenant seemed to have fired Imogen up about our journey to Hiwassee Garrison. She kept up a whispered tirade behind me: "That *jerk*... the *nerve* to show his face here... *not* get away with this... *so* unfair!" To my surprise, Imogen's every word expressed how I felt about it. Sure, I'd read about things like this in history class – native Americans forced to leave their homes unfairly and all. But now it was happening to *real* people ... people we'd danced and laughed with ... the McKays and Grasshopper's family. For once, I felt Imogen had the right of it: Lovegood *had* to be stopped.

"*Stop!*"

I halted so suddenly that Imogen rammed into the back of me. Apparently, we'd both been so caught up in our thoughts, we hadn't even noticed Wattie leave the road. He waved from behind a row of bushes growing up beside a cabin with a swinging sign hanging from the porch that read Trade Store followed by some swirling Cherokee letters.

Once we'd crouched down behind the hedge, Wattie

gave orders. "I'll go first and unlock the door, then whistle once for you to follow."

"Ok," I whispered. A second later, the whistle came, and Imogen and I tiptoed up the steps to the porch and darted through the shop door. Wattie closed it quietly, then spun around, his eyes bright in the moonlight beaming through the window.

"Katie Fire-Hair, with me. Dilli, stand guard at the window and watch to see if anyone's coming down the road."

Imogen rolled her eyes, but did as she was told without even complaining about the nickname.

I followed Wattie around a long counter covered in furs and fabrics. He took a piece of some kind of animal hide and threw it out flat on the floor. "Put the things on that." He nodded towards the hide, then started rummaging through barrels, baskets and crates along the shelves that lined the store's back wall, handing me the oddest assortment of things, from gunpowder to hollowed gourds. "Oh yes, I almost forgot." He reached under the counter and pulled out a narrow, woven basket, about the length of a soda bottle, and offered it to me.

"What is it?" I asked, taking the basket from him and holding it up to the moonlight to appreciate the red and green zig-zag designs woven around its middle.

"It was my first dart quiver. My mother made it for me when I was just learning to shoot."

"She made it?" I said impressed. "It's really lovely."

"The blowgun's inside. Only a small one, but useful. It's yours now, sharp shooter."

I looked up, not knowing quite what to say. "Mine? But … I couldn't …"

He grinned crookedly. "'Course you can. I've moved on to bigger guns." He patted the rifle sling on his chest. "I bequeath it to you as your teacher. You've earned it."

I smiled. "Well then, you'd better show me how to use it properly."

He took the basket from my sweaty hands. "You sling it over your shoulder, like so." He looped the strap over my head and I situated it across my chest, feeling somehow taller with the quiver on my back.

"You'll make a good warrior, Katie Fire-Hair," he said with a sharp nod.

Before I could thank him for the gift, Imogen gasped. "Oh my gosh, it's *him*. No, it's both of them!"

"Who?" Wattie and I asked in unison, both dropping everything and hurrying over to the window. The window had a view of the road and the thicket on the other side of the road where an unmistakable officer sitting on an unmistakable grey horse was having a conversation with an enormously tall, broad-shouldered Cherokee man. If the size of him wasn't giveaway enough, his long, black hair and the glinting tomahawk dangling from his belt brought the terrible memory back sharp as a knife edge. The man who'd come out of the shadows in the cave. Black Fox.

15

THE FOX AND THE STONE

*W*e kept throwing glances over our shoulders as we followed Wattie through the village, across some vegetable patches and into a dense forest of cornstalks. Only when we were deep into the maze of tall, swaying stalks did I feel I could breathe again. Wattie wound his way through the rows and rows of corn, following a path only he could see, and at last brought us out onto a river bank.

Grasshopper was waiting at the water's edge beside a long canoe that looked more like half a hollowed-out log. He greeted us with a low bird call. "What took so long?"

"Ambushed," Wattie said, and explained how we'd watched Lovegood and Black Fox from the shop window until we were certain they'd gone and the coast was clear. "You know Black Fox," Wattie added. "He can make himself invisible when he wants to."

That thought sent a shiver down my spine, and Imogen started casting her eyes around frantically.

"He didn't follow us," Wattie said reassuringly. "But best not to linger here and give him the chance."

He and Grasshopper loaded the rolled-up tarp into the canoe, then grabbed hold of its sides and pushed it into the water. Wattie kept a foot on the stern, keeping it steady. "You navigate first," he said to Grasshopper, clearly waiting for his cousin to climb into the canoe. But Grasshopper didn't budge.

"I have to stay in Nickajack," he said at last, his eyes falling to his feet.

Wattie looked taken aback. "I don't understand. We agreed to do this together … for Crow Feather."

"That is just it," Grasshopper said, sounding sorrowful but determined. "With Crow Feather hurt, my father has no one to help him. He was once a great warrior, but now he grows old. He cannot bring in the harvest and defend our home on his own."

The two cousins stared at each other for a moment, both with a look of stern determination on their brows. At last, Wattie held out his hand, and they clasped arms. Wattie spoke up first. "Look after them and my family too. Tell my mother and father not to worry."

Grasshopper nodded solemnly, then turned to me and Imogen. "Tell the Governor what you saw. Get justice for Crow Feather. For all of us. I believe you have come to Nickajack for this purpose."

His words hit me like a punch in the stomach. "Do you really think so?" I asked, wanting desperately to believe him.

Grasshopper gave me a crooked smile, which made him look younger and less stern, and pointed to my head.

"It is a sign, Katie Fire-Hair. As long as the fire burns, there is hope for the Cherokee." Next he turned to Imogen. "And that goes for Dilli also."

Imogen rolled her eyes, but only half-heartedly. "Tell Little Beaver I said goodbye," she said. "And ..." – she seemed to be struggling with herself – "tell her I hope I see her again soon."

Once again, Grasshopper nodded. "*Donadagohu'I*," he said.

"Until we meet again," Wattie answered.

We watched as the sea of cornstalks swallowed Grasshopper. Then I climbed into the canoe followed by Imogen, and at last Wattie waded out and climbed into the stern.

"Without Grasshopper, we will all need to paddle," he said, indicating the short-handled paddles in the canoe's keel between us. I handed one to Imogen, then situated myself so I was sitting on my shins, and followed Wattie's lead as he dipped his paddle into the dark water.

We didn't talk, just paddled, watching the shore. I could tell Wattie was feeling deflated about Grasshopper staying behind. I could only guess what Imogen might be thinking. I could hardly believe what she'd said – that she hoped to see Little Beaver again. I was sure she'd wanted nothing more than to leave Cherokee Country far behind and get back to her own world. Was it possible she was actually worried about what might happen to these people?

My own mind was churning with a dozen questions about Lovegood and Black Fox and what awaited us down the river. I kept coming back to what Grasshopper had said, that we were here for a purpose. I didn't know if my red hair had anything to do with it, but I hoped deep down that it was true, that this journey would lead us to the reason we'd come, and then home.

I was startled from my thoughts when the canoe suddenly lurched forward. The water was moving more quickly. The river was getting wider, and up ahead something jutted out across the water with a little, glowing light at the end of it.

Wattie pulled in his paddle and twisted around in his seat. "It's the ferry crossing up ahead, where this river runs into the Tennessee. Those waters are too treacherous to navigate by night. We'll just crawl past the ferry, then bank for the night, just over there in those trees." He pointed to the distant shore.

As we drifted silently closer to the ferry, I could make out the silhouette of the ferryman in the light of his lantern, leaned against a rope barrel. As we edged past, all was quiet except the river lapping against the pier and the ferryman's snores that carried across the water.

Once clear of the ferry, we put our paddles back in and steered to shore. Once we'd pulled the canoe up on land, Wattie collected up some of the bundles from the keel and threw us each a rolled-up piece of animal hide. "Here. For sleeping on."

"Thanks," I said.

Imogen was looking at the furry bundle miserably. "I will never complain about having to sleep in a tent *ever* again."

I sat on my mat and watched Wattie work away at trying to start a fire with just a couple of sticks and a little ball of kindling. Neither Imogen nor I spoke while he spindled a stick between his hands, his face screwed up concentrating. Then finally, a little ribbon of smoke appeared. He wrapped the smoking embers into the ball of kindling, held it to his lips, then blew on it gently. After what seemed like a lot of blowing, the first flicker of flame shot out, and in no time, we had a full-grown fire to warm us. Wattie leaned back on his elbow, admiring his work and looking very pleased with himself.

I didn't give him much time to bask in his success. There were too many questions that needed answering. "So what do you think they were talking about? Lovegood and Black Fox?"

Wattie frowned. "Maybe they were arguing?"

Imogen and I looked at each other with raised eyebrows. "They definitely weren't arguing," she said. "Did you hear raised voices?"

"I agree. It looked more like conspiring." Imogen nodded. "But that doesn't make any sense," I said. "If Black Fox hates white settlers, why would he conspire with Lovegood, the biggest bully of them all?"

Wattie squinted into the flames as if he was looking for answers. "I don't know."

"Why does he hate white people so much anyway?" Imogen asked, pulling her bear skin tight around her shoulders so she looked like some sort of very strange forest animal. "What did they ever do to him?"

Wattie kept his eyes on the fire. "I don't rightly know, but I have heard rumours ..."

"What rumours?" I asked when it seemed like Wattie wouldn't continue.

"Some years ago, Black Fox joined with the Chicka-maugas on a raiding campaign on some settlements a little further west on the frontier. They say he came back with innocent blood on his hands, and not a drop of shame. In fact, he and a band of young warriors who ran with him thought Black Fox should be the next Principal Chief. They claimed the old chief was being too soft on the settlers, and Black Fox thought he could do a better job."

"What happened?" I asked, horrified at the idea of that menacing man leading the Cherokees.

Wattie shrugged. "Their plan was found out, and the Council put a stop to it."

I had to be missing something. "But why is he still allowed to stay in Cherokee Country, after all that?"

Wattie considered the question. "He had a lot of supporters who thought he had the right idea. So the Chief forgave him and gave him a seat on the Council. I guess he thought that way Black Fox could speak his mind rather than getting into mischief. You know what they say: Keep your friends close and your enemies closes."

I felt the last thing I'd ever want to do was keep Black Fox close.

"And then there's the other thing," Wattie added.

"What other thing?" I asked, watching him chew on a twig.

"The Chief would've had a hard time getting rid of Black Fox because of his family. His great grandfather was the most powerful medicine man who ever lived, Agan-uni'tsi."

My mouth dropped open. "Wait, you mean *the* Agan-uni'tsi who killed the Uktena and took the stone?"

Imogen groaned. "Oh Katie, you are *such* a nerd. You two can stay up having geek chat. I'm going to sleep."

I ignored her and got up on my knees to have a better view of Wattie over the fire.

"That's the one," he answered. "Black Fox always wanted the stone. Thought it belonged to him, along with all the power that came with it. Some say if the stone hadn't disappeared when it did, Black Fox would've killed for it. Then there would've been no stopping him from rallying followers who would make him their Chief."

"But it's so unfair! Old Grizzly might've saved the day by stealing that stone before Black Fox could get to it. Black Fox is the one who should be banished from Cherokee Country, not Jim Weaver."

Wattie smirked. "I wouldn't bring it up with Old Grizzly when you meet him. He doesn't talk about what happened. Not to anyone."

"Why not? Doesn't he want to tell his side of the story?"

Wattie shrugged again. "I guess it's too painful. Some speculate that the reason Ramona ran away with the stone was to save her husband's life. Otherwise, Black Fox would hunt the man who had his precious stone, no end."

"Do you think Ka-Ti is safe?"

"It's been eight years, and Black Fox hasn't tried anything yet. I reckon that means Ramona's plan worked."

I stared at Wattie, letting this new information sink in.

"I told you that stone was more trouble than it's worth," he said, stretching out on his mat. "Well, best be getting some sleep. It's a long leg of river tomorrow."

Imogen gave a muffled groan. "I'm not going to get a

wink of sleep on this piece of fur." But in less than a minute, I could hear her snores over the crackling fire.

I stared into the fire, thinking. Here was the Uktena stone again, rearing its head like the giant serpent in my dream. It had to be a piece to the puzzle, but how? But there were more urgent questions that needed answering now. What could Lieutenant Lovegood and Black Fox possibly be plotting together? Only one thing was sure. Whatever it was, it couldn't be good news for Nickajack.

16

MUDDY WATERS

a hand gently shook my shoulder. I opened one eye to see Wattie's face hovering above me.

"Are you awake, Katie Fire-Hair?"

I opened my other eye and blinked. Above Wattie and the treetops, the sky was a pale pink. "I'm awake," I croaked, sitting up and taking in the pile of ashes from last night's fire and Imogen lying sprawled out on her mat with her mouth hanging wide open.

"I'll let you wake Dilli," Wattie said, eyeing Imogen warily.

"I thought you were supposed to be the brave warrior," I joked.

Wattie gave a quick, flat laugh. "Not that brave."

It took some doing, but I finally managed to shake Imogen conscious. She started with a snort, then moaned, "But I've hardly slept at all."

I caught Wattie's eye, and we both stifled a laugh.

Once Imogen was up, we rolled up our mats, munched down some bean bread that Wattie had pinched from the kitchen when his mother wasn't looking and were pushing the canoe down the bank within minutes.

"I don't know how much more of this my bum can take. It's already aching," Imogen complained as she teetered into the boat and settled herself down on her bottom.

I had to admit, the dugout canoe wasn't exactly designed for comfort. I knelt on my knees to begin with until they got sore, then transferred to my backside 'til it got sore, then carried on switching between the two. But in spite of my sore knees and numb bottom, all burdens seemed to lift off my shoulders in those first glorious moments on the river. As the sun rose and sparkled on the water and a flock of geese flew overhead, I felt convinced that, after horseback riding and dancing, canoeing down a river through woods and mountains must be the most wonderful experience in the world.

NONE of us spoke for the first while, all either lost in our own thoughts or just too exhausted after the little sleep we'd gotten the night before. But that suited me just fine. All I wanted to do was look and listen and feel the movement of the canoe, sliding silkily through the moving water.

The waking wilderness was putting on a breathtaking performance. A great blue heron stalking fish in the rushes lurched himself into the air, spread his enormous wings, and swooped across the canoe before taking to the sky. A little way down as we turned a bend, a duo of beavers flapped their tails against the river and disappeared beneath their dam. A shower of canary yellow poplar leaves swirled on a gust of wind, then drifted down onto the water's surface like confetti. Meanwhile, a redheaded woodpecker drilled into a dead pine tree on the bank.

I breathed it all in and felt a smile bubbling up my whole body. I could just imagine if my dad were there. He'd say "Isn't this just paradise?" and I would have to agree that it was.

Before long, though, I had to turn my full attention to manning the canoe. Just as Wattie had said it would, the smaller river we had come up soon joined up with the much wider, much muddier Tennessee River. We stayed close to the shore, avoiding the rough open water, but that meant constantly having to paddle around fallen logs or pieces of rock jutting out from the shore. It took so much concentration, I completely lost track of time, so it came as a surprise when my stomach made a loud grumble and Wattie announced it was time to stop for midday rations.

We dragged the canoe up a pebbly bank and found a flat, sunny rock to stretch out on. Wattie unwrapped packs of venison jerky and corn cakes which we all attacked like a pack of starving wolves.

"How much further to Old Grizzly's place?" I asked, ripping off a piece of venison jerky in my teeth.

"We've covered about half the distance," Wattie answered cheerfully, as if this was *good* news.

"Half?" Imogen gaped at him. "We've been canoeing for absolutely *ages*. How do you people stand such long journeys?"

Wattie chewed a mouthful of corncake, looking

thoughtful. He swallowed. "I suppose we tell stories to pass the time."

"Go on, then," I said, feeling much happier now my stomach was full. "Tell us one."

Wattie looked bashful. "It's Grasshopper you want. He's the storyteller, not me."

"Well Grasshopper's not here, is he?" Imogen said insistently.

"Very well." Wattie leaned over on his elbows and peered out over the river with his eyes narrowed, as if he were looking for something far off in the distance. "You see that place, just a stone's throw further down the river, where the rocks form a sort of bowl?"

Imogen and I both craned our necks. "I see it," I said. "Where the bowl makes a sort of whirlpool?"

"That's it. Well," Wattie continued, "that whirlpool is the home of Dakwa, a giant fish whose appetite is as enormous as he is. So large is Dakwa, it is said he can throw over a canoe of warriors and swallow them whole." He went on to describe several of the monster's skirmishes with some Cherokee warrior or other who'd brought back to his village tales of its viciousness.

Imogen waited until he'd finished, then rolled her eyes. "Rubbish," she said, leaning back on her hands to bask in the sunlight. "Surely nobody actually believes that stuff?"

Wattie raised one of his thick, black eyebrows. "Plenty of people do. Perhaps in tame England, no more monsters remain. But Cherokee Country has been untouched since the beginning of time. You never know what you may f—"

He was interrupted by a scream so loud it sent a flock of roosting blackbirds squawking from the branches overhead. With the speed of a squirrel chased by a fox, Imogen had flown to her feet and darted behind Wattie for protection. She was pointing near the place she'd just been sitting, where water collected in a dip in the rock. "There's some kind of monster *right THERE!*" she squealed.

Wattie courageously approached the place Imogen had indicated. Straddling the little pool, he bent down, flipped over a rock and made a sudden lunge.

"It's got him! Oh my gosh, OH MY GOSH!" Imogen screamed.

But the next second, Wattie was standing up with a triumphant grin across his face, and holding tightly with both hands what looked at first like a large, slimy catfish with legs. He held the creature up for Imogen to see.

"What. Is. That. THING?" She sounded as if she was going to be sick.

"In Cherokee, we call him *menopoma*, but you can call him hellbender or a mud puppy. It's all the same to him." Wattie leapt nimbly over the rocks to where Imogen watched with her hands now over her mouth. She squeezed her eyes tight shut, but Wattie seemed determined to make peace between her and the disgruntled beast.

"Nothing to worry about. He doesn't have a tooth to his name. See for yourself." He held the slimy, wriggling creature right up to Imogen's face. She opened one eye and, finding herself nose to nose with the mud puppy, gave a shriek and sprang backwards, toppling over Wattie's water gourd. "Ow!" she cried, landing splat on her backside on the rock.

I ran over to give Imogen a hand up. Wattie stood

paralysed looking shocked and guilty, still holding the now thrashing mud puppy.

"I think that thing wants its freedom," I said over my shoulder as I hauled Imogen back to her feet.

"Of course," he said, snapping into action and, to my relief, returning the mud puppy to its water hole where it promptly wriggled itself back under a stone away from all the prying eyes.

"Ow!" Imogen suddenly stumbled forward and grabbed my arm for support. She was wincing and holding up her right foot. Through her gritted teeth, she said, "I think I sprained my ankle."

I looked at Wattie, who looked guiltier still. "I told you I shouldn't try to tell stories."

17

ON TOP OF RACCOON MOUNTAIN

*B*y the time we banked the canoe again that evening, Imogen's ankle had swollen to twice its normal size and had taken on a deep purple hue. Wattie, anxious to make up for the accident that he felt was his fault, did everything he could to help. He cut strips of hide from his own sleeping mat and tied them with twine like a bandage around the sprain, then chopped pieces of wood to make a crutch.

I couldn't help feeling that Imogen was enjoying the extra attention. She was certainly being nicer to Wattie then she had been the whole trip.

I, on the other hand, was getting worried. With Imogen having to sit back with one foot propped up in the canoe, it had taken us much longer to arrive at the base of Raccoon Mountain than it should've. The sun was sinking fast, and the Tennessee River had brought us to wilder country now. The river narrowed into a ravine between steep, woodsy mountains, and one peak in particular stuck its head up above the rest: Raccoon Mountain. Hiking up there to meet Old Grizzly would not be a walk in the park, especially in the dark. And then there was the problem of Imogen's ankle. However good she was at sports, there was no way she was getting up that mountain on one leg.

Wattie left Imogen to try out her new crutch and came up beside me. I was expecting him to say that with Imogen injured, we'd have to push on to Hiwassee Garrison and forget about going up the mountain. But I couldn't afford to lose my chance of meeting Old Grizzly and his daughter.

For reasons I still didn't fully understand myself, I knew this meeting was extremely important... that I was *meant* to speak to them. I'd had that feeling ever since that strange dream, and nothing could shake it off. But how was I supposed to explain that to Wattie? I was already searching for an answer when he opened his mouth.

"Ready to climb up?"

I was caught off guard. "But Imogen—"

"She'll have to stay behind, of course."

A sudden image of Black Fox running off with Imogen over his shoulder flashed into my mind. "Will she be safe here by herself?"

Wattie was trying to choose his words carefully before answering. "I do not think it would be wise to leave her on her own for long. But I think we could risk just long enough for me to show you to Old Grizzly's cabin. Then I can run back down to Imogen while you speak to him."

My stomach lurched. I'd always imagined meeting Old Grizzly with Wattie and Imogen at my side. But if this was the only way... I took a deep breath.

Wattie must've seen the nerves on my face. "Don't

worry, Katie Fire-Hair," Wattie said with a reassuring smile. "Jim Weaver might be an old grizzly, but I don't reckon he's got any claws."

I breathed out and tried to smile back. Wattie was right – what was I so worried about? I had been all alone when I'd faced the Queen of England and her Court last summer. What was an old mountain man after that, even if he was a convicted criminal? "I'll be fine," I agreed.

But Imogen was not fine with being left behind while Wattie guided me up the mountain.

"Why do you even want to meet this mountain man again?" She was sitting against a fallen log with her swollen foot propped up on a pile of furs, a crumbly pile of *selu* cake in her lap.

"It's hard to explain," I said, bending over to take one of the sticky balls.

She pulled her hands away out of my reach. "Well you better come back with something good, Katie. If I get attacked by some wild animal all for nothing …"

"You won't get attacked. Wattie will only be gone an hour. And here," I unslung the strap over my shoulder and handed her the little basket quiver. "You can keep my blowgun while we're gone."

She eyed it suspiciously. "Like *that's* gonna help against a grizzly bear."

"There are no grizzly bears in these mountains," Wattie called up from the bank below where he was filling up several gourds at the water's edge. "Except for the one who lives in a cabin at the top of *this* mountain. But you're right." Wattie grabbed the gourds by their ropes and leapt up the shoals. "Those darts will only protect you against a vicious rabbit ... maybe a squirrel if you're a quick shot."

Imogen gave me a snotty look that meant, "I told you so."

"Unless...", diving into his knapsack, he came up a second later with a little drawstring bag. From the bag, he took a small, silver vial.

"What on earth?" Imogen asked impatiently.

"It's snake venom."

"Oh my gosh," she exclaimed, dropping the remainder of a corn cake into her lap as she covered her mouth with her hands.

"Is it for the darts?" I asked.

He nodded. "We Cherokee never use poison darts, but my father got this on a trading expedition to South America. I've never tried it, but they say it will tranquilise a full-grown wildcat for up to an hour."

He knelt down and offered the little bottle to Imogen. "If you're in *real* danger, just dip the end of the dart into the venom ... and be sure not to touch it to your lips."

"I'm not touching that at all," Imogen said, looking away from the bottle as if were something offensive. "I'll just take my chances." She handed me back the quiver and crossed her arms over her chest.

"Here, Katie Fire-Hair," Wattie held out the vial. "You keep it, just in case."

I tucked the little bottle into the pouch hanging from my belt. "Hopefully I'll never have to use it," I said, patting the pouch.

Wattie nodded, then cupped his hand over his eyes and looked up at the sun's position in the sky. "We'd better get going. It'd be terribly easy to lose the trail if you try coming down in the dark." He slung the strap of his rifle over his shoulder.

I gulped, but tried to sound upbeat as we said goodbye to a grumpy Imogen and started up the trail.

The path wound its way up the mountain through dense, evergreen forest, trickling streams and soaring, lichen-covered boulders. Crows cawed overhead and we crossed paths with a few deer, but, thankfully, we didn't encounter another living soul all the long hike up.

"Nearly to the lookout now," Wattie announced as the path turned suddenly very steep, and we were forced to climb with hands and feet over boulders to reach the flat rock surface jutting out above. At the lookout, Wattie used a bandana to mop the curly hair off his sweaty brow, then took a great gulp from his water gourd.

When I finally got to the place he was standing at the edge of a jutting out rock, gazing out at the fast setting sun, he handed me the gourd. I eagerly accepted it, letting several long gulps flow over my parched throat.

"Can you go on, Katie Fire-Hair? We haven't much time before the sun sets."

I would have given my biggest riding trophy to sit down and rest at that moment, but I took one more swig of water and answered, "Yea, let's go."

It took my full effort to keep up with Wattie to the top of the mountain. He hardly seemed to break a sweat, but my legs ached and my chest was on fire before he finally stopped at the bottom of a stone stairway carved into the mountainside.

"Old Grizzly's lodge is just at the top of these stairs. I'll take you to the door. Remember, you've only got about an hour to get back before sunset. With these clouds moving in, I wouldn't put too much store in making it down by moonlight."

"An hour should do it," I said, doing my best to sound confident, but feeling my heart skip a beat at the thought of being alone with the mountain man.

With my last ounce of strength, I pushed myself up to the top step and stopped in my tracks, my breath catching in my chest. I could never have imagined the scene in front of me. It was almost like something from a fairy tale. The mountain top clearing, though not particularly big, was a world all of its own, all the more magical for its loneliness. The setting sun lit up the leafy yellow and orange canopy so that it felt like being inside a golden, glowing lantern. A stone path had been laid from the stone stair to a little log cabin which sat on a rock outcrop right at the mountain's edge with a sweeping view of the valley below. From a distance back, it looked as if it had been built on the very edge of the world.

Wattie led me up the path and onto the porch where, besides the usual baskets and drying herbs, there were hung rustic pipes and wind chimes made of river cane. As the breeze passed through them, some jangled together, making a woody, tinkling melody, while others, like pan flutes, whispered soft, breathy notes. I was so mesmerised by the dreamlike feeling of the place, I forgot for a moment to feel frightened … until Wattie knocked on the door. The sound made my stomach jump and start dancing to the jangling chimes.

What felt like a long moment later, soft footsteps

approached the other side of the door. It opened just a crack, just enough for two enormous, long-lashed dark eyes to peer out. They landed on Wattie and sparkled. The next instant, the door was swung wide open and a girl with silk black hair down to her waist had thrown her arms around Wattie's neck. He hugged her back like a long lost friend, and I knew this was Ka-Ti.

I don't know what I had expected a girl raised by a mountain man to look like, but it certainly wasn't anything close to reality. She must have been only a couple of years older than I was, but Ka-Ti was as beautiful a girl as I'd ever seen, even in books or films. If the mountain top was a scene from a fairy tale, she was the perfect fairy princess. She made even her simple white cotton dress look like a princess's gown.

Wattie spoke to her in Cherokee, and I heard him speak my name. Suddenly both sets of eyes turned towards me, and I realised I'd been gawking. Ka-Ti didn't seem to notice. Her whole face lit up in a smile that matched the golden sunset, as if she'd been longing to see me. She reached out and grabbed my hand, the way Sophia had done when we first met, as if we were old friends.

I glanced at Wattie, who looked bemused by Ka-Ti's familiar behaviour towards me. "Well, I'll be going. If you're not back in an hour, I'll know to come looking for you, Katie Fire-Hair." His eyes quickly moved back to Ka-Ti, and he dipped his head in a gentlemanly bow before turning to go.

Ka-Ti closed the door behind us and walked—though it looked more like dancing—across the room on bare feet to a hearth where a kettle hung over a small, crackling fire.

Bending over the hearth, she looked back and gestured to a thick, woolly rug on the floor in the shape of a bearskin.

I made my way to the rug slowly, taking in the cabin's interior as I went. It was just one room with a rough wooden table near the hearth, one low, lumpy bed in the back corner and a ladder leading up to a loft. All sorts of tools, weapons and rope hung from pegs on the walls, and a long-barrelled gun hung over the fireplace mantel. It was dark and warm, and the room had an earthy, smoky smell.

But there was magic within the walls of this cabin as well as outside of it. Every surface had been painted in deep, vibrant colours—the chair legs, the wood-slat walls and support beams, even parts of the floor. There were vines, flowers, birds, a river of colourful fish... I looked up. There was even a blue sky with swirling clouds painted on the ceiling. A shaft of sunlight spilled through an open window and brought to life a pair of deer painted on the opposite wall above the table.

I sat on the hairy rug, unable to stop staring at the painted world all around me, until Ka-Ti handed me a mug of hot, sweet-smelling tea.

She folded her legs beneath her on the rug beside me and took a sip of her own cup.

"Blueberry?" I asked, inhaling a breath of fruity, sweet steam.

She nodded.

I waved a finger around the room and asked, "Who painted all of these?" Then, remembering Wattie had said to ask only "yes" or "no" questions, quickly said, "I mean, your mother was a painter, right?"

She smiled and nodded, but I thought her smile seemed a little sad.

Not wanting to upset her, I changed the subject. "I'm Katie, by the way. Our names are almost the same."

She nodded again and pointed to a painting on the wall above the fireplace where a blue and orange bird sat on a tree branch with a pointy beak.

"Is that a Kingfisher?" I asked. "Oh, is that what your name means? Ka-Ti means Kingfisher?"

She looked pleased that I'd understood. I glanced again at the bird, and something caught my eye on the mantelpiece just below it—a small picture frame with a brownish-tinted photograph inside—but I couldn't quite make out who the subject was.

Ka-Ti must've noticed me squinting at the little frame because she got up and went to the mantel for it. Kneeling down once again, she held it out for me to see.

With a sharp breath, I took the frame from Ka-Ti's hand. One look had sent a shiver travelling up my whole body, making the hair stand up on my arms and scalp. And for the first time, the thought flashed across my mind: *this must be a dream.* How else could I know so well the faces looking back at me of a beautiful Cherokee woman with a plump, black-haired baby in her arms.

"Ramona?" I asked in a whisper. My voice had all but disappeared.

Ka-Ti was watching me with a look of intense interest. How I wished she could speak! I had so many questions for her, I didn't know where to start. I opened my mouth, waiting for my voice to return. But before a single word was out, the door was flung open. I swung around and my eyes met a bear-sized man filling the doorway. He was dressed head to toe in deerskin and wore a rifle slung over his shoulder, a long knife on his belt and in his fist, he held a rope from which dangled two dead rabbits.

His face was shaded by his broad hat brim, but I could just make out the claw-mark scar down the left side of his face and see the firelight reflected in his deep-set eyes. With a gulp, I realised those eyes were fixed like a predator's on me. He didn't so much as blink as he took two heavy steps nearer. "Kingfisher, hadn't you best be gittin' down to that spring 'n fetch some water fer supper?"

Without a moment's hesitation, Ka-Ti stood up, took a bucket from the hearth and disappeared through the open door, leaving me alone and shivering, face-to-face with Old Grizzly.

18

THE GRIZZLY AND THE GIFT

*W*as it the floor shaking under his treetrunk-like legs as he stepped closer, or was it me? Whichever it was, I didn't dare move at first, not until he was so close that he hulked over me and I was looking right up into his face. His eyes frowned at me down his long, crooked nose.

Old Grizzly bent down so his face was right beside mine. My heart thumped loudly. I could smell tobacco on his bushy, greying beard. I wanted to close my eyes. Holding his gaze felt threatening, like looking an angry bear in the eye; somehow *not* looking felt more dangerous.

Without a word, he reached out a big, rough hand and took the picture frame I didn't even realise I was still clutching. Standing up, he thudded over to the hearth and set the frame gently back on the mantelpiece.

"Wattie knows I don't like visitors," he mumbled under his breath. Then, with his leather-covered back still turned towards me, he asked, "Who are ya, anyway?"

"I'm—" My mouth had gone dry. I gulped and tried

again. "I'm Katie. Katie Watson. I'm a friend of Wattie's. He thought you might be able to help me."

Old Grizzly turned to face me, his bushy eyebrows furrowed. His jaw twitched from side to side, as if he were chewing something. "Help you with what?"

I got to my feet, feeling I'd rather look those stern eyes straight on than from down on the floor. "I just wanted to ask… I thought you might …" I searched desperately for words. Now face to face with Old Grizzly, I couldn't bring myself to mention the stone or Ramona. Wattie had warned me to avoid those topics, and I was beginning to see his point. Desperate for something to say, I made a wild leap. "I'm looking for my uncle, Tom Tippery. He's a painter, and I thought you might—"

"Never heard of him," he growled before I could even finish. Then stomping to the door, he jerked it open. "Now you can tell Wattie we don't need no more company. Not even little girls."

I stayed frozen where I stood, shocked. I'd hardly gotten a word in, and I was being chucked out! I swallowed, trying to think of something, anything I could say. Deciding this might be my one and only chance, I took a deep breath and spoke. "I wanted to ask you about the stone."

The look on his face told me I had made a terrible mistake.

When he next spoke, his voice had a low, dangerous growl. "Get outta my house." There was nothing to do but obey. Stiffly, I hurried out the open door and felt it slam behind me. I didn't stop until I'd reached the top of the stone stairs.

Ka-Ti was just coming up them with her pail of water propped on one shoulder. Our eyes met for just a moment. I tried very hard to smile, but I couldn't hide the terror on my face. She looked truly sorry, perhaps because of her father's unkindness; but I wondered if partly she was sorry to see me go because she would be left all alone again with nobody but her grumbling old grizzly of a father for company.

"Kingfisher!" came the growling voice from the cabin. Ka-Ti dropped her eyes, walking quickly past me to the house without another glance. Old Grizzly didn't spare another glance either. He ducked inside and shut the door again, leaving me standing there alone in the shadows.

The mountain top had lost its magic now that the sun had dipped below the distant hills. It was cold, dark and lonely. An owl hooted somewhere off in the trees, and a bat narrowly missed my head as it dived after an insect. And I just stood there, too bewildered to move at first and fighting the lump that had grown in my throat. I bit my lip, determined not to let the mountain man's rudeness get the better of me.

I wished Wattie were there to guide me back down the now shadowy mountain path. But I would work out the way on my own. Taking my chances was better than risking Old Grizzly coming out to find me standing there crying. I could just picture him raising his rifle and giving me the count of ten to get off his property.

My tired legs smarting, I took the first three steps down and froze, listening. Had I heard another pair of footsteps, or had I imagined it?

Those were footsteps without a doubt. I scrambled

back up the stairs and found Ka-Ti waiting at the top of them. Her eyes kept darting over her shoulder towards the cabin as if she was afraid her father might be watching.

"I'm sorry I caused you trouble," I said, not sure what else to say.

Ka-Ti shook her head vigorously as if to say it wasn't my fault. She spared one more glance at the cabin, then took a rectangular package bundled up in cloth from behind her back and offered it to me.

"For me?" I asked, and she smiled. "Thank you." I took the package and held it tight to my chest. "I hope to see you again, Ka-Ti."

She reached out her hand and squeezed my arm, smiled the saddest smile I'd ever seen, then turned and ran back to the cabin.

"Katie Fire-Hair? Is that you?"

With a rush of relief, I looked up to see Wattie looking back at me as I stumbled into the clearing at the bottom of the mountain. I had got back down the trail on my own, but the shadows were growing longer by the minute, and my legs, still shaking from my encounter with Old Grizzly, were threatening to give up on me.

"Why have you come down so soon?" It was nice to hear the concern in Wattie's voice after being barked at by the mountain man.

"Turns out Old Grizzly has claws after all," I said, and told him the whole story as we picked our way across the shoals toward Imogen.

As he listened, he rubbed his forehead and looked thoroughly put out. When I'd finished, he looked downright angry. "Well that's some way to treat a friend of mine, after all I've done ... I didn't have to trade with him when nobody else would. And maybe I just won't bother anymore." He spoke upwards as if his voice would carry all the way back up to the top of the mountain.

"But what about Ka-Ti?" I reminded him. "You can't stop trading with him. She'll have nobody if you do. She likes you a lot. I can tell."

Even in the dark, I could tell Wattie was blushing. Quickly changing the subject, he pointed to the package pressed under my arm and asked, "What is that?"

"Oh, I almost forgot. It's a gift from Ka-Ti." I stopped, about to unwrap the mystery object when Imogen shouted my name.

"I guess I'd better see what she wants," I said, sticking the package back under my arm. Wattie shrugged and went off in search of more firewood. I took a deep breath. Imogen was not going to take the news well that my mission had failed. I felt a sneaking suspicion that when she found out we were still no closer to finding a way home, she would either blow up or melt down. Either way, I was dreading it.

"So?" Imogen's eyes were wide and fixed on me as I sat down on the log she was using as a backrest, setting Ka-Ti's gift down beside me. "Did you find anything out? Did they know about the painting in the cave, or who brought us here, or how we're supposed to get back?"

I avoided her glaring, expectant eyes by looking down at the blisters on my palms earned from so many hours' paddling and shook my head.

Just as I suspected, Imogen let out a burst of hot, angry air. I didn't have to look. I could easily imagine the murderous look on her face. "I knew it!" She sounded almost happy to have been proven right. "I knew this was all a waste of time. Now what are we supposed—"

"But it wasn't all a waste of time," I interrupted, then quickly dropped my voice as Wattie reappeared at the treeline, close enough to overhear us shouting. "I saw a photograph of Ka-Ti's mother, Ramona, and she *is* the very same woman from my dream. I'm sure of it. But before I could ask any questions about her, Old Grizzly threw me out!"

Imogen glared. "Even if you did somehow see this woman in your dream, so what? Why would she want us to come here for nothing? Face it, Katie. You were wrong. It was just a dream, and it didn't mean anything." She made a growling sound in her throat. "I can't believe I let you drag me out here all because of some stupid dream."

I didn't answer. Whatever Imogen said, I was positive it *had* been Ramona in my dream. It had been more than a dream. It felt so very real … the colours, the meaningful look in her eyes … and the danger had felt as real as anything.

My stomach gave a sudden jolt. I'd almost forgotten about the striking serpent. If the dream *had* been real, if it had been some sort of message, then the serpent must be part of that message too. Was it a warning? I'd been sure in the dream that Ramona wanted me to come nearer, but what if I'd gotten it wrong? What if she'd actually been warning me to stay away from some lurking danger? Something to do with the Uktena … the stone.

There it was again. Somehow that stone linked everything together, but if Old Grizzly refused to speak to me, would I ever be able to work out how?

I didn't have a clue what I was supposed to do now, except to press on with our other mission to see the Governor and pray some answers came up along the way.

I woke up in the middle of the night, sure I'd heard someone call my name. Wattie lay still on the other side of the fire, one hand resting on his rifle. And there was Imogen, curled up against the log and snoring as usual. I was just about to lie back down and pull my furs up close to my chin when my eye caught sight of a large lump on the log. Ka-Ti's gift! I had been so preoccupied with my own thoughts and Imogen's icy attitude that I had completely forgotten about it.

Now, pulling on my moccasins, I tiptoed over to the log as quietly as I could, reached over Imogen for the package, and returned to my mat with it. I untied the bit of twine and peeled back the layers of cloth. Inside was a soft, leather journal, about the size of a photo album and tied with a leather strip. I unfastened it and folded back the leather cover.

I stared motionless at the picture in my lap. Was it my sleepy brain or just the dark making my eyes play tricks on me? Pushing myself up, I walked on my knees closer to the dying fire and held the open journal up to the embers. My hands began to shake as I slumped down onto the ground.

I was wide awake. This was no dream. In my hands

was a painting of a girl sitting on a giant black horse. My shaking hand reached up for the chain around my neck. I prised open the locket. The tiny painting inside showed the same horse. And the girl, well, I'd have known her anywhere. She was me.

19

JOURNEY TO THE GARRISON

*W*hen dawn came, part of me wanted more than anything to hold the painting in front of Imogen's face and say, "What did I tell you?" But I fought back the urge. Instead, I carefully rolled up the painting in its leather wrapping and tucked it safely and secretly away in my quiver.

I needed to work this one out by myself. *I can't tell Wattie, and Imogen wouldn't understand*, I told myself. She'd probably just get stroppy and tell me to march back up that mountain and demand that Old Grizzly tell me everything. The thought of doing that turned my blood to ice. I could just imagine that bear of a man would probably shoot me for trespassing before I got so much as a word in.

I just needed to think ... to make sense of the painting. If Ramona had left Nickajack eight years ago, when could she have painted it? How could she have known about Vagabond ... about me? I'd spent ages the night before examining every inch of the painting for a date or any kind of clues. All I'd found was a tiny, ink kingfisher in the bottom right-hand corner. I guessed it must've been Ramona's signature. She obviously had a thing for the birds, naming her daughter after them.

If I could only speak to Ka-Ti again, I thought. Then I reminded myself, *if she could only speak at all*. But maybe, just maybe with Wattie's help, I could see her in private ... try to get more information about her mother. We'd be coming back past Raccoon Mountain in a couple of days. I'd have time to think of a plan before then.

Meanwhile, we still had our mission to Hiwassee Garrison, and no time to lose if we were to prevent Lovegood from whatever horrible attack he was planning on Nickajack. I'd just have to keep my eyes open for any clues along the way.

I tried hard to feel hopeful as we pushed off in the canoe that morning through a cold, dense mist. The weight of the secret painting was bearing down on me, and Imogen's bad mood certainly wasn't helping. Her spirits had remained in the doldrums all that morning as we packed up camp, her scowl never budging even when Wattie helped her into the canoe and cushioned her foot with furs and sacks.

Though I wasn't making such a show of it, my spirits were feeling pretty stuck in the mud too. I had been so sure I'd find answers, and all I'd come away with were more questions. I felt as though something had been snatched out of my hands; what was more, I had to admit to myself that Imogen and I really were in a pickle now, and it was all up to me to fix it.

The weather matched Imogen's temper all that morning. The fog fell so heavy across the river, sometimes we couldn't even see one another clearly in the canoe, let alone what lay ahead. We were forced to crawl along at such a slow pace that there was no time to stop for rations.

"Was that your stomach or mine?" It was the first time Imogen had spoken to me in hours.

"What?"

She gave an exasperated sigh. "That rumbling. Was it your stomach? Because I for one am starving and I just wondered if other people were too."

"It wasn't mine ... wait a second." I listened and heard a definite low rumbling noise, but it wasn't coming from inside the boat at all. It came from the sky where a mass of black clouds was careening in our direction like a herd of wild horses.

"Um, Wattie?"

He turned and followed my eyes towards the menacing storm headed our way. "Lord, help us," he whispered and started paddling as fast as he could. I stuck in my paddle and tried to keep up. All the while the cloud mass drew nearer, the rumblings louder. We were just a stroke away from the shore when the clouds broke loose. Bullet-hard raindrops pummeled us as lightening flashed across the sky with an ear-splitting *crack*. Wattie was out in the water in a flash, dragging the canoe to shore, throwing all its contents onto the bank, then lifting Imogen out and setting her down in the mud.

"We've got to turn it over!" Wattie shouted over the deafening rainfall.

I followed and grabbed both sides of the canoe. Then, on Wattie's count— 1-2-3! —we lifted it, flipping the bottom up over our heads and sitting down. It felt like being inside a giant's helmet in battle. The canoe was taking a mighty beating, but we were safe.

For a second, we were silent. Then Wattie began to laugh and hoot as if he were enjoying a theme park ride. I found myself smiling and looked over at Imogen. She was hugging her knees in to her chest, sniffling, her teeth chattering. She wiped her face on her wet sleeve, but I could swear more droplets were falling from her eyes. I looked away with a guilty twist in my stomach. Something told me it wasn't the storm that had got to Imogen, but the real and growing fear of never getting home.

The storm passed as quickly as it had sneaked up on us, leaving a muggy mist behind it. Imogen never said a word as we shook the water off our bundles and pushed back off down the steamy river as if nothing had happened.

The mountains soon flattened into meadows, and the river broadened out into marshland. Out of the clearing mist up ahead, an enormous flag on a tall pole was furling and unfurling itself. It had red and white stripes, just like any American flag, but the stars were arranged in a circle instead of in rows against the blue.

"What's that flag doing there?" I asked Wattie.

"It's marking the Garrison," Wattie shouted over his shoulder. And then I saw, getting clearer and clearer as we paddled nearer, the lookout towers and tall tree-post walls rising up out of the fog, and my stomach did a somersault as I realised I was about to meet the Governor dripping wet and covered in mud.

20

A BLUNT AUDIENCE

*W*e did our best to freshen up before approaching the Garrison, scrubbing our faces and arms in the river. Wattie unrolled a bundle of clothes he'd packed especially for meeting the Governor and disappeared with them behind a bunch of shrubs.

"Why didn't we bring a change of clothes?" Imogen moaned. She was leaning on her crutch and looking down with a grimace at her mud-stained, soggy dress. I looked her over and had to admit that she did look terrible. And not just because of the sopping clothes. Her blonde and black hair hung in limp strands around her face which had gone a shade paler than normal. But what really startled me were her eyes. They weren't bored or sarcastic anymore. All the confidence, all the fiery temper had drained out of them. They were just … hollow.

"Are you all right, Immy?" I muttered.

Her hollow eyes looked into mine. "What do you think?" Then she looked away again.

For a fleeting second, I thought about showing her the

painting, then imagined the rant that might follow and decided against it. Instead, I said, "I haven't given up, you know. I'll find a way home."

She made a noise that sounded something between a sigh and a laugh.

Just then, Wattie reappeared in a smart—if slightly damp—suit. He looked much older dressed like that, and suddenly I was feeling a little self-conscious too. "Do you think they'll let us see the Governor dressed like this? I mean, you look fine, but we look like a couple of lost orphans."

He looked at the two of us a moment, biting his lip, then shrugged. "Governor Blunt knows my father. He'll see us, clean clothes or not." He became suddenly sombre. "He has to see us. He has to put a stop to Lovegood today, before that scoundrel descends on Nickajack and starts driving people from their homes."

I knew what he was thinking. None of us had said it, but we each knew painfully well that it had been three days since the Stomp Dance. Today, the people of Nicka-jack would be faced with a decision between remaining in their homes or facing a new onslaught of attacks unless we could put a stop to it first. It was all down to this moment. We *had* to persuade the Governor that Lovegood was a crook, or… I shuddered at the thought of Ulma and Little Beaver shivering in the cold night air as their home went up in flames. "Let's do this," I said with a sudden rush of urgency. "There's no time to lose."

Wattie led us up the bank to the broad road that ran to the Garrison. We had to stick to the muddy side as a steady stream of carriages and men on horses passed us by.

"I've been to the Garrison many times before," Wattie said as a large black carriage pulled by a team of four horses drove past, spraying us with a fine mist of mud. "But I've never seen the road quite so busy."

We soon found out the reason for all the traffic when we arrived at the tall, wood-post gates. Two guards were just pulling them shut and about to drop a heavy cross-beam to lock them.

"Wait a moment!" Wattie shouted, quickening his pace. "We need to enter the Garrison!"

"Name and business?" one of the men in a navy coat and flat black cap demanded.

Wattie cleared his throat. "I'm William McKay. My friends and I are here to speak with Governor Blunt."

The guard didn't move his head, but his eyes scanned each one of us before he answered. "Governor Blunt's a busy man. What matter of business do you wish to discuss with him?"

Wattie's face hardened. "It's an urgent and a private matter, one intended for the Governor's ears only."

The other guard, an older man with a handlebar mous-tache, sauntered up to Wattie. "Now look here, boy. You ain't gonna see the Gov'ner today. He's entertainin' a whole bushel of delegates over from England and don't have time for a bunch of younguns, so you can just be gettin' on your way, you hear?"

"You don't understand." Wattie sounded angry. His face was so close to the guard's that their noses nearly touched.

"I don't think *you* understand," the guard said through his teeth and laid a hand on the gun at his side. I froze, debating whether to jump in or not, when, to my surprise, Imogen took a step forward on her crutch and cleared her throat.

"Listen, you numpties."

All four of us turned to look at her with the same surprise on our faces.

Imogen continued with a roll of her eyes. "We know all about the delegates, *obviously*. I'm the daughter of one of the delegates."

"Which delegate?" the older man demanded with some uncertainty.

Imogen pursed her lips and gave him a withering look. "*Lord* Humphreys is my father. Advisor to the Queen... ahem, I mean the *King* of England," she answered coolly. "Father's busy with all these tiresome delegation meetings, so I decided to go off for a bit of an explore. Only, I injured my leg, as you can see." She raised her bandaged foot a little higher and both guards glanced at it. "Thankfully, I met these kind peasants."

She gestured towards Wattie and me. He and I exchanged a look but didn't dare interrupt.

"If they hadn't mended me up and brought me back, who knows what would've happened to me in this God-forsaken wilderness?" As sudden as a snap, she dropped the pitiful tone and took on a commanding voice. "Now, will you please let us pass? I'm in a lot of pain, and I need to see my father immediately. I'd hate to tell him that the American guards had behaved in an ungentlemanly way."

As if a general had just barked an order at them, both

the guards sprang into action and pushed open the gate. The younger of them doffed his hat as we passed. "Beg your pardon, Miss. We didn't mean any disrespect."

"Hmph," Imogen replied, and with the air of a queen, she stuck her nose in the air and hobbled through the gates with Wattie and me following in her train.

"That was incredible," I whispered once the gates closed behind us. I had to admit it, Imogen's performance deserved an award. In fact, it *had* earned an award: a free pass into the Garrison.

"Mum and Dad sent me to drama camp last summer," she whispered back. "I hated it."

"But at least it paid off," I said.

She shrugged one shoulder and, with a slight smirk, answered, "I never said I wasn't good at it."

Once inside, Wattie took over, leading the way down the middle of a big, rectangular sandy courtyard. Long buildings with many doors ran down the right side. The other side looked much less official. There were greenhouses, a tanner and blacksmith's shop, and... I stopped in front of the farrier, the familiar sound of snorts and stamping hooves grabbing my attention. A tall, grey horse was stamping temperamentally while the farrier tried to get hold of his foot. The farrier was getting nowhere, leaping backwards each and every time the horse stamped. I knew the horse the instant I saw him, tall and proud, just like his rider.

"Wattie," I whispered, and gestured to the horse. "Lovegood's," I mouthed, then glanced around, nervous at the thought that if Lovegood's horse was here, that meant Lovegood himself might be anywhere. At least that meant he wasn't right that minute terrorising Nickajack, but undoubtedly, he'd be on his way soon. And if he found out the three of us were there to spoil his plans...

Shaking off the thought, I turned my attention to where Wattie was taking us. We were passing the stables on our right. Just on our left was a small rock building. Metal bars covered its one small window, and out in front there were wooden stocks with holes for prisoners' heads and hands and dangling chains. I caught up with Wattie and whispered, "Is that the jailhouse where they kept Old Grizzly for three years?"

He glanced left and shook his head. "He did a few nights there, just until they sent him off to a workers' prison."

I grimaced at the thought of spending a night in that cold, stone shed. But just ahead of us was a much nicer sight. We'd reached the very end of the Garrison, which was filled entirely by a big brick house decorated with red, white and blue swags on the windowsills. The enormous American flag swayed above its chimneys.

We passed a man splitting wood and another tending to a flower bed as we reached the elegant stairway that led up to a double door with a brass knocker in the shape of an eagle.

"Is this the Governor's office?" I asked, impressed by just how grand it was. Not exactly the rough, frontier fort I'd imagined.

"It's the Governor's mansion," Wattie corrected. "But it's also the headquarters for the Indian Agency, where most of the delegations between the United States and the Cherokee Nation take place." Wattie smiled, and a look of relief spread across his face. "This is it, Katie Fire-Hair. We've made it, and now we can put everything to rights." And with that, Wattie lifted the eagle and knocked three times.

The door opened and a stout maid with grey curls beneath her little cap stepped out on the landing, her hands folded in front of her stomach like she was about to recite a poem. "Can I help you?" she asked, casting a suspicious glance at Wattie, then grimacing outright at the sight of Imogen's and my mud-spattered clothes.

Wattie again gave his name, and again explained we'd come from Nickajack on urgent business with the Governor. The woman pursed her lips, and Wattie hastily added, "The Governor knows my father, John McKay. He has joined him on several delegation trips to Washington." The woman's expression didn't change, but she told us to wait and closed the door. When it opened again, she smiled and said with a polite nod. "Governor Blunt will see you now."

Wattie and I shared a hopeful look. I was sure we were thinking the same thing. If the Governor was so quick to make time for us, then surely he was the sort of man who would take immediate action to defend Nickajack. Lovegood's game would soon be up.

The maid escorted us down a corridor lined with paintings of military heroes and battle scenes. At the very end of the corridor, she stopped and laid her hand on the shiny doorknob. "Wait here," she ordered, and disappeared through the door.

When she didn't immediately come back, Wattie turned to me. "I'm glad the two of you are here. I feel certain that when Governor Blunt hears your testimony first-hand, he'll believe it."

I gulped. I had imagined my job would be to nod and agree with the story that Wattie told the Governor. I hadn't realised I was to be the spokesperson.

Wattie must've noticed my face fall. "You'll do just fine," he said reassuringly. "Just tell him what you saw that day in the woods."

I nodded, reminding myself of Grasshopper's last words to me— "I believe you have come to Nickajack for this purpose"—and felt courage lift my head a little higher.

Next thing, the door opened and the maid showed us inside a large room. We walked across a soft carpet and stood before a polished wooden desk in front of a picture window hung with yellow satin curtains.

The man at the desk had to push back his chair to stand up. He leaned back to support the weight of his bulging belly and lightly touched the desk with his fingers, posed in just the same way as many of the war heroes and presidential-looking characters in the hall paintings … only the Governor looked more like a prize pumpkin than a war hero. His fluffy grey hair was pulled back in a little pony-tail with a ribbon. His face, like his belly, was round, double-chinned, lit up with a jolly, welcoming smile. I smiled back, wondering what on earth I had been so worried about. There was nothing intimidating about Governor Blunt. After facing Old Grizzly the day before, this felt more like meeting a teddy bear.

"Ah, young Mr. McKay." Governor Blunt held out a

plump, white hand to Wattie, who shook it. "And who might these elegant young ladies be?"

"Miss Katie Watson of the State of Pennsylvania and her cousin from London, Miss Imogen Humphreys. Both guests of my family."

Imogen made a face as the Governor kissed her hand, then took mine. He must have noticed how grim we looked and probably smelled, but he certainly didn't show it.

"And I understand you've travelled all the way from Nickajack to speak to me?" He tutted. "Children, children, rest yourselves!" He showed us to a settee by the fireplace and sat himself down beside us in a spindly chair, then crossed his legs and laced his fingers around one knee. "Now, tell me. What is this urgent business that brings you all this way?"

Wattie cleared his throat and began. "As you'll be aware, sir, the Cherokees in Nickajack and nearby villages have suffered a number of rampages lately. Livestock have been stolen or butchered, crops destroyed ..."

The Governor nodded while Wattie made his list, his fat face sombre with sympathy. "Well do I know of these troubles, son." His voice rose and fell, as if he were reciting a tragic poem. "The woes of Nickajack are the very reason I applied to Washington to issue a cavalry guard." He laid his podgy hand on his heart. "Though my passion for Cherokee wellbeing is boundless, I am just one man and cannot possibly prevent every villainous act of lawlessness within Cherokee borders ... as much as I would like *personally* to see justice done. But you have my word, I will send Lieutenant Lovegood to Nickajack this very day to hunt down the perpetrators and see that they get their full comeuppance."

Wattie and I exchanged a quick glance. This was it. The ball-dropping moment. "I'm afraid, sir, Lieutenant Lovegood isn't interested in setting things to rights."

The Governor looked so taken aback that a third chin appeared above his collar. "Why ever do you say such a thing?"

Wattie took a deep breath. "Because we believe… we know, sir, that Lieutenant Lovegood is behind the attacks on Nickajack. Just days ago, he led a party of horse thieves on the village, then personally struck down my cousin Crow Feather. Miss Watson and Miss Humphreys are eye witnesses. They can tell you just what happened."

Wattie looked to me. "Yes, we saw everything," I began and launched into the story yet again. The Governor listened, leaning back in his chair with his eyes closed, either trying to concentrate on every word or because the news about Lieutenant Lovegood was so distressing, I wasn't sure.

When I'd finished retelling everything that had happened in the woods, Wattie took over again. "I'm afraid it gets worse, sir. Lieutenant Lovegood is using you to carry out his own schemes."

The Governor raised a doughy hand to his lips and whispered, "No."

"Yes," Wattie confirmed. "Just three days ago, he and a couple of officers interrupted a sacred festival and announced that you were giving Nickajack three days to sell our homes or face more attacks. As if those were *your* orders, sir!"

Governor Blunt didn't speak for a long time. He put his fingertips together beneath his chins and gave each of us a long, thoughtful look. At last, some of the jolly smile returned to his face as he spoke. "My dear boy, those *were* my orders."

My mouth dropped open, and at the same time I heard Wattie's chest deflate. We were both speechless.

With a sickly smile, the Governor continued. "Children, children. You are young. You couldn't possibly understand the complexities of government ... the greater picture. I must think of the future posterity of this nation."

"What about *my* nation?" Wattie demanded.

The Governor actually tutted. "I'm thinking of them too. This is for everyone's good. Why would the Cherokees want to risk their own safety and wellbeing by staying here when they could start fresh on a new land? I'm offering to buy their land in exchange for a new life. It's a very generous offer, if you really think about it."

"But it's not an offer," I blurted. "Lovegood made a threat. He said if the people didn't sell their homes, they could expect attacks. That's not giving them any choice."

The Governor raised his hands as if calling for peace. "My dear, you're quite right. Lieutenant Lovegood may have misspoken. I'm sure he didn't mean to make any threats. After all, he is a faithful servant of the Cherokee people. I will speak to him, and I'm sure we can clear up this little misunderstanding."

Imogen spluttered. She'd been silent up 'til now, but apparently she'd heard enough. "Misunderstanding? A servant of the Cherokee people? Whatever!"

The Governor looked startled by her outburst. "I'm... sorry," he stammered.

"Weren't you listening to anything we just said? Love-good *shot at us*." She enunciated each word. "Where I come from, that's called a felony. And besides that, we *saw* him conspiring with Black Fox, so if that's not criminal activity..."

The Governor stood up abruptly. "Black Fox? I'm sure I've never heard of him," he mumbled as he dabbed his forehead with his handkerchief. He seemed almost distracted as he carried on talking very quickly, as if to himself. "Well well... it is very unfortunate. Lovegood must have mistaken you for an animal... a deer perhaps. I will tell him to take more care in future. Now," he said, pulling down his waistcoat that had crept up over his belly, "I'm afraid we must say farewell. I'm very busy, as you can see. Delegates to host. Important business... Very good of you to come all this way." He was pushing us towards the door. "Give my respects to your father, William, and I'm going to have my cook pack up a nice knapsack for your journey home." He patted Wattie on the shoulder with one hand while opening the door with the other. Then, with a little shove, he pushed Wattie into the corridor.

"We don't want a knapsack!" Wattie tried to protest, but the Governor wouldn't hear it.

"It's no trouble at all," he said with a wave of his hand, and next thing we knew, he slammed the door in our faces. A second later, a lock clicked.

We all stared at the door. I glanced at Wattie. His face had gone bright red, and he looked stunned.

I resisted the urge to ask the first question that arose in my mind: *What do we do now?*

Imogen, on the other hand, spoke her mind. "What. A. Jerk. You know, I really do hate this place. I don't know how you stand it, Wattie."

Wattie wasn't listening. With the same stunned expression, he turned away from the door and began to walk slowly back down the corridor. Defeated. For me, the blow was still sinking in. We had failed.

21

THE PEDDLER'S POTION

*W*attie didn't speak as we made our way to the Garrison gates. His shoulders slumped, but a fire still raged in his eyes.

"There must be another way... someone else we can go to," I said, wanting to encourage him. But if there was another way, I sure couldn't see it.

Wattie stopped in his tracks like something had just struck him. He smacked himself on the forehead. "I forgot to ask the Governor if he knew of your uncle. I...I'll go back—"

"It doesn't matter," I said, grabbing his arm and turning him back towards the gate. "He won't let you back in. You saw how desperate he was to get rid of us. And I doubt Blunt has any information about our uncle anyway."

"But you've come all this way to help me, all for nothing. I just can't believe the Governor dismissed us like that," Wattie fumed. "Wait until my father hears—" His face dropped again, as if he would be sick. "How can I face my father? He'll be furious. He forbade me to come here, and now I've crossed him with nothing to show for it. If anything, I've made matters worse."

Before I could think of anything worth saying, Wattie staggered off and slumped down on a wooden barrel near the stables with his head in his hands.

Imogen, who had kept her mouth shut since we'd left the Governor's mansion, couldn't keep her thoughts to herself any longer. "Well, he's right about one thing. This was all an idiotic waste of time. Like the Governor was ever going to believe *our* testimony against the word of his precious Lieutenant."

My face went hot. "Well we couldn't do nothing! Do you really want Lovegood to get away with what he's done to Nickajack?"

Imogen pressed her palms over her eyes. "I don't care. I don't care what happens to anybody. I just want to go home." And without another word, she stormed off as fast as she could go on her crutch towards the gate, leaving me to stand alone in the middle of the Garrison yard.

I looked back at Wattie on his barrel, not sure whether to follow Imogen or hang back. That's when I saw the grey horse at a mounting post outside the stables. Just heaving his leg over the horse's back and sitting up proudly in the saddle was Lieutenant Lovegood.

Lovegood tipped the brim of his hat with the two gold sabres to the groom and turned the horse about. I stood fixed to the ground as horse and rider cantered past. He slowed slightly, and for the briefest moment, I felt his cold gaze. Did I imagine it, or had a sinister smile flashed across his face?

I watched the guards salute Lovegood as he rode out of the Garrison, probably on his way to Nickajack. Once again, everything inside me was screaming and kicking to *do* something. But I could do nothing. *You've failed everyone,* a nasty voice in my head chided. I was no sign of hope. Just a regular, red-headed kid lost in a dangerous world that was too big for me.

THERE WASN'T any point in starting the journey back that evening—the sun was already sinking below the foothills, and none of us had the heart to turn back for Nickajack. Back at the canoe, Wattie put on his Cherokee clothes and strapped his rifle over his shoulder. I could tell he was doing his best to play the part of brave leader.

"If we turn up Chickamauga Creek, just there where it runs off the Tennessee, it'll take us to a Cherokee outpost in about a mile's distance. We can get supplies and make camp there."

Back into the canoe we all climbed, my backside smarting as I lowered it back down into the dugout's rough wooden keel. But in no time, we were banking again in a swampy grove. My moccasins slurped and sunk deep into the mud with each step as we dragged the canoe up the bank. At last we reached higher, dryer ground, and went through the routine of covering the canoe with branches and vines to hide it from any would-be thieves.

"The outpost isn't far, Katie Fire-Hair. You can come with me and bring a basket to gather some hickory nuts or pecans on the way."

Imogen hobbled forward on her crutch and snatched a

basket out of Wattie's hand. "I'm not staying guard again. I'm coming with you."

The pines grew close together as we crunched through the wet straw. The forest smelled musty and had a murky, wild feeling about it. When a loud voice not far ahead of us broke the silence, Imogen and I both started. At first I thought it was someone howling in pain. I picked up my skirt to catch up with Wattie and reached him just as he stepped out of the trees and onto a wide dirt road. Then I saw what had made the howling ... or singing, as it turned out. Two men with their arms draped around each other's necks and bottles swinging in their free hands stumbled out of a log shack, belting at the top of their lungs in different keys. Another man was clumsily hitching up a cart to a mule out in front of the shack, but he leaned back every few seconds to rub his belly and let out an echoing belch. All three looked as though they'd never seen a bathtub in their lives.

Wattie watched the scene across the road with a disapproving look.

"What is this place?" I asked.

"It *was* the outpost," he answered darkly. "Looks like a tavern these days. There's a growing trade in Cherokee Country for liquor. It's brought nothing but trouble to our people." As the three drunken men moved on down the road, Wattie crossed over the road to the shack.

"I'm not going in there." Imogen had caught up with us on the road, but she wasn't budging a step closer to the tavern. "Not if it's full of people like *them*." She gestured towards the singing trio.

Wattie peered around at the trees, then pointed.

"There's an old walnut tree, just there, overhanging the road. Why don't you girls gather up some nuts while I sort out the supplies? Whatever you do, just don't get separated."

With a roll of her eyes, Imogen hobbled off in the direction of the walnut tree. As we filled up our baskets, I stood up sniffing the air. "Do you smell a fire?"

Imogen nodded, and we followed our noses around the tree. Through the bushes was a clearing, and right in the middle of it, the three drunken men were roasting what looked like a squirrel on a spit over a smoky fire. One of the men spotted me through the bare branches and called out, "Hey there, little lady! How'd you like to buy some Indian goods?"

My heart skipped a beat as I realised the three men were getting up.

"Let's get out of here," I whispered hoarsely.

Imogen was peering around the tree now. "What do *they* want?"

"Let's not stick around to find out." I waved her to come faster, but the three men were surprisingly quick considering how poor their balance had been a few minutes earlier. Two of them were on the road between us and the outpost in an instant, the third leading the cart just behind.

A scrawny one with a scraggly blond beard and several missing teeth held up his hands. "Now look here, no need to get yer bonnets in a tangle. We're just poor, humble peddlers. But we got some mighty fine treasures you won't find no place else. Now just you have a look here." He stepped aside to reveal the cart with a flourish of his hands, like a painter revealing his masterpiece. Meanwhile, a short, stocky one chewing on a pipe threw off the canvas that covered what was inside. There was an array of barrels and crates overflowing with the strangest assortment of objects, from raccoon tails to jars of what looked like pickled frog's legs, and many bottles of some kind of clear liquid that I doubted was water.

The man with the blond beard spoke up again. "Now, fer two beeeauteeful young lassies like yerselves, how 'bout some o' these fine Injun beads?" He picked up a basket that was full of ropes of every coloured beads and started stringing his fingers through them. "Wouldn't those look perty on yer little necks?"

I glanced sideways at Imogen, who had clearly seen enough. Her arms were crossed over her chest in a challenging pose. "Look, we don't want your beads or any of your junk."

The man blinked in dumb surprise at her response.

"Unless one of those bottles is filled with magic potion that can take us through time, then we're *not* interested." She pushed right between the salesman and the cart, turning sideways so as not to brush shoulders with the unkempt peddler. I swallowed and followed quickly behind her, the three men gawking silently as if they didn't know what had hit them.

"It's the only way to handle hecklers. With a firm hand. That's what my mum says whenever we go abroad."

"But I can't believe you said that about traveling through time," I whispered.

"Oh, for heaven's sake, Katie. It's not like they understood what I was talking about."

We both turned our heads at the sound of footsteps scurrying up behind us.

"Hey!" It was the voice of the bearded peddler.

Rolling her eyes, Imogen turned around with impatience written all over her face. "WHAT?"

The man stepped closer, glancing side to side, as if he wanted to be sure nobody was listening. "You said yer lookin' for somethin' that'll take ye back in time?" he asked confidentially.

"More like *forward* in time," Imogen grumbled.

"Yea, that."

"But she wasn't serious," I said. But Imogen cut me off.

"Go on."

"Well," the man licked his lips and lowered his voice to a whisper. "I've got what ya need." And he pulled a bottle of some swirling, gold-flaked liquid out of his coat. "It's an old Cherokee secret brew. Real rare. Ain't hardly any of 'em left as know the recipe. I oughtn't to sell it at all, but fer the right price…"

"You can sell your goods to the devil." Imogen and I both whirled around to find Wattie standing right behind us, his dark eyes fixed on the man in a hard stare.

"Look here, young'n. That ain't no way to talk to a God-fearin' man. I was just—"

But Wattie didn't let him finish. "What kind of a God-fearing man tries to swindle young ladies? Now take your counterfeit goods and get off Cherokee land."

The man held up his hands again as if in surrender and walked away.

"It's scum like that who corrupt good trade between the settlers and the Cherokee," Wattie said, shaking his head as he watched the ragtag team of peddlers disappear into the woods. "Secret Cherokee recipes. As if any Cherokee would sell our secrets to the likes of them!"

"We didn't need your help, Wattie," Imogen snapped. "We were handling it fine without you."

Wattie's jaw tightened. Without a word, he hoisted his sack of goods over his shoulder and turned back to the road.

"He was just trying to look out for us," I muttered, shifting the basket of walnuts under my arm.

Imogen didn't answer. She was too busy brooding, although several times she looked back over her shoulder, as if expecting to see someone following us.

22

MISSING

I needed some space from Imogen. This fruitless journey would have been difficult enough without her bad mood, which seemed to get worse by the hour.

"I'll just be cracking the nuts," I said, and snatching up the basket Imogen had dropped beside the fire pit, hurried off to find a quiet place to be alone. I found a couple of hard, flat stones for nut cracking and straddled an old fallen log. It felt good to smash the walnuts between the stones. At least I was taking my frustration out on them rather than on Imogen.

No sooner had the thought entered my head than I heard her walk up behind me. *Couldn't she just give me one moment's peace?*

Imogen stood there waiting for me to stop smashing nuts. I could tell she wanted to say something.

Whack! I brushed another pulverised walnut shell onto the dirt, then looked up.

With a glance towards Wattie who was preparing the

fish he'd caught for dinner, she leaned in. "I say let's go back and find those peddlers."

"What?" I was all ears now and couldn't believe what I was hearing. "You're joking, right?"

"No. Listen to me. This could be our ticket home!"

I hadn't seen Imogen this excited since the time she'd found a Wi-Fi hotspot at a gas station on the way to Tennessee. She was actually serious. And insane. "You heard Wattie. He says they're untrustworthy. They probably shouldn't be on this land—they're not even Cherokee!"

"Of course, we *have* to believe every word Wattie says, don't we?"

"No," I said defensively. "But obviously he knows a lot more than we do about Cherokee Country. That's why *he's* our guide, and we should do what he says."

"You know what I think?" Imogen said, tossing her hair over her shoulder. "I think Wattie just wants what's in it for him. You heard him at the Governor's. He forgot all about us!"

"Never mind Wattie," I argued. "*You* didn't trust those men either. You told them to scram even before Wattie got involved."

"That was before they told us about the time-travel potion."

I sighed. "Even if that *was* really time-travel potion, which I *highly* doubt, we couldn't just leave now, just like that."

Her eyes narrowed. "Why not?"

"Because... because I still think... we're here for a purpose. We've got to find a way to help the people in

Nickajack. They all believe we can do something." The words sounded pathetic as they spilled out of my mouth.

Imogen gave me a look that made me feel like I'd shrunk to half my size. "Good grief, Katie. Isn't it time to grow up? You're not a hero; you're a twelve-year-old girl. You can't change history."

I opened my mouth, but no words came out.

"Besides," she pressed, "once we get back to our own lives, it won't matter what happens to them. They'll all be in the past. Dead."

The word struck me hard, like a punch to the stomach. Imogen had said the very thing I had fought so hard to avoid thinking about for the past four months. Before I could stop them, tears flooded my eyes. I got to my feet, walnuts spilling off my lap in every direction, and exploded. "You are the most horrible, selfish human being I have ever met. You don't care about a single person but yourself. It's no wonder your parents sent you away so they wouldn't have to deal with you."

Imogen's mouth opened. I thought she would shout back, but she just shook her head with a wounded look in her eyes and limped off into the pine grove.

I watched her go, thinking vaguely about the danger that might be lurking among those trees, but my blood was still pounding through my temples with hurt. *Let her look after herself*, I thought, and turned away.

When it came time to bed down, Imogen made a show of picking up the end of her mat and pulling it to the other side of the fire, as far away from me as she could get.

Suit yourself, I thought, pulling the deerskin up over my shoulder and rolling onto my side to face the creek rather than Imogen's back. I could just as easily ignore her as she could me.

I didn't sleep well that night. I dreamed I was tied to a stake. Lieutenant Lovegood, with a smug smile on his stony face, lit the pyre with his torch. But the flames licking my ankles burned icy cold instead of hot. When I looked up from the flames, Imogen was beside me, looking right into my eyes as if begging me for help. With a choked gasp, I sat up, still breathing fast. It had just been a nightmare, not like the dream about Ramona.

It wasn't real, I whispered. Everything was quiet except the burble of the river. There was a soft glow in the lower sky that meant it must be nearly dawn. Smouldering embers were all that remained of the fire. I shivered as the dewy morning air touched my shoulders and pulled the deer skin up under my chin. Reluctantly, my eyes wandered over towards Imogen's mat, off on its own.

She must be freezing, I thought. After all, she'd left all the blankets behind. My stomach lurched. It wasn't so much hunger as my conscience prodding me. I should never have said what I did to Imogen. She might be selfish and spoiled, but she couldn't have known that her words would cut me so deeply. I had no idea that what I said about her parents would hurt her that way. Maybe there *was* more to Imogen's story than what met the eye. Who knew? What I did know was just how frightening it was to be stuck in the past without much hope of a way home. Could I really blame Imogen for being just a bit desperate? For wanting to snatch at the dim ray of hope those peddlers had offered her?

I got to my feet, taking the deerskin with me, and

tiptoed over to Imogen's mat. "Imogen," I whispered, taking a step closer. Something was off. I went right over and looked down. The mat was empty.

Kneeling down, I laid my hand on the mat. There was no warmth at all. She hadn't been in bed for at least several minutes. My eyes darted in every direction. I listened intently for the sound of a crackling pine straw. It was so horribly silent, all except for the voice in my head that told me exactly where she had gone.

23

HANDS TIED

*W*ith the feeling of a stone sinking down into the pit of my stomach, my eyes turned where I hadn't dared to let my thoughts go: down the road to the old walnut tree where we had encountered the peddlers.

Wattie came to my side with a small lantern held above his head. The moment I'd awakened him and told him Imogen was gone, he had sprung into action like a well-trained soldier. He had immediately suggested we each search the road in different directions. Now as we met back at the starting point, he shook his head. "Nothing. You don't think she …?"

With a sickening feeling, I nodded. "Last night she told me she wanted to go back to the peddlers' cart. She wanted … something she thought they had." I paused, trying to piece together what could have happened to Imogen. "She didn't run away," I said at last. Imogen might be selfish and as temperamental as a mule, but she wasn't stupid. She'd seen enough of this wilderness to know better than to turn herself loose in it without a guide.

"That only leaves one alternative," Wattie answered hesitantly. "We need to track down those peddlers before they sell her off to the highest bidder."

My eyes widened with the horror of what he'd just said. Sell her? That possibility had never entered my mind. "But they were old men and drunk," I protested, willing myself to hold out hope. "We can outrun them."

"We go back and get our weapons," Wattie said. "Then we return to the place we met the peddlers to look for any signs of struggle." Wattie could see how anxious I was. He reached out and gripped my shoulder. "We'll track them as far as it takes until we find her."

WITH SHAKING HANDS, I turned my little quiver upside down. The blowgun, darts and little vial of venom fell out on the ground along with the folder with Ka-Ti's painting inside. "Oh no!" I breathed as the painting shifted out of its leather cover onto the mud. I reached down to gather it up and discovered more painted pages fanning out across the ground. How had I not noticed before? It wasn't just one painting, but a whole portfolio. Carefully, I turned over the top painting – the one of me on a black horse. What I saw made a painful lump grow in my throat. The painting showed two girls with arms linked. One of them looked just like me and the other was, without a doubt, Imogen.

Like the thud of a falling tree, it hit me. All the time we'd been in 1828, I'd been thinking of Imogen as a problem... just the accidental tag along on *my* journey through the cave painting. *I* had to help Nickajack because it was *my* purpose. *I* had to be the one to solve the mystery of the Uktena stone ... it all came down to *me* to get us home again. Even after all the times she'd proven herself – like the time she saved me from Lovegood's bullet, or when she persuaded those guards to let us into the Garrison.

All the time I'd been resenting Imogen for not pulling her weight, she hadn't been to blame. When had I ever included her or asked for her help?

I should've known! Great detectives never solved mysteries alone. Even Sherlock didn't go it alone. He needed Watson. But instead of working together with Imogen, I'd ignored her, keeping my thoughts about the stone to myself. And—the realisation stung my conscience more than anything—had I only shared the painting with her, it might've given her enough hope that we were getting close. She might never have felt the need to do something so desperate as chasing after those peddlers.

I looked down at the painting again. It was so clear now. This wasn't just my story. It was hers too. Ours. All the time I'd been wishing for Sophia, I'd missed the friend right beside me. Well, I wasn't going to ignore Imogen anymore. Whatever it took, I would find her and tell her how sorry I was.

THERE WAS no sign of the peddlers' camp except ashes and cartwheel ruts in the mud. With his bow in hand, Wattie squatted low and made zig zag patterns as he searched every inch of ground. After a few minutes, he straightened up, holding something invisible between his thumb and index finger.

"I think this is one of Dilli's," he said, apologetically.

I ran over to see the thing he'd found: a long, bleached blonde hair, dark brown at one end. I gulped to keep from being sick. So they had taken her.

"With a kidnapped hostage, they may be avoiding the roads. We need to know which way they left the clearing. You check for signs on the south and east. I'll go west and north, back towards the road."

"Got it," I said, trying to sound in control while my heart beat itself into a frenzy.

Once out of the clearing, I tried zig-zagging the way Wattie had done, looking for some clue, maybe a footprint or wheel rut. I hadn't got far when I heard a piercing yelp from behind me followed by shouting. My breath caught in my chest as I spun around and ran back to the clearing, just in time to see someone disappear behind the walnut tree. As quickly as my wobbly legs could take me, I shot off towards the tree, but my foot slid in what must've been a mule patty, and I fell with a wet smack onto my back, knocking the air out of my lungs.

As I lay there, chest heaving, world spinning, I could hear voices on the other side of the bushes. "William McKay, you're under arrest." I recognised Lieutenant Lovegood's flat, cold voice immediately.

Wattie answered, his voice cold with spite. "Arrest for what?"

"For threatening to start an uprising against the Governor of Tennessee."

Sucking in shallow breaths, I crawled on my hands and knees to the base of the walnut tree, peering around its trunk. "*No*," I breathed. Lovegood's posse of two had dismounted from their horses and were tying Wattie's hands behind his back with thick rope.

"You're lying," Wattie spat.

"I have the warrant right here," Lovegood said, unscrolling a piece of paper and giving it a flick. "Now where's the girl?"

I nearly choked.

"What girl?" Wattie growled.

Lovegood chuckled as if it were all a game. "The red-headed one."

"She ran off," Wattie said in a carrying voice and turning his head ever so slightly in my direction. "I haven't seen her since I left the Garrison."

He was warning me not to give myself away, but it was all I could do to stay hidden. To do nothing.

"She's probably been et up by a cougar," the scruffy officer holding Wattie's ropes said. The other man laughed.

"Enough!" Lovegood shouted. "I'll take him back to the Garrison. You look for the girl."

"And if we find her? Can we take her and sell her like them peddler boys got to do with the other girl? The English one?"

"I want her brought to me," Lovegood responded in a commanding tone. "At no cost can she be allowed to reach

Nickajack. If she's on the road, I'll find her. I've got business in the Injun village tonight."

Imogen was being sold and Wattie arrested under false accusations. I wanted to scream. To fight. But I couldn't do either. With my fists clenched, forcing myself to stay quiet, I watched Lovegood lead Wattie away.

24

ALONE

J was alone. How had this happened? Imogen kidnapped. Wattie arrested. The Governor behind all of it. And there I was, the only one left free, in the middle of the woods and completely helpless.

There was Wattie's family, but they were all back in Nickajack, miles and miles away, and Lovegood's men would be patrolling the road.

Stay calm. Think of something. I tried to force my panicked brain into cooperation. *The canoe.* It was a wild thought, but it was the best I had. The canoe was too big for just one person to operate, but if I could just manage to get it back up Chickamauga Creek and into the Tennessee, at least the river would be flowing in my favour. Maybe with the help of the current, I could paddle back to Nicka-jack through the night and be there by the next evening. *Which will be much too late,* the voice in my head jabbed. I didn't have time to argue with it. I took off running to the creek.

As I skidded to a halt in what had been our camp, my

heart sank from ground floor to basement. Someone had already been there. The furs, the mats, the cookery knives and kettle, everything that had been of any value was gone. The rest had been thrown aside. But the canoe ...

They'd found it too. Whoever took it must have watched us cover it. The camouflage vines and branches were strewn all over the ground. With my hands clutching the sides of my head, I peered down the creek. Somewhere, right that minute, someone was making a getaway in my last hope.

"Thieves!" I said out loud and gave the water a kick with my mud-spattered moccasin. I'd never make it to Nickajack now. I ran muddy hands through my hair trying to think. I hadn't a clue where Imogen might be, but I knew Lovegood's men were taking Wattie to the Garrison. If I followed, there was a chance I might just find Imogen too. It was as good a next step as I could come up with.

The first thing to do was to cover my head. Lovegood's men would be looking for a girl with red hair. Looking around, I spotted the cloth Ka-Ti had wrapped around her paintings. I brushed it off and tied it around my head, carefully tucking away any straggling pieces of hair. There was nothing then but to choose my path. The road must lead back to the Garrison. Lovegood had gone in that direction. But it would be risky if anyone should be riding past.

My other option was to follow the creek back up to its meeting point with the river. I would not likely be seen among the reeds and pussy willow, but one look at the murky, swamp-like waters made taking my chances on the road seem a much more tempting option. Besides, the road would be quicker.

No sooner had I made up my mind than I heard the sand-grinding sound of wheels coming from the right. *The peddlers* was the first thought in my mind, and I raced to the edge of the road to wait and see, squatting down behind a mulberry bush. But it was only an old man driving a cart full of pumpkins. Probably taking them to the Garrison to have them cooked up for the Washington delegates the Governor had said were on their way.

The Garrison! This could be my ride, I realised with a flutter of excitement. But I'd have to act quickly. I squatted down on the ready as close to the road as I could get without being seen. At least the farmer didn't appear to be in too much of a hurry. He was leaning back, giving the reins an occasional flick and singing 'Turkey in the Straw' to nobody in particular.

I counted out the *clop clop, clop clop, clop clop* rhythm of the horse's hooves as he trotted past, then leaped onto the road, grabbed the wooden side of the cart and hoisted myself up. A few pumpkins rolled down the pile to knock me on the head, but I had made it! *I was officially a stow-away*, I thought with a sense of pride.

I must have heard at least eight different verses of 'Turkey in the Straw' before the pumpkin cart rolled up to the gates of Hiwassee Garrison. The farmer pulled the cart to a halt. "Fer the Gov'ner's harvest banquet," I heard the old man drawl, and my heart took off. Supposing the guards wanted to search the cart? There was no running now. I folded my legs, kept my head down and pulled the biggest pumpkin I could get my arms around into my lap, hoping to my very bones those guards wouldn't take any notice of me.

A second later, the cart was moving forward again, the guards returning to their watches without so much as a glance in my direction. I let out a chestful of air, then hastily pushed the pumpkin off my lap and slid off the cart onto the sandy courtyard, just outside of the stables. But the courtyard was much busier than it had been yesterday, and there was a pretty regular flow of people in and out of the Governor's headquarters. If I could just find a way to blend in.

Two ladies brushed past me, giggling and with their arms full of baskets piled with linens which they carried up the steps of the brick building. They disappeared inside.

I spun around. *Where had they just come from?* A drying line of linens gave me my answer. There was an open covered area just before the stables that appeared to be the Garrison laundry.

I took quick stock to make sure no one was watching, marched over and seized an empty basket, quickly filling it with sheets and tablecloths from the drying line. With my best effort at acting natural, I perched the basket on one hip as I'd seen the other maids do and bee-lined across the courtyard in the direction of the mansion. But instead of ascending the stairs, I veered right and floated over towards the stone shack prison.

"Lookin' fer sommat?" belched a burly guard with an underbite that reminded me of a bulldog.

"Oh!" I tried to appear startled, as if I'd drifted towards

the prison unawares. "I … um … just wondered what was inside this little building?"

The burly man spat on the ground. "Ain't nothin' but outlaw scum inside o' thar."

I widened my eyes, trying to fake interest. "Really? What kind of outlaws? Any Indians?"

The man's already grumpy face turned into an outright scowl. "Don't see as it's any o' yer business." As if to make quite clear he'd had enough of my questions, he snorted and spat out a huge ball of phlegm in the dirt at my feet before turning away.

I stumbled backwards to avoid the spit and bumped against someone. Spinning around, I looked up into the fierce face of the Governor's housekeeper.

This is it, I thought. I'd blown it. The housekeeper was sure to recognise me from the day before. Did she know the Governor was looking for me? Either way, she'd tell him I was snooping around the Garrison and that would be the end of it.

"You must be one of the new girls," she snapped. "Dreaming and dawdling when there's a heap of work to be done." And with that, she pinched my shoulder and marched me right up the mansion steps and into the front door. She released my shoulder inside the foyer. "I catch you taking your sweet time again and I'll dock your wages, you hear?" she scolded just before turning on her heels and marching down a hallway so that I was left standing there with my basket of linens and giggling maids bustling back and forth around me.

As relieved as I was that the housekeeper had *not* recognised me and turned me in to the Governor, this was no time for catching the breath I'd lost in my terror a moment earlier. I was standing in the middle of my enemy's front doorway with a decision to make.

My instincts told me to turn around and run, run as fast as I could away from that perilous place. *But then what*? I'd be alone again in the woods, no closer to helping Wattie or Imogen.

You call yourself a detective, Katie, a braver voice in my head reminded me. *And detectives don't run from danger; they walk straight into it. That's how they stop criminals: by spying on them, not by hiding from them.*

I knew that voice was right. It was the voice that had coached me to ride Vagabond through the church doors to Sophia's rescue last summer. That memory filled me with a reckless energy, and without another thought, I dumped my basket of laundry behind a pedestal with a bust on it and made straight for the long corridor with the Governor's office at the end of it. Nothing was going to stop me now. My feet, silent on the long hall rug, carried me steadily to the Governor's door and didn't stop until I reached it. It was ajar. Holding my breath, I leaned my ear close to the open door when a voice spoke out from inside the room.

It was the Governor's voice, but not even a hint of jolliness remained to warm it. Now it was cold, biting, as if he was speaking a curse. "Joseph McKay has been a thorn in my side for too long now. There's simply no competing with the man. He always makes a case for the Cherokee in Washington. Fought with the President at Horseshoe Bend, you know, and now he can do no wrong. The Indians regard him as one of their own, as they did Jim Weaver before I removed him. The McKays have to be crushed." He paused. I clamped a hand over my mouth, afraid they had heard the gasp I had let escape.

But a moment later, Blunt continued his tirade. "I can't have them getting in the way of the treaty with Black Fox. And speaking of that savage man, you must be more careful. Those children told me they saw you conspiring with him."

"They're harmless—" It was Lovegood who spoke, but the Governor cut him off.

"They are *not* harmless, Lieutenant. If Nickajack found out about that treaty, everything we've worked for could be ruined."

"I thought everyone to be at their little powwow, or I would not have—"

"Well it turns out those two wretched little girls were not, were they, Lieutenant? Have you found them both?"

"Jed's men have one of them. We're still searching for the red-headed one. It's only a matter of time."

"Let's hope you're right, Lieutenant." Blunt's voice was venomous. "I don't have time for mistakes."

"What are your orders, sir, when I find the girl? Prison?"

"I told you before. We don't know who these girls are or what their connection with the McKays is, but they've seen too much. They suspect the conspiracy between Black Fox and yourself. As I haven't any warrant for locking up children, just make certain that the red-haired one, like her cousin, ends up somewhere far away where she can't pose any problems to the plan. I trust tracking down a little girl won't prove too arduous a task for you, Lieutenant. Now if you'd do your job and allow me to get back to mine …"

"Good day, sir."

My heart sprang into my throat as heavy boot steps approached the door. Scuffling to the next closest door down the corridor, I prayed, *please be open. Please be open.* I laid my hand on the knob. It turned! I fell inside and closed myself in just as I heard the Governor's door swing wide open on its hinges. Then I held my breath. The Lieutenant's steps sounded hesitant for a brief moment that felt like an eternity. But then his boot steps retreated down the hall. It was music to my ears, but there was no time to bask in relief. I had to get out.

There was a picture window behind a desk on the far wall, like the one in the Governor's office. I tiptoed across the floor, threw back the sash and brushed aside the papers on the desk before climbing on top. With one knee already up, I stopped. My hand was resting on a map. I recognised it immediately as the map of Cherokee Country Wattie and the others had used to chart out our journey from Nickajack to Hiwassee. But there was something definitely different about this copy. I traced down the Tennessee River with my finger until it pointed at the spot I was sure was Nickajack. But this map didn't say Nickajack at all. What should have been Nickajack was labelled in bold black letters: *Blunts Town.*

I heard a movement in the Governor's office next door. In a flash of panic, I hastily rolled up the map and stuffed it under my arm. Then, with both knees on the desk, I heaved the window open, swung my legs through and dropped to the ground.

OUTLAW

I braced my hands on my knees, allowing myself just a couple of deep breaths. I wasn't safe yet, but at least here on the backside of the Governor's mansion, no one was coming and going. But someone might spot me from a window at any moment. With that thought in mind, I pressed my back against the wall and looked around for my next way of escape.

There was only a narrow pathway between the building and the outer wall of the Garrison. *If only I could climb it*, I thought. But the logs were tall as trees and spiked at the top. There was no chance.

I heard what I thought was a faint snorting sound away to my left. Of course! The stables were just on the other side of the building. Maybe I'd be able to sneak behind them without anyone noticing and climb into another cart. It wasn't much of a plan, but I had to do something other than stand there right under the Governor's nose.

I crept along, keeping close to the wall, rounded the

corner and could've jumped for joy. Behind the stables, cut out of the wall, was a corral door! And what was more, it was open to allow some of the horses out for grazing, the afternoon sun spilling through. I was no more than ten or so yards from freedom!

Squatting low but moving fast, I scampered and ducked behind a horse's stall, inched along and peeked around. I could hear men's voices down at the other end of the stable, but the coast seemed clear. With a deep breath, I sprinted towards the fence ready to hurdle it, but skidded into it instead. There, tethered to a watering trough was a tall, sinewy grey horse with a silvery mane. Lovegood's horse. He had lifted his head to watch me out of one startlingly blue eye.

"You deserve a better master," I said, holding out my palm to the horse's probing nostrils. I touched his nose, and an idea rushed through me like an electric shock. It was more a feeling than a thought, a surge of complete recklessness all the way down to my toes. I'd escaped the guards, taken the Governor's map, jumped out the window. What was stopping me from riding off on Lovegood's horse? I was a fugitive. What did I have to lose? Ok, I had a lot to lose, starting with my freedom if I got caught and thrown into prison. But at that moment, it didn't matter. Nothing mattered but getting out of that Garrison crawling with enemies.

With a wave of giddiness, I untethered the reins, stuffed the map into the saddle bag, and hoisted myself up onto his back. He didn't seem to question what was going on, but answered immediately to my lead. I trotted him to the back of the corral. We turned, then I whispered, *Now!*

With a lunge, we careened forward towards the fence. It was a big jump, but this was no time for caution. I leaned in close as his front legs left the ground. For a moment, I felt completely weightless. Then his hooves hit the ground, and we were galloping again.

"Hey! Come back here!"

I heard the shouts, but I didn't look back. I had to reach the river, and then … I knew exactly where I had to go. It had come to me when the Governor mentioned his name: Jim Weaver. Raccoon Mountain was just a few miles south. Old Grizzly was my only hope.

IF ANY THOUGHTS entered my mind on that long ride, I can't recall a single one of them. I focused on the path ahead as if my life depended on it. The path along the river soon narrowed. The further we went, the steeper the bank became until mountains rose up on either side.

The stallion was well trained and never once reared back when I led him over rocky shoals or even down into the water where the river rapids sometimes beat against his legs. I could tell he was as glad as I was when at last we'd hit a patch of sandy bank where we could pick up speed a little. Every second that passed felt precious, and I had no idea just how many were passing. It might have been an hour. It might as well have been days. My stomach felt hollow, my mind was getting numb and my backside was sorer than ever.

I was just beginning to feel I would have to slide off and rest when I recognised the flat shoals and little pools where Imogen had met the mud puppy. I'd made it! I could've cried with happiness and exhaustion.

The horse could take me as far as the lookout. Then I'd climb the rest of the way on my own.

"Go on, get a good drink," I told the horse, leading him to the water and patting his sweaty neck as he lowered his head. It should have been a peaceful moment's rest after such a wearing journey, but something made me tense up, the hair standing up on the back of my arms. The sun was still out— I wasn't cold. *You're just tired and hungry* I reassured myself. But it wasn't just me. The birds even seemed unsettled. A blue jay swooped down and landed in the branches overhead, screeching like an alarm bell. The stallion sensed it too. He lifted his head from the water, his eyes wide, nostrils sniffing the air.

My pulse thumped in my ear. Something … or *someone* was watching.

I clicked to get the horse moving, then turned back up the bank. A minute up the trail, the river was out of view, which meant that we were out of view of whatever hidden creature had been lurking there. Yet the eerie feeling of being watched didn't go away.

The mountain's tall, flat rock face rose straight up on my right, like a fortress wall. Wondering how far we had to go before we reached the lookout, I craned my head back to look up. My eyes met with the predator-like stare of Black Fox. He was crouched low on a rock outcrop above, like a wildcat about to spring on its prey. His black hair hung like a curtain of camouflage on either side of his face so that his eyes stood out, glowing with a ravenous light. Then his eyes narrowed into a savage smile. The predator had his victim cornered.

Or so he thought.

"*YA!*" I dug my legs into the horse's side, and he shot off like an arrow. The climb became steeper, but I urged him forward with every muscle in my body, depending totally on his sure footing. As he made a sharp turn around a bend, I threw a frantic glance over the rocks and boulders for any sign of Black Fox. Meanwhile, the horse reared up with a scream. I screamed too and clung on for dear life as his hooves slid and scuttled on the narrow ledge. Then I saw what had frightened him.

Black Fox dropped down onto the path right in front of us, baring his teeth. I surged forward to bowl right through him, but he was too quick. He leaped to one side, threw out his arm and grabbed the horse's reins, wrapping them once, twice, three times around his boulder of a fist, nearly unseating me. I yelled and snatched up fistfuls of mane. The horse jerked its head, trying to pull free from Black Fox's grip and roaring with frustration. Then, with that raving smile, Black Fox used his other hand to pull the tomahawk from the strap across his bare chest.

The sight of the blade glinting in the sunlight sent an electric shock up my spine. There was a flash of a moment when we met each other's eyes, and I knew he was going to kill the horse to get to me. Without a second thought, I flung myself off the horse. My forehead smacked hard against a tree limb, and I landed hard on my knees. The world spun, but I scrambled to my feet. I had to keep moving. I was running up hill, pushing off jagged rocks and stumbling over roots, my every muscle heaving me upwards, never daring to look behind me where I knew Black Fox would be gaining like a wolf outrunning a mouse. I could hear his steady breathing, the pounding of his moccasined feet getting closer.

As I turned sharply around a boulder, I threw myself into the undergrowth and crawled on my elbows and knees under a thorny shrub. Sitting back on my heels, I slung my quiver around to my front and jabbed the blowgun between my knees. I had only seconds to get this right. I had to concentrate. I took a dart and put it between my teeth. Then I reached into the quiver, found the vial of snake's venom and uncorked it. Hands shaking, I plunged the dart's tip in. Black Fox's heavy pants were audible just around the bend. With a thrill of terror, I stuffed the dart into the blowgun, put the pipe to my lips and drew in a deep breath, just as my hunter's feet came into view. He stopped at the bend and appeared to be squinting up the path, listening.

I froze, my breath held and my chest on fire. If he would just take one step further up the path, I might have a chance of hitting him. But instead, in a horrific instant Black Fox turned and looked directly at my hiding place. His hate-filled eyes narrowed on mine just before he lunged. I didn't think. I just blew with all that was in me, then squeezed my eyes shut.

A heavy thud on the ground made me open my eyes. Black Fox was on his knees, hardly more than an arm's length from my hiding place, one hand gripping his neck where my dart had struck. He ripped out the dart, looked at it, then his eyes rolled up and he fell, face down, his silver earring swinging from his ear.

MEZ BLUME

I stared at the fallen giant in shock. But he was only knocked out. I had to get out of there. Had to reach the top of that mountain. Still shaking, I fixed my quiver to my back before crawling out from under the bush, careful to skirt around Black Fox.

I don't remember running up the trail. My mind was so numbed from my narrow escape, I didn't feel the ache in my legs or notice the pain from the steadily bleeding cut in my forehead. As if transported by magic, I found myself standing on the porch of Old Grizzly's cabin, hand lifted to knock. But I didn't have to. The door opened all on its own. The last thing I saw were a man's dark grey eyes. They were not full of hatred like Black Fox's, but full of worry.

26

IN THE GRIZZLY'S DEN

When did I fall asleep in the forest? was the first groggy thought to form in my throbbing head. The pain was so strong that I had to be really awake, but all I could see looked like a hazy dreamland. I rubbed my eyes and blinked. I wasn't in the forest at all. I was in a bed, in a cabin, staring up at wooden rafters. Tree branches laced with autumn leaves were hung like a canopy from the ceiling. There was a giant papery bee hive suspended right over my head.

I tried to hoist myself up on one elbow, but the pain through the left side of my forehead blinded me. I gasped and fell back, my hand automatically bracing the side of my head. It was bandaged.

Soft footsteps came near. I felt a cool hand on my burning forehead. I blinked until my sight came back and saw, in the dim light, Ka-Ti's kind and beautiful face smiling back, but her eyes were full of concern.

My mouth opened, but my throat was so dry that no words would come out. It went dryer still when Ka-Ti rushed away. Next thing I knew, I heard the floorboards creak as the mountain man lumbered over to the bed and stood towering over me. He still wore a scowl, but something was different. He looked much more human than grizzly now with his long, dishevelled strands of greying hair and his shirt sleeves rolled up to his elbows. Ka-Ti was holding one of his massive forearms and smiling from him to me.

The mountain man lifted one of his huge hands and patted his daughter on the head, then walked around the bed and creakily sat down in a wooden chair. We eyed each other for a moment. At last he gave a sniff and started talking.

"So, girl. How'd you wind up back at my door in such a sad state? I thought you were with Will McKay. Ain't he lookin' after you?"

I shook my head, then winced from the movement. Why did it hurt so bad again? I had a vague memory of hitting it … when I jumped off the horse. "Horse!" I tried to sit up and saw stars from the pain.

Ka-Ti laid her hand on my shoulder and pushed me gently back.

"Your horse is safe. After you turned up, I went out scoutin' to try and figure out what'd happened to you. I found your horse at the lookout and took him down to the valley on the other side of the mountain. He's happy as a lark, grazin' with our own horses."

"He's not really my horse," I mumbled, lying back down. Ka-Ti exchanged a look with her father.

"You mean you stole him?" Jim Weaver asked, giving me a hard, squinting stare.

I hadn't meant to say as much, so I didn't say anything.

"Is that why you were chased up here? 'Cause you stole somebody's horse?" There was anger in his voice.

"Nn... no. It was Black Fox. He followed me. I was worried he'd kill the horse. I shot him with a poisonous dart. That's how I got away." I was beginning to wonder if I was making any sense at all. Whatever I'd said, it seemed to make an impression on the mountain man. His face darkened.

"Black Fox, you say?"

I nodded.

"What the devil's Black Fox doin' up on my mountain? He knows better'n to come up here." He scowled towards the window, his jaw twitching. "And you say you shot him with a poisonous dart? Well, he'll be out there somewhere feeling rougher'n you do right now. That's fer sure." He squinted at me again. "How'd you go and get on ol' Black Fox's bad side anyhow?"

"It's Governor Blunt whose bad side I'm on. I think Black Fox is just working for him."

A light flashed in Jim Weaver's eyes as soon as I mentioned the Governor, and deep lines appeared in his leathery forehead. "I'd trust the bear that gave me this scar before I'd trust Blunt. But what bone's he got to pick with a little girl like you?"

"He's arrested Wattie." With a stab of panic, I remembered Imogen. "And my cousin's been kidnapped. They might've already sold her to somebody!" How could I lie there when Imogen was in the hands of kidnappers? I tried to kick off the blankets so I could get to my feet, but my legs got tangled up.

"WHOA. Whoa, now." The mountain man was standing over me with his hands out like a traffic policeman. Ka-Ti braced my shoulders again.

"What'd you say your name was?"

"Kk.. Katie," I said, trying to steady my breath. "The Cherokee call me Katie Fire-Hair."

"Right. Well I'm Jim. You already know Kingfisher here."

Didn't he hear me? This was no time to make introductions. "I need to find my cousin *tonight*," I said, flailing frantically until I almost fell out of the bed.

"Now look here. You ain't goin' no place tonight," Jim said as Ka-Ti hurried away to the fire. "Now just you calm down and tell me what all this is about, the Governor kidnappin' and arrestin' people."

A blinding pain forced me to lie back, gripping my sore head.

Ka-Ti was back. She handed me a bowl of some steaming liquid. It smelled like the blueberry tea she had served me before. I took a sip and felt my muscles relax, then another, and the throb in my head seemed to ease up just a little.

"If I tell you everything, will you help me?" I asked the mountain man.

"Well I reckon I can't tell you that until you've told me why it is you need my help." He struck a match and lit up a pipe, clearly planning to sit right there until I'd explained the whole story.

"all right," I said, giving up. I started with the stampede on our first day in Cherokee Country and all the events that had led us to our journey to Hiwassee. I told him about the peddlers and Imogen's disappearance, and how Lovegood had arrested Wattie. I told him every word I'd overheard between the Governor and the Lieutenant. When I got to that part, I remembered something. "He mentioned you. Governor Blunt. He said he had to remove Joseph McKay the way he'd removed you … something about the Cherokees liking you too much."

To my shock, Jim Weaver actually laughed, though it sounded bitter. "That's Blunt all over. Can't stand to see nobody else going up in the world without feelin' he oughtta club 'em down."

"But why did he have to remove you? Remove you from what?" I asked.

Jim Weaver whistled. "That's a looong story, little lady."

"Well, you said I'm not going anywhere tonight."

The mountain man frowned, finding himself cornered.

With a quiet smile, Ka-Ti got up and went to the door, her long curtain of black hair swishing behind her.

I looked at Jim Weaver, waiting for him to speak. He was still frowning, deep in thought.

"I told you my story," I reminded him.

"all right," he said gruffly. "I'll tell you what happened. But it don't mean nothin'. It's all in the past now, understand?"

I nodded.

He sat back, eyes fixed out the window, took a few puffs of his pipe and began. "I was a fur trader as a younger man. Travelled all across the frontier, met with all manner of dangers." He tapped the scar on his cheek.

"While I was out Oklahoma way, I met a beautiful Cherokee woman."

"Ramona?" I asked, and thought I saw a slight wince at the name.

He nodded. "Sounds like you heard some of this story."

"Wattie told me a bit," I admitted.

"She'd come from Cherokee Country originally, but her family'd gone west when the government bought up the land she called home. She was the only one of 'em left when I met her. The others'd all caught disease or some such. She'd taken to paintin' as a little girl, and made a livin' of travellin' around sellin' her craft to other tribes, traders and the like, so she was used to the wanderin' life." He gnawed on his pipe and looked out the window again. Though I had questions, I held my tongue. I could tell the words caused him pain.

He set the pipe in his lap and carried on. "I married her and took her out West with me on the trade route. It was a rough life for a man, let alone a woman. But my Ramona never let that bother 'er. She was happy. We were happy. But it was no place to raise a family, of that you may be sure."

"You mean Ka-Ti?" I asked.

He nodded. "When we found out Ramona was on the nest, we decided it was time to settle down. She wanted the baby to grow up knowing Cherokee ways, so it seemed the best place was right here, in the old country. So here's where we came. It wasn't easy at first for Ramona. She'd never been like the rest of the Cherokee wives, staying put in one place. But she kept up her paintin' and looked after the baby, and helped me get a good trade going among the Cherokee. Horses mostly. Ramona's got a real way about her with horses. They come to her — even the wild ones — and do whatever she bids 'em. You ain't never seen nothin' like it." The slightest hint of a smile made the whiskers twitch at the corner of his mouth.

"I wish I could meet her," I said quietly.

He looked at me a moment, then cleared his throat. "Me too."

"But what did Governor Blunt have against you and Ramona? You were just earning a living, minding your own business ..."

"Well now we come to that," he said, straightening his shoulders which had become slumped over during the course of his story, as if he'd been bearing a heavy weight. "The American government decided to send an agent down to the Cherokees to help 'em learn agriculture and husbandry and such."

"And they sent Governor Blunt?"

He shook his head. "He wasn't Blunt back then. And he wasn't 'governor' yet neither. They sent a fella called Meeks. A good man. Cared deeply about the Cherokee and always tried to do right by 'em. But he didn't understand 'em at first. Couldn't communicate with 'em."

"That's where you came in?" I asked.

"Yup. I helped him as much as I could, translatin', mediatin'. Even travelled up to Washington with him and a handful o' Cherokee delegates to meet the President. That's when I got made an official delegate of the United States of America to the Cherokee."

"So what happened to Meeks?" I asked. My head was

clearing, but my stomach ached. I could smell the stew boiling on the other side of the cabin where Ka-Ti was cooking. But I was just as hungry to hear the rest of the story.

"He died," Jim Weaver said plainly. "He was an old man when he started the job. Then Washington named a young land prospector the new Indian Agent and things changed."

"Blunt," I said, and he nodded again.

"Blunt never got on very well with the Cherokees. Problem was, he didn't want to understand 'em. He hated it when they'd come to me with their troubles and complaints that he was chargin' 'em too much for the goods the government had sent 'em. I told 'em I'd make their worries known to the President next time I was in Washington. Well, Blunt got word of it. Said I was trying to turn the Cherokees against him ... that I was more Cherokee than white man and was therefore not fit to represent the interests of America. Of course, the thing that really got his goat was that I was competition. I got right in the way of his dirty business deals."

"So he had you sacked?" I asked.

"He tried to, but the President refused to give me the boot. So Blunt took matters into his own hands."

"What did he do?" I was leaning forward on my knees now.

"He did just what he accused me of doin' to him. He contrived a way of turning the Cherokees against me."

"The Uktena Stone." The words left my mouth before I could think.

Jim Weaver sat back with a shrewd grin on his face.

"Sounds like you already heard the next part of the story too."

My cheeks went hot. "Only that you were accused of taking it and causing all kinds of bad luck for the Cherokees."

Silence. His intense eyes stayed glued to my face as he took slow puffs of his pipe. I felt suddenly hot and fidgety. Keen to get the conversation back in motion, I cleared my throat. "It's just a story, right? About the monster snake and the magic stone? I mean, it can't be real."

The sly smile came back. "Oh, the stone's real enough. The Cherokees kept it hidden for generations in a sacred cave just over'n them hills." He nodded towards the view out the window. "'Til it got stole."

I waited another fidgety moment before getting the nerve to ask, "And ... did you ...?"

"That's common belief, Miss Fire-Hair. But there's more to the story than what you've heard, and that's 'cause there ain't nobody 'at knows it 'cept for me and Kingfisher."

I looked over my shoulder. Ka-Ti had just come over to join us, a smile on her face and a painted tray with three steaming bowls. My stomach gave an audible rumble as she handed me one of them.

"Good," Jim Weaver said, taking a bowl from his daughter. "Maybe this'll hush you up long enough so's I can finish this story."

I flinched and took a quiet sip of the stew.

"All that's left to say is that Blunt cooked up a way to frame me for stealin' that stone. And no, I didn't never so much as lay eyes on it, let alone steal it."

"But I don't see why your Cherokee friends, like Terrapin Jo, would believe Blunt's story over yours."

I saw the scowl on his face and bit my lip.

"As I was sayin'," Jim grumbled, "they never found the stone, but Blunt used his power to have me arrested by the Tennessee militia. I served three years in prison. Ramona and Ka-Ti were on their own. Meantime, Blunt started a rumour that Ramona had the stone hidden. That she was using it for some kind of ..." he hesitated, and I felt Ka-Ti stir beside me. "For somethin'."

I sat up, ignoring the stew that sloshed onto my dress. "You mean the stone didn't have anything to do with Ramona?"

Jim gave me a hard look before answering. "'Course not. She didn't give a monkey's uncle 'bout that old rock."

Could it be true? I wondered. *The stone was just that – a plain old piece of rock?*

Jim's voice broke into my thoughts, deeper and softer than I'd heard it before. "Ramona had to leave due to Blunt's rumours. When I got out of prison, Kingfisher and I had to leave Cherokee Country for good. So we set up home here in the mountain, away from everybody, whites and Cherokees alike, but close enough for Kingfisher to have some knowledge of her land and people." After a pause, he turned his attention to his bowl of stew.

A question remained burning on my mind, but did I dare to ask it? I cleared my throat and, in a voice rather smaller than my usual, said, "I still don't understand why Ramona had to leave."

The hand holding the spoon he had just lifted to his mouth dropped back down into his bowl. His whiskery jaw twitched a minute before he answered gruffly, "Because she had to."

I didn't dare ask any more questions about Ramona after that. Oh, I had plenty more coming, but at that moment, there were more pressing matters than the Uktena Stone ... even more pressing than getting home.

I sat quietly and waited for the mountain man to finish his stew. Only when he'd set down the bowl and wiped his mouth across the back of his arm did I dare to ask one and only one question. "So I was wondering ... Seeing as we've got the same enemy, will you help me?"

27

AN UNLIKELY ALLY

*J*im Weaver didn't answer for what felt like a long time. He seemed to be struggling with himself as he sat there, puffing his pipe and blowing smoke rings. Meanwhile, all I could think was how Imogen was out there at that very moment, no doubt scared out of her wits. The shadows in the cabin grew longer as the sun sank below the windowsill. I couldn't wait much longer.

A glance at Ka-Ti told me that she too was holding her breath to see what her father would say.

"Right." Both Ka-Ti and I jumped slightly when Jim Weaver spoke, breaking the silent tension. "Here's the thing, Miss Fire-Hair." He leaned forward and rested his elbows on his muscular thighs. "This mountain? This is my kingdom. If your cousin's captors are anywhere near my mountain, I'll help you track 'em. If they've gone on further, which I doubt since you said they was drunk, but if they have, then I'll set you on course, give you rations, weapons, whatever you need, but then yer on yer own."

My heart sank, taking my ability to speak with it. I could only manage to stutter, "But … Blunt … how could you … everyone in Nickajack …?"

He stood up, towering over me again. "Because, Miss Fire-Hair, helpin' people never helped me or the people I care about." He stomped over to the window and looked out with his back to me, bracing himself with one forearm against the wall. "I don't like what Blunt's doin' any more'n you do. But it ain't my fight."

"But how can you say that when he did the exact same thing to you?"

He frowned over his shoulder. "I told ya. What he done to me … it's in the past. It don't constitute nothin' anymore. I can't undo it. I can't change what's happened."

"But you can make a difference to what *will* happen," I said, pleading for him to hear me out. "The past doesn't just disappear, you know. You can't run from it and hide away up in your mountain forever."

He turned around to face me, then slowly circled around the bed. His eyes narrowed so he looked dangerous again. "What do you know about the past? You're just a little girl. You don't know nothin' about losin' people you love. Well, let me tell you somthin'." He leaned so close, I could smell the tobacco on his breath. "If yer past ever comes a hauntin' you, you'll wanna run and hide from it too."

As he stomped away, I called after him, "Is that what Ramona would want? To know you were spending your life a coward?" His footsteps stopped. My bones froze. Ka-Ti's eyes closed in her seat beside me. I had done it now. I'd gone too far, and Old Grizzly would throw me out and leave me to the wild animals and Black Fox. I waited for the rage to break loose, but it didn't. A second later, I heard the cabin door open and swing shut again.

I PULLED on my moccasins and got to my feet to fix my quiver over my shoulder. Even real bears could be tamed into doing circus tricks, but trying to persuade Old Grizzly to do anything was like trying to move a mountain. I had made up my mind the minute he'd walked out of the cabin — I was going alone, and I was leaving tonight. How could I stay another second when people *I* cared about were out there in danger?

I gathered up the last of my belongings and walked out of the cabin onto the front porch. Ka-Ti was standing there with a shawl wrapped around her shoulders and a lantern in her hand.

"I need to get to my horse," I said so Old Grizzly could hear me from where he stood sulking in the shadows of the trees.

"And just where d'ya think you're goin'?" he challenged, folding his arms.

"To find my cousin, then do whatever it takes to rescue Wattie."

"Look at you!" he waved his hand and laughed once. "You've still got a bandage on yer head. You mighta got lucky with Black Fox, but don't go gettin' cocky and think you can take on a whole army of full grown men with that little gun of yers."

"Well I have to do *something*," I said angrily. "They would do the same for me."

But it was hopeless. Old Grizzly stood there shaking his head when a voice beside me, soft as the wind, spoke up. "I will go with her."

Old Grizzly's mouth fell open, and I looked at Ka-Ti with amazement as she put her arm around my shoulder. "She is right, Pa. Wattie would do the same for us."

The mountain man's mouth opened and closed several times. He sniffed and turned his head away, wiping his eyes on his sleeve before walking up onto the porch. But in the lantern light, streaks of tears glistened on his cheeks as he looked down at his daughter. "I knew you had a voice, my Kingfisher." He cupped her face in his big, rough hand, then heaved a sigh and said, "What're we waitin' fer? We best be gatherin' up some supplies."

Ka-Ti's face broke into a smile. She threw her arms around her father's waist as he patted her hair, then hurried into the cabin.

Old Grizzly watched her go. "I never thought I'd hear her again," he said, almost to himself. "She ain't spoke a word since her momma left." He turned to me. "You were right, what you said back there. This ain't what Ramona would want, me sittin' up here, keepin' Kingfisher locked up in a cage when she's got wings that need spreadin'." He walked over to a wooden trunk beside the door and squatted down to rummage through it.

I bit my lip, hoping what I was about to say wouldn't sound too … hollow. "I do know a little about the past … and losing people. My best friend … she's … well …." I couldn't say it, not only because I didn't want to admit it. It still didn't feel true.

Jim Weaver stopped rummaging. He was watching me

thoughtfully, bent down beside the trunk. "She's part of your past?" he finished for me.

I nodded.

He got up and sat on the corner of the trunk, scratching his whiskery chin. "There's an old Cherokee sayin', goes somethin' like 'Don't let yesterdy use up too much of today.' You were right, what you said about hidin' from the past. I reckon it's comin' with us whether we like it or not. But you can't live there. You gotta keep on keepin' on."

I let the words turn over in my mind as he unrolled a large animal skin and started laying objects on it from the trunk, one by one.

"Maybe," I hesitated. "Maybe if the truth comes out about Blunt, things could be different for you and Ka-Ti. Better than they are now."

He started rolling up the skin with all the objects inside it. "Could be I'll wind up back in jail." He laughed a dry laugh as he tied some twine around the rolled-up knapsack. "But as for Kingfisher ...." He turned his eyes toward the cabin where Ka-Ti was busily packing up food. I could hear her singing happily as she worked. "Will McKay's been a good friend to her. Her only friend, up 'til you came along. Could be if I go to prison ... or worse... his folks'll take her in again. Maybe one day she'll be one of the family. Things could be better for my girl."

Just then, Ka-Ti appeared in the doorway. She had changed out of her skirt into deerskin breeches and braided her long hair. She had a bundle tied to her back and a smile on her face.

Jim Weaver stood up and looked me up and down, as if

just seeing me for the first time. "You don't mean to go trackin' kidnappers and rescuin' people in a dress?"

I looked down at the filthy, tattered dress Ulma had given me what felt like ages ago. "Well I'd rather not, but I don't have much choice. This is all I've got."

He shook his head. "Kingfisher, get this girl some decent trackin' clothes. Then let's get huntin'."

28

A CHILLING RESCUE

*T*he grey horse greeted me with a friendly whinny.

"What do you call him?" Ka-Ti asked above a whisper as she stroked the nose of her beautiful black-and-white paint horse.

"I don't know what Lieutenant Lovegood calls him, but I suppose I should think of something." I looked into the horse's eye, trying to get inspiration for a name. "What should I call you?" I mumbled.

"How 'bout callin' him Giddyup?" the mountain man grumbled as he threw a blanket over his big, buckskin stallion's back. "This ain't no pony show. We got work to do."

Ka-Ti and I exchanged a look, both of us trying not to smile. Ever since Jim Weaver had agreed to lead this rescue mission, he seemed as eager to get going as if it'd been his idea.

The other two mounted their horses. I swung myself up onto the still nameless grey horse, grateful for the soft deerskin breeches Ka-Ti had loaned me. Then, with Jim in the lead, me in the middle and Ka-Ti in the rear, we trotted out of the small paddock at the base of Raccoon Mountain and into the almost pitch-black forest.

In the dark, my senses sprang to alert. The forest was wide awake. I could hear the river gurgling and lapping the rocks in the distance, an owl's *hoo hoo ho HOO* in the treetops, a toad's croak, some small creature scurrying through the underbrush, and all the while the gentle, steady fall of the three horses' hooves.

Every now and again, I would hear Jim's horse slowing pace just before his hand shot up for us to halt. Then he'd jump down and spend any number of minutes walking in circles, sniffing plants, getting right down on his knees to examine the dirt in a tiny patch of moonlight. Eventually, he'd mount his horse again and carry on confidently, as if the forest had told him exactly what he needed to know.

It went on for ages like this, stopping and starting, nobody speaking. I was beginning to find it extremely challenging to hold up my drooping eyelids. Gravity seemed to have a hold on my head too. It kept dipping to one shoulder, then jerking back up with a painful throb. Just when I thought I couldn't fight it any longer, Jim turned his horse to a new trail down a steep hill through the trees. At the bottom, rippling like a giant black snake, was the river. He rode right down the bank until his horse's front legs stood ankle deep in the water, then jumped down and went straight to inspecting the ground again. Out from under the trees, I could see his outline, lit up blue in the moonlight, as he stood, gazed out over the water, nodded and turned back. This time he didn't mount his horse but waved for us to dismount and join him on the river's edge.

"What do you see?" I whispered, squinting into the darkness.

He pointed to the opposite bank of the river towards a flickering light.

"What is it?" I asked.

"Ain't you never seen a fire before?" Jim unstrapped the rolled-up animal skin and heaved it off the horse's back. He laid it on the ground and rolled it out. Taking two little pewter cups, he handed one to me and the other to Ka-Ti. "Get yerselves some water, and water them horses too."

I took the cup, but stood there for a second, feeling confused. "But what about the fire? Do you think it's them?"

He sat back on his heels and wiped his brow. "Only one way to find out, and you leave that to me. Now drink up."

We all filled our cups in the river. I splashed my face with the icy water so I was wide awake. Then Ka-Ti passed around the dried meat and apples. We fed the horses the apples and sat around tearing off chewy bites of meat in silence. Jim finished long before the two of us and got up. Before I knew it, he'd pulled off his rifle, hat, deerskin coat and set to pulling off his boots. I looked at Ka-Ti. She was watching her father too with a worried expression.

"You gals should get some rest," Jim whispered, laying the things he'd just shed on a rock. "I'll be back before first light."

"But where—" I began.

"Can't wait for sunup to find out if them there's the scum that snatched yer cousin, now can we?" And before I could answer, he waded out into the river and disappeared under the surface.

I looked at Ka-Ti again, speechless.

She gave a small smile back, but her eyebrows gave away that she was anxious. She took blankets from her horse's back and gave me one, then found a nook between two rocks and curled up in her own. I laid out my blanket and curled up inside it.

I had been aching to sleep for hours, but now I couldn't do it. With every little gurgle or splash, my eyes opened to see if it was Jim coming up out of the river to say whether he'd found Imogen on the other side. What if they didn't have her anymore? Or she was hurt? What if it wasn't the peddlers at all, but some of Blunt's men out looking for me? If they caught Jim … I refused to finish the thought. I just lay there and listened.

Somehow or other, I must've dozed off. The next thing I knew was the sound of the mountain man's deep gravelly voice. I opened my eyes and rolled over. The world had that dim, misty greyness of first light, and I could make out much more of our surroundings now. Ka-Ti was putting a blanket over her father's shoulders. I sat up as he walked over to my mat and sat down on a stone, dripping wet. He didn't immediately speak. He was busy fumbling with a little leather pouch which I soon realised was his pipe bag. It took him a minute to light it up, his hands were shaking so much, but he managed and took several long draughts while I waited, holding my breath, for the news.

"Yer cousin." His teeth rattled. "Has she got kinda yeller and brown hair, 'bout so long?" He touched the side of his shoulder.

"Yes. Yes, that's Imogen!" I was on my feet in a flash. "Is she ok? Did she look all right? They didn't see you, did they?" My heart was racing. I stared with all my might across the river as if I could see Imogen for myself.

"Just hold yer horses there, Miss Fire-Hair. She looks just fine, as far as I could tell in the dark. In fact, I think she heard me creepin' up on 'em. Looked sceered to death, but she was the only one awake, hands and feet all tied up while th'other four all slept flat out. Bunch of bottles of moonshine lying 'round the campfire, so I reckon they won't be too quick gettin' up this mornin'." He stood, throwing the blanket off his shoulders. "Still, we ain't got no time to lose sittin' here."

"How're we gonna get her across the river?" I asked. After all the Uktena stories, I felt pretty sure Imogen would rather suffer her kidnappers than brave swimming across those murky waters.

"They got a canoe over there. Looks like a Cherokee dugout."

My eyes popped. "That's Grasshopper's canoe. So the peddlers stole that too …,"

"Peddlers? More like professional thieves." He was rolling up the animal skin again with everything inside it. "I'd be willin' to bet my horse those men are workin' for Blunt."

I frowned. "They had a whole wagon full of Cherokee goods. Probably payment for doing Blunt's dirty work."

Jim grunted, then got to his feet and looked at me as if he were sizing me up. "You any kind a swimmer?"

I glanced at the river and gulped, remembering the shock of icy water on my face. "I can swim all right."

"Then here's the plan."

By the time he'd finished explaining, I was already shivering with the anticipation of what I had to do, but determined to grit my teeth and go through with it. I took off my moccasins, my quiver and hip pouch, bundled them up in one of the blankets and handed the bundle to Ka-Ti. She braced my arm and looked into my eyes, a look that said all the encouragement I needed.

Jim was already up to his knees in the river, waiting for me. I stepped lightly over the smooth, cold river rocks and dipped my first foot into the water. A rush of ice travelled up my veins, right to the top of my head, but I bit my lip, determined not to gasp. Jim nodded to Ka-Ti, then turned and shrank into the water until only his head floated on the surface. I closed my eyes, took a staggered breath and walked forward.

It was like hundreds of needles prickling my skin all at once. My throat closed off, but I took short, quick breaths through my nose until at last my body was submerged. My toes just touched the slimy river bottom. I inched forward, my arms circling in a frog-like stroke. By the middle of the river, I'd almost got used to the cold. Jim was waiting just beyond.

"Now remember, you take this knife and cut yer cousin free. Get her into that canoe without so much as a sneeze. Then wait for me." I nodded and followed him as he slowly, silently raised himself out of the water and crept, crouched low, up the bank. He stretched his head up, had a look around, and waved me to go forward. The idea was that Imogen would be less likely to scream out if she saw me first. At least I hoped, after all she'd been through, she still had enough sense to stay quiet.

I took the knife from his hand and forced my frozen fingers around its handle, then crept up the bank, squatting low as he had done. When I reached level ground, it was just as Jim had said. The men lay around the smoking fire snoring, their mouths hanging open, arms flung in every direction. Smashed glass and half-empty bottles were everywhere. My eyes travelled just beyond the mess.

There she was, tied to a tree with her head slumped down on her chest, fast asleep. Carefully stepping over chunks of glass, I reached the tree, lowered the knife and laid my icy hand on Imogen's bare arm.

With a gasp, she lifted her head. She blinked wide eyes, but I didn't need to hush her. The peddlers had already seen to that by tying a gag in her mouth. As I picked up the knife and started carving away at her ropes, I glanced up to see silent tears streaming down Imogen's cheeks. I squeezed one of the hands I had just freed and smiled at her, trying to convey the silent encouragement Ka-Ti had given me at the river.

As soon as I got the gag off, waterfalls started pouring from Imogen's eyes. I helped her up to her feet, and, hand in hand, we tip-toe ran around the sleeping thieves and climbed down the bank. Jim Weaver, crouched down just out of sight, gave me a wink as we reached the canoe and disappeared up the bank. Imogen climbed into the canoe, and I pushed it halfway out before climbing in after her.

We held each other's hands, waiting, listening, Imogen still crying silent rivers. A second later, Jim slid down the bank with his arms full. He quietly dumped what I then recognised as four pairs of boots and a couple of shotguns into the canoe. Jim winked again as he pushed us off and jumped in. Within minutes, we had paddled down river, out of sight of the peddlers' camp.

29

WHAT IMOGEN LEARNED

*I*t was a wonderful sight that rose up out of the mist in front of us: Ka-Ti standing out on a rock with the three horses to greet us. We banked the canoe in a little pool just before the river took a plunge over a small cataract. The whoosh and crash of the rapids below drowned out all other sounds — the very reason Jim had chosen that spot for our rendezvous.

As soon as our feet touched the ground, Ka-Ti was there, draping blankets over Imogen's and my shoulders. She motioned for us to follow her a little climb up the rocks from the waterfall where she'd set up camp on a flat shoal. Already she'd a built fire and over it, a little teepee structure made of sticks from which a kettle hung.

After I'd pulled on a pair of dry breeches and a fresh tunic, I sat down crosslegged beside Imogen near the fire and happily took the mug of steaming tea Ka-Ti offered me. The warmth of the flames on my face and the tea going down my throat felt like magic, thawing me right down to my frozen bones.

As Ka-Ti took a basket and wandered off into the trees, probably to gather nuts, I glanced at Imogen. Ka-Ti had given her a dry, clean cotton dress in exchange for her tattered, mud-splattered one, put ointment on Imogen's arms where the ropes had rubbed them raw, and put her hair up in a tidy braid like Ka-Ti's own hair. She looked like a new person, though her eyes were still a little puffy as she sat sipping her tea, staring into the fire in a far-off way. I didn't know quite how to begin saying the things I'd been mulling over ever since she'd disappeared.

"How's your ankle?" I began casually. "I guess you lost the crutch Wattie made you."

She pulled her skirt up a few inches and wiggled her foot. "Hardly hurts anymore. I almost forgot about it while I was being dragged around behind that wagon full of weirdness."

I snickered. "I'm glad it's better and … and I'm really glad you're ok, Immy. I could never have forgiven myself if something had happened to you."

She turned to look at me, but with a very different look in her eyes than I'd seen before. "It wasn't your fault, you know." Tears were welling up in her eyes again. "I'm surprised you even came after me, after the way I ran off on you like that, even after you'd warned me. I totally asked for this."

I opened my mouth to contradict her, but she carried on. "It's not an excuse for the way I acted, but I hope you know I only did it because I was so scared and … and angry."

"I don't blame you for being scared," I said. "This

whole thing is ... well ... really scary. But why were you angry?"

Imogen wiped her eyes with the corner of her blanket and stared down into her mug. "I guess it was because I was kind of jealous."

"Jealous?" I was gob-stopped. "Jealous of who?"

"Of you," she said as if it was obvious. "You seem to be getting along fine, like you belong here. Why does it have to be so much harder for me?"

"It's been hard for me too," I insisted. "I've just gotten good at hiding it, I guess."

She was shaking her head. "The truth is, as much as I've been wanting you to find a way home, I've been starting to realise that I don't belong there either. That's what made me so angry. I don't belong anywhere or in any time." Two giant tears plopped into her tea.

"What do you mean you don't belong at home? Your parents—"

"My parents are way too busy to care about me. I mean, they care that I nearly failed my first year of secondary school, but—"

"Nearly failed?" I hadn't meant to sound so surprised. "But you've always made top grades. That's how you got into that really good school."

"Yea, well, I guess I didn't work hard enough once I got in. I just felt really ... really lonely at boarding school. And even in the holidays, my mum and dad would rather hire private tutors and send me to see a shrink, when all *I* want is just to spend some time together as a family... like your family."

For the first time, I was beginning to see beneath the

shiny surface of Imogen's perfect life. "I guess that's why you weren't very excited about coming to America for autumn break," I muttered.

She sniffed and swivelled her mug. "I knew the only reason they sent me was because… they thought you'd be a good influence."

"Me?" I felt like I'd just been smashed with a wrecking ball of guilt.

"Oh, you know. Mum and Dad are always saying things like 'Why can't you be more like your cousin? She doesn't get into trouble.'"

"But that's not true," I protested. "I make mistakes all the time. Like the way I've been a selfish, terrible cousin to you ever since you got here."

She shook her head. "You haven't been. And none of that matters now, anyway. I just want to see them again."

"You will," I said, looking straight into her watery eyes. "We'll find a way together, and when we get back, things are going to be better."

We hugged, sloshing tea on my dry pair of breeches. It didn't even matter. I felt lighter than I had in days. With a gasp, I released her. "Im, you *do* belong here!"

"You're just being nice."

"No, I'm not." I smacked myself on the forehead. "I can't believe I forgot."

"Forgot what?"

"You have to see this." I scrambled over to the heap of clothes where my quiver rested on top, pulled out the leather folder and brought it back to Imogen. "Now brace yourself," I said as I turned open to the painting of the two of us side by side.

She stared at the painting as I explained how I'd thought there was only the one painting of me, then how I'd accidentally found the others after she'd been taken by the peddlers.

"I don't understand what this means," Imogen said, her eyes still transfixed on the picture.

"It means Ramona knew we'd be here. We were meant to be here *together*."

"But *how* did she know? And how did she mean for us to get back? Have you asked them?"

"I've been a little distracted rescuing you," I admitted. "But I did ask about the stone, and I was wrong. Ramona didn't take it. It's got nothing to do with her magic."

"But if Ramona painted those horses in the cave, then she has to come back some time. I mean, the painting isn't there yet, right? Don't they have any idea where she is?"

I shook my head. "Wattie told me that Ramona might've run off with the stone so that Black Fox would leave Jim and Ka-Ti alone. But Jim swears she didn't take it, and I believe him."

Imogen scrunched up her face, thinking. "Still, if Black Fox *thought* Jim had taken it, Ramona might have pretended to take it away just to throw Black Fox off the scent."

I looked at Imogen, impressed by the sleuth skills I never knew she had. "Yea, I suppose she might've done that. In which case, the stone is still out there somewhere."

Imogen's eyes grew wide. "Maybe if we could find it, she could come back." She frowned. "Only, how would she know, even if we did find it? I mean, it's not like we can send her an email."

"I don't know," I said, and my eyes dropped to the painting of Imogen and me. "Maybe the same way she knew about us, even though we've never met her. Maybe she'll just know."

Imogen made a face to warn me that Jim was approaching. With a grunt, he lowered himself onto a stump beside the fire, took out his knife and started picking at his fingernails with the tip of it. We watched him, neither of us speaking.

"What's the matter?" he asked, holding his hands out to the flames. "Wildcat caught yer tongues?" When neither of us said anything, Jim tried a more direct approach. "What's yer name again? I-ma-jeen?"

"It's *Imogen*," she corrected.

Jim tried again. "Eem-o-gin?"

"Oh, never mind. Just call me Dilli. All the others do."

"Dilli?" Jim scratched his head and chuckled to himself. "Well it's easier to say, I'll give you that. Well now, Dilli, I don't reckon you happened to overhear anything interestin' from them thugs while they was draggin' you around?"

Imogen knitted her eyebrows, thinking back. "They talked a lot about Governor Blunt."

"Go on." Jim was all ears.

"He's been paying them to steal things from the Chero-kee. Like horses," she said, giving me a meaningful look. "Oh, and something about a treaty Blunt is making. They said they'd get the rest of their pay day after tomorrow once the Governor made the deal … that they'd get first pick of the land."

"Blunt's Town," I said at once.

Both Imogen and Jim looked at me.

I got up, ran to the grey horse and found the rolled-up map I'd stuffed into his saddle bag. "Here," I said, handing it to Jim. "I found this in Blunt's mansion. I forgot to show you."

Jim unrolled the map and scratched his chin. "Well I'll be …"

"Blunt's making a treaty with Black Fox," I told Imogen. "That's why he got so flustered when you mentioned his name. He's buying Nickajack *illegally*."

Imogen looked outraged, then perplexed. "How do you know all this, Katie?"

"Long story," I said, and explained briefly how I'd followed the officers who had taken Wattie, then sneaked into the Governor's mansion and spied on his conversation with Lovegood.

"How'd you get away without being caught?" she asked in a mix of amazement and horror.

"I … uh …"

Jim answered for me. "She rode off on Lovegood's horse. That one, right there." He nodded at the grey horse and clapped his hands together.

Imogen's face had gone from horrified to impressed. "Katie! Now *you're* a horse thief!"

I shrugged. "Only in the Robin Hood sense of the word."

"There's a fittin' name for that horse," Jim hollered. "Why don't you call him Robin Hood?"

We all laughed for one golden moment. Ka-Ti returned with her basket and put her arm over her father's broad shoulders.

But Jim quickly steered the conversation back to deep waters. "There's somethin' about this whole treaty story that don't sit right. I know Black Fox. He's as red-blooded a Cherokee warrior as ever you'll meet. I just can't see him sellin' his people's land to a man like Blunt."

Something Wattie had said leapt to mind. "Unless Blunt had something Black Fox really wanted."

"Like what?" Imogen asked.

"Wattie told me he'd do anything for the Uktena Stone. Even kill for it." I glanced at Jim, whose eyes were fixed on the fire. "What if that's what Blunt is bargaining with? The stone for the land?"

"I always suspected Blunt had the stone," Jim said at last. He sounded as if he was only just controlling the angry grizzly bear inside of him. "He didn't just accuse me of stealing it. He arranged the whole thing. But he's gonna reap what he's sown."

"What do you mean?" I asked.

"Just wait 'til Black Fox gets his hands on that Uktena Stone. He believes it'll make him invincible, and his gang of followers'll believe it too. He'll make himself Chief and lead his warriors in a war against the settlers, you mark my words." He shook his head. "Blunt don't have the slightest idea of what he's getting himself in for. You pick a snake up by its tail, and the other end's bound to bite you."

"If we could just find that stone, we could put a stop to this," I said, jumping to my feet. "Without the stone, Blunt has nothing to bargain with."

Jim was shaking his head. "Gal, you done been in that

cold water too long. Don't you know that ol' chunk of rock could be anywhere? Why, it could be in Blunt's pocket."

I sank back down beside Imogen again, but she was looking at me with a strange light in her eyes. "Of course!" she said, almost laughing. "Katie, we know where it is! Don't you remember the first time we ever encountered Black Fox?"

I shivered. "How could I forget?" I grabbed Imogen's arm. "Oh! The cave! Of course."

In a rush of excitement, Imogen and I told Jim what we had overheard between Black Fox and the guard that first terrifying night in the cave.

"Where was this cave?" asked Jim.

We looked at each other, both trying to remember some useful point of reference.

"Somewhere near the Federal Road?" I offered.

"And it's behind a waterfall," Imogen added.

To our amazement, Jim gave a sharp nod. "I know the place." He stood up and, thrusting his knife back into its sheath, said, "Drink up, gals. We're goin' on a treasure hunt."

30

A SHOT IN THE DARK

"*B*ut what about rescuing Wattie?" I murmured to Jim as we dismounted our horses. I was beginning to worry about what Blunt might do to him when he learned we'd foiled his plans.

"We get that stone first," Jim answered. "Then we got somethin' to bargain with."

We tied the horses a little way off and followed Jim on foot up a steep, winding path through the woods.

"That's the entrance to the cave just there." He was nodding towards the other side of the ravine we'd been hiking along where, sure enough in the rock face, almost hidden behind the rhododendron bushes, was the black outline of a cave opening. When we got closer, Jim lit a couple of lanterns and handed one to Ka-Ti. Then he ducked his head and disappeared into the dark sliver in the mountainside. Jim led the way, Imogen and I following after him and Ka-Ti taking up the rear, holding her lantern up to cast a beam of light on the steps just ahead of us.

I could never have imagined what strange worlds exist

in the belly of a mountain. The lantern lights lit up walls and a ceiling that looked like dripping wax. Sometimes we had to squeeze around a corkscrew pillar of the waxy stone or duck under a great blob of it like a giant bee hive, or step over little streams that cut across the slippery floor and disappeared down mysterious holes.

Imogen grabbed on to the back of my tunic as we squeezed past a particularly narrow gap, shuffling sideways as the walls almost touched each other, then opened out again. Then the ceiling came down to meet the floor like the two halves of a hamburger bun, and we had to drop to our hands and knees and crawl across the clammy surface. The tightness made me feel as if I were choking. I closed my eyes, breathing slowly and forcing myself to imagine that I was in a vast, open cavern. When I heard the sound of rushing water, I opened my eyes and my imagination had come true.

Jim's lantern swung in his raised hand, shooting beams of light in every direction of the enormous room that was as wide as a circus tent and as tall as a cathedral. My jaw dropped as I got to my feet, my head tilting back to take in the waterfall spilling from the rock ceiling down into a clear pool.

"Wow," Imogen breathed when she'd got to her feet beside me, followed by Ka-Ti.

"Heh. So this is where Blunt hoards his loot. Ain't he a right magpie?" Jim said, walking a circle around the cave.

Only then did I take my eyes off the waterfall to notice the dozens and dozens of crates and barrels littering the cave floor. Jim rifled through them, picking up a beaded belt here, tossing aside some cloth there. It dawned on me that these must be the stolen treasures of countless Cherokee villages along the Tennessee River.

"But the stone could be anywhere," Imogen said despondently as she half-heartedly started searching through a crate of knick-knacks.

"Miss Fire-Hair, Dilli, you two take my lantern and start huntin' on that side." Jim pointed to the opposite side of the cave as he handed me the lantern. "Me and King-fisher'll start over here. Look for smaller boxes first. I don't reckon even Blunt would just toss the stone into a crate of petticoats."

Imogen and I searched every small box, basket or pouch we could find. We found silver earrings, beaded necklaces and even a purse made out of a bear's paw, but no stone.

I sat back on my heels and scratched my nose – I'd just been sifting through a basket of feathery headdresses. "I feel like we're wasting time, looking in all this stuff."

Imogen tossed a pair of moccasins aside. "You mean you don't think the stone is even in here?"

I chewed on my lip. "It *has* to be in here. At least it was when Black Fox came sniffing for it, or why else would the guard have turned him away? It just seems like it would be hidden somewhere all on its own. Somewhere special."

As if drawn by a magnet, my head and Imogen's both turned at that second towards the waterfall.

"Can't hurt to try," Imogen said. "We do tend to find interesting and unexpected things behind waterfalls."

Together we meandered through the maze of stolen goods until we came to the pool fed by the waterfall. We walked gingerly around the slippery edge, grabbing hold of the cave wall as soon as we reached it. I held up the lantern, making a sparkling mist appear before our eyes. But what else appeared were stones, smooth and flat, spaced out across the pool leading behind the waterfall. Stepping stones.

It was slow work, hopping from stone to slippery stone. I went first, turning to shine the lantern for Imogen each time before going on. Twelve stones later, I could feel the shower of mist wetting my face and hair. We were nearly under the waterfall. With the next leap, I landed on a stone floor. Grabbing Imogen's hand as she leaped behind the waterfall, I held up the lantern.

We were in the belly of a colourful alcove. Yellow stalactites dripped down like weird, waxy chandeliers from the domed ceiling. A sort of stone shelf jutted out in the middle of the alcove. We tiptoed closer, light held high. There on the shelf was a single, smooth oval stone. It glistened green and pearly white in the light, and when I leaned in closer, I could make out the spiral design etched into its surface: a snake.

I didn't lay a finger on the stone until Jim and Ka-Ti came to see it for themselves.

"Is that it?" Imogen looked at Jim, whose eyes were glued to the thing with a grim expression.

Without ungluing them, he nodded. "That's the little rock that cost me everything I had." With that, he reached out and grabbed the stone with a vengeance, then slipped it into the pouch at his hip. "Let's get outta here." He stepped across the stones again, the rest of us following him.

I brought up the rear and had just reached the last step when a voice echoed around the cavern walls.

"WHAT'S GOIN' ON IN THERE?"

Jim turned and ordered, "PUT THAT LIGHT OUT AND TAKE COVER!" I put out my lantern just as Jim put out his. The cave went black as we scattered like mice. I felt Imogen whip past me just as I ducked down behind a box.

The pitch blackness lasted only for a second before another light flickered in another passageway on the opposite side of the cave. It grew larger and brighter as a guard scurried into view, his lantern in one hand, a pistol in the other.

I ducked a little lower as he held up his lamp, swinging it this way and that. It stopped. My heart stood still as I looked down its beam. It had landed on Imogen's foot just as she'd pulled it in behind her barrel. I watched, horrified, as the guard set down his lantern and took aim with his pistol at the barrel behind which Imogen lay huddled, unaware she'd been seen. *Where was Jim?*

Then I saw him. Jim's hulking figure rose up from behind a pile of crates behind the guard's back. Just as the guard cocked the pistol, Jim threw something hard and round at him. It caught the man in the shoulder. He hollered and spun around, ready to shoot at Jim.

I jumped out from behind my box. *"OVER HERE!"* I shouted.

The guard swung the gun around to point it at me, and at the same time Jim ran up behind him and threw his muscular forearm around the man's neck in a chokehold, while another hand reached around and grabbed the pistol. The guard kicked his lantern in the struggle and, in an instant of shattering glass, all light went out followed by a deafening *Bang!* that made the cave walls and floor shudder. I dropped to the ground and covered my head with my arms as bits of rock and sharp stalactites crumbled and plummeted from the cave's ceiling.

For a minute, I was deaf and blind, groping around on my hands and knees, terrified to learn what had happened when the gun went off. With a sharp breath, I pulled my hand back in pain – I must've cut it on a piece of broken lantern glass — but as I did, my fingers brushed over something smooth and round. Getting shakily to my feet, I slipped the object into my pocket. A sound, like faint grunting, made me stop and listen.

A second later, there was the unmistakable sound of a match striking and, blinking into the lamp light, I could make out Jim Weaver's broad shoulders. He had the guard pinned to the ground with his knee and the man's hands bound up with rope.

"I lost the stone, but I caught us a rat," Jim said. His lip was bleeding.

"Katie, you're insane." Imogen appeared from behind her hiding spot. "You nearly got yourself—"

A chunk of the rock the size of a tombstone landed about an arm's length from where Imogen stood, crushing several barrels and sending shock waves through the room.

"Y'all *RUN!*" Jim yelled, but he didn't have to tell us twice. As more chunks of stone thundered down from above, we bolted for the passageway on the other side. Jim and his captive stood at the doorway waiting as Imogen, then Ka-Ti, then I made it through. We didn't stop, but ran through the blackness, hands out to feel the way forward. I'd got about ten strides in when I heard a yell behind me that could only mean pain.

"Stop!" I screamed into the darkness ahead of me. "Jim's hurt!"

I heard Ka-Ti's and Imogen's heavy breathing beside me.

"Pa!" Ka-Ti panted, moving past me.

"Ya'll get outta here!" Jim growled. But none of us listened. Imogen took the prisoner's rope — he was too scared to put up a fight — while Ka-Ti and I each grabbed Jim under an armpit and dragged, dragged until I was sure my face had turned blue, dragged until the passage started to lighten.

"There's the way out!" Imogen called from the front. And with another few heavy steps, we were dragging Jim right out into the daylight. Ka-Ti and I stumbled to our knees, exhausted, but she didn't even catch her breath before taking the bandana she wore around her arm and tying it around her father's leg where the deerskin had been soaked through with blood. She took a flask from her jacket and gave it to him to drink.

Jim took a swig and winced. "You gals ain't too good at followin' orders," he grunted.

None of us apologised.

Jim's leg was badly hurt. There was no doubt about it. We had come out of the mountain into the open alcove behind the enormous waterfall that Imogen and I had now visited three times. After scouting the place for any more guards and finding it deserted, we propped Jim up against the stone wall and tied our prisoner to a root that had wormed its way through the rock. Once Ka-Ti had tended to all of our scratches, even the prisoner's, we washed our hands and faces in the runoff from the waterfall and plopped down, exhausted.

It was Imogen who asked the question I'm pretty sure we'd all been thinking: "Now what?"

Nobody answered. Then Jim shook his head. "Without that stone, I reckon our hands are 'bout as tied as that fella's over there." He nodded his head towards the militia man who hadn't made a peep since the shock of his narrow escape from the cave.

A faint recollection, like a fading memory of a dream, came into my head. "Wait a second ..." I reached my hand into my hip pouch and pulled out the object I'd found in the dark. The stone glistened green and pearly white in my hand.

"Well I'll be ..." Jim clicked his tongue. "I'd take my hat off to you if I hadn't lost it in that there avalanche."

31

PAINTED HORSES

*I*mogen and I sat crosslegged on the ground, chewing on some dried meat from the guard's rations we'd found in the alcove and tried with all our might to think. Time was running out fast, and now with Jim unable to move, our options for rescuing Wattie *and* stopping Blunt before daybreak were looking pretty slim.

And now it was all down to me and Imogen ... and Ka-Ti, of course. Though she had her hands full looking after injuries. As we tried to think of a plan, she was busy about her work with such focus that she almost looked like she was in another world. I watched her as she filled several clay pots she'd found in the alcove with water from a little stream that ran down the rock and carried them back to the deepest part of the alcove. There she took tiny bottles from her bag and shook some sort of powdery stuff from them into the water, then stirred it with a stick. I wanted to ask her what she was doing. Probably mixing some kind of Cherokee medicine, I thought. As I watched her, something niggled at my memory ...

"How long do you think we have?" Imogen's question jolted me back into the important conversation of what we were to do.

Jim squinted at the patch of sky that was just visible between the waterfall and the rock. "I reckon it's about noon already. Governor's treaty signin' is set for daybreak, so that means …"

"Probably between fifteen and sixteen hours, assuming the sun rises around six o'clock in the morning."

I stared at Imogen.

"What?" She shrugged. "It's just simple maths."

I turned back to Jim, who was trying to hide the fact that he was still wincing from pain by pretending to itch his nose. "But we have the stone," I said hopefully. "Black Fox will never sign the treaty without the stone."

Jim took a sharp breath. "That's prob'ly true, but what's to stop him shootin' us and takin' it? Last I heard, Black Fox has got good reason to be sore with you, Miss Fire-Hair. Prob'ly got a welt in his neck the size of a groundhog's mound to remind him."

"Then we hide it," Imogen said, raising her open palms in a 'what's the big deal' sort of way.

"Huh," Jim shook his head. "You could hide it, sure. But Blunt'll just find another bargainin' tool. It won't stop him from makin' life difficult for the Cherokees. And if you hadn't noticed, I ain't in much of a state for playin' hide 'n' seek just now."

Imogen sighed and rested her chin on her fist, scrunching up her face to think some more.

But I was thinking about what Jim had said. "You're right," I said. "Blunt needs to be stopped for good. People need to know what he's really like, what he's really up to. If we could only speak to the President—"

"Sure! You wanna ride up to Washington tonight and have a word with him?" Jim slapped his knee, then grunted in pain. "They should'a called you Katie Head-in-Clouds, instead of Fire-Hair. It's a nice idea for a story book, but that ain't how things work in the frontier. Blunt's a powerful man. He's got powerful people on his side. Trust me. I've tried goin' behind his back once before. He'll snap his fingers and have me right back behind bars for plottin' against him, just like last time."

I squeezed my fists, willing an idea to land in my head. If only we had help. If only Joseph McKay and Terrapin Jo and the rest of them were there to stand beside us ... that was what we needed. I got onto my knees and looked Jim straight in the eye. "We *need* to tell everybody in Nickajack the truth about Blunt. We need a protest. We need them to come here and stand up to the Governor so he knows he can't get away with his tricks anymore."

Jim gave me one of his silent hard stares that I'd almost gotten used to by now. "And just how do you suggest we're a'gonna get word to Nickajack, then get all them folks up here before daybreak?"

"They will ride."

I jerked my head around, completely surprised to find Ka-Ti had been listening to the conversation.

"But Blunt stole all their horses," I reminded her. "They won't have anything to ride."

Ka-Ti hadn't turned around. She still knelt facing the rock wall in front of her, her head to one side as if she were examining something. "They will ride," she said again in the same quiet, confident voice.

I pushed myself onto my feet. There was something so strange about the way Ka-Ti spoke. What *was* she looking at on that wall?

I walked slowly up behind her with a prickling sensation in my skin, like something was about to happen. I peered over her shoulder and saw now what she had been doing all the while. It hadn't been medicine she had been mixing, but paint. She had used it to decorate the cave wall with dozens of running horses.

DREAM WEAVER

*R*ealisation rushed over me, as strong and heavy as the pounding waterfall rushed overhead. "It was you?" The words came out in a breath. "It wasn't your mother. It was you who brought us here?"

Ka-Ti turned her head and peered into my eyes, her brow knitted as if she were trying hard to remember something she'd forgotten.

Things were starting to make sense. I took the leather folder from my quiver and, dropping to my knees beside Ka-Ti, pointed to the Kingfisher at the corner of the first painting. "You painted this, didn't you? But how did you know? How had you seen me on that horse?"

Her brow knitted; a memory flashed in her eyes. "A dream," she whispered, as if it was all coming back to her. Her voice was like the softest breeze as she explained, "My mother speaks to me in dreams. She sends pictures of faraway places ... and people."

"And you painted them all?"

She nodded. A smile lit up her face as another memory

came into her mind's eye. "I used to dream of a girl with fire for hair." She rested her hand gently on mine and looked very earnestly into my eyes. "I knew you were that girl," she breathed. "You came to us across many suns and moons."

"Yes," I answered, and quickly added, "but not on purpose. We fell into your painting … *this* painting," I said, nodding towards the cave wall. "It brought us here."

I felt a hand on my shoulder as Imogen knelt down beside me, her mouth open and her eyes sweeping over the painted horses. A whispered "Oh my goodness" was all she could say.

Ka-Ti was positively glowing. Taking the painting of me and the horse, she threw back her long hair and rushed over to her father. "Pa, my dream friend has come."

Jim Weaver looked at the painting, then up at me, then he did the same several times more. "Come closer," he mumbled, and I obeyed. He stared at me with a strange, almost frightened look in his eyes. "Who are you?" He said it as if he'd seen a ghost. "Where'd you come from?"

I rubbed my bandaged hand awkwardly, not sure quite how to answer. "We came from … from a long way away. From—"

"Another time," Imogen finished for me.

I nodded, and looked at my hands again, avoiding Jim's eyes. They looked so pained … yet so hopeful. "Have you seen my Ramona?" he asked, his deep voice nearly cracking.

I shook my head, a knot tying itself in my stomach to see the disappointment on Jim's face as he closed his eyes and let his head fall back against the wall.

"But I think I know where she's been."

His eyes opened again with a flicker of hope.

"Last summer I met a painter," I began. "Tom Tippery was his name. He told me he had bought some paints from a woman at a market. It must have been Ramona."

"Where'd you meet this Tom fella?"

I winced as I told him the truth. "In England, over 200 years ago."

Jim looked in shock. He rubbed his hand over his chin, his eyes fidgeted around as if looking for an explanation; then he hung his head in his hands. It was a long moment before he found his voice again. "Ramona used to tell me stories … of faraway places. Other times. I always wondered how she knew so much. She didn't read English, but she sure knew things … knew 'em like she'd seen 'em with her own eyes." I was startled when Jim looked up at me with pleading in his eyes. "Will I ever see her again?"

"I … don't know," I whispered. I had only one small flicker of hope to offer this broken-hearted man, but it was something. "I did see Ramona," I said, "in a dream last week. She was holding you, Ka-Ti, when you were just a baby."

Ka-Ti smiled and wiped a single tear from her eye.

"I think she wanted to come home, but there was still some danger in the way."

"What kinda danger?" Jim asked, a bit of his old gruffness coming back.

"It was a snake. The Uktena." Jim looked taken aback. This was the time to tell him Imogen's and my theory. "We thought maybe Ramona left because people thought she had the Uktena Stone, and she didn't want to put you two in danger. So we've been thinking, now we have proof that Ramona never took the stone, that … maybe she can come back somehow."

"How?" Jim asked.

Imogen and I exchanged a helpless look. "We don't know."

"We don't even know how *we're* supposed to get back," Imogen said. "We only know that we came through your painting, Ka-Ti."

Ka-Ti got gracefully to her feet. She took one of my hands and one of Imogen's in hers. "I remember a song my mother sang when she mixed her paints. A song that belongs to travellers. When she sang, her paints came to life. I remember every word of it." She released our hands and ran to the alcove where her painted horses were still drying. "Maybe I can sing them to life."

Imogen and I each let out a breath of disbelief. I had buried my fear of never getting home deep down until it was nearly forgotten in my race to rescue Imogen. But now, a fountain of hope was bubbling up inside of me and threatening to burst out at the corners of my eyes.

Jim cleared his throat, and I forced the tears back down with a deep breath. His voice was gruff again, but kind. "If you girls wanna get back to where you come from, can't nobody blame you for it. Y'all done what you could here, but this ain't yer time. It ain't yer fight. Y'all get on back and let fate do what he will with the rest of us."

I wanted to protest, to say that we would see it through … whatever *it* was. But I took one glance at Imogen, sniffling and wiping her eyes and runny nose on her sleeve, and kept my mouth shut. I couldn't ask Imogen to risk her life again. Not after all she'd been through already. I made up my mind and opened my mouth to agree with Jim that it was time to go home.

But before I could get the words out, Imogen spoke up in a stuffy-nosed but strong voice. "Of *course* we're not leaving *now*! Not when it's just getting exciting." She sniffed at me through her puffy eyes. "Sorry, Katie, but I'm not missing out on seeing the look on Blunt's face tomorrow morning."

I threw my arms around Imogen's neck and gave her the biggest hug my sore arms could muster. Now the die was cast. We were in this adventure together to the end, for better or for worse.

THE AFTERNOON SUN was already high in the sky. The waterfall kept pouring down into the pool below, like sand in an enormous hourglass. Time was running out. We needed a plan.

"What was that you were saying before, Ka-Ti?" It was Imogen who posed the question. Now that she had taken a stand to stay and fight, she was applying every cell in her brain to coming up with an idea. "About Nickajack? You said the people could ride here."

Ka-Ti nodded.

"But where will they get the horses?" I asked again.

"I will show you."

Ka-Ti did not want to leave her father, but Jim waved us away. "Y'all get on. I've been wantin' to have a talk with this young guard here. See if he has anythin' interestin' to say about this treaty business." So we left the guard still tied and propped up next to Jim, who appeared to be sharing a pipe with the man as we followed Ka-Ti along the ledge that took us out from behind the waterfall.

From there, we left the path and climbed, hands and feet, up the side of the mountain, grabbing onto rocks, roots, branches, whatever we could grip to pull ourselves up the steep slope. Ka-Ti reached the top first and gave us both a hand up. Then she pointed down the slope on the other side.

I couldn't believe my eyes. At the bottom of the hill was a grassy gorge, and grazing on the grass were dozens of horses!

"So *that's* where Lovegood's been keeping all those stolen horses." I turned to Ka-Ti. "How did you know they were here?" I asked in awe.

She was looking out over the horses with a serene smile. "I saw them in my mind. That is why I painted them."

Imogen and I exchanged another awed look. Then she asked, "But how are we going to get all of these back to Nickajack?"

Ka-Ti gave Imogen an almost mischievous look. She tossed her curtain of hair back, raised two fingers to her lips and gave a whistle that echoed all around the gorge. Like magic, the horses' heads rosed, their ears perked. They snorted, stamped, and trotted, every one, into a neat semicircle facing the mountain, as if waiting for Ka-Ti's next command.

I shook my head in disbelief. "So you've got your mother's horse-whispering gift as well, huh?"

Ka-Ti nodded. "They will follow me to Nickajack."

It seemed at least part of our problem was solved. Ka-Ti could lead the horses back to their masters in Nickajack. We agreed she would go straight to the McKays' house and take the Uktena Stone with her in hopes that Nickajack would rally behind her when they heard how Blunt had deceived them and saw the proof with their own eyes.

Jim kissed his daughter's forehead, but couldn't say much more than "You come back to me, Kingfisher, you hear?" She nodded and kissed his whiskery cheek. Then Imogen and I climbed back up to the ridge with her. At the top, she hugged us both, then climbed, as easily as a squirrel scurries down a tree, down the gorge to where the horses were grazing. We watched them gather around her, as if listening to her instructions. One chestnut stepped forward. She mounted it bareback and, with the whole herd falling in line behind her, kicked off into a gallop.

A minute later, a cloud of dust was all we could see of them, but Imogen and I didn't turn back. While we'd been discovering the horses with Ka-Ti, Jim had discovered from the guard that the treaty was to take place in Hiwassee at sunup the next morning. Lieutenant Love-good was to meet the guard at the cave in the early hours to retrieve the stone, then carry it back to Hiwassee where, so the guard said, the treaty would be signed in secret.

If Ka-Ti succeeded in rallying Nickajack, there was still a chance of throwing water on the Governor's plot. But whatever happened, we had to rescue Wattie first, or who knew what Blunt might do? With Jim's injury, breaking Wattie out of prison all came down to Imogen and me.

We had no plan, just each other and a rough map Jim

had sketched onto a piece of paperbark. We'd go down the mountain for Robin Hood, then follow the river back to Hiwassee. With one more good look at the map, we started off across the mountain ridge, just as the sun started its journey downward. The race against time was on.

PRISON BREAK

"You know you don't have to hold on *quite* so tight," I grunted over my shoulder to Imogen behind me in the saddle. Her arms were squeezed so tight around my waist, I was seeing spots. "Just use your legs a bit more to grip the horse."

"Sorry," she whispered, loosening her grip a little. "It feels a lot faster in the dark. And you never know when we might just ride off a cliff or something."

"We won't ride off a cliff," I whispered back. "Jim's directions were simple. We follow the Federal Road all the way into Hiwassee. We can't possibly go wrong. Now just try to relax. I'm going to get us back into a gallop. No time to canter."

"Sure, I'll just relax then," Imogen answered sarcastically as she wound her fingers tightly around handfuls of my tunic.

The road was lonely and lit only by a pale sliver of the moon, but we kept up a steady pace. With every stride we were getting closer to Wattie. I tried to think of that and ignore the other fact – that we were also getting closer to our enemies.

We dismounted at the edge of the forest and crept towards the Garrison to spy out our prospects.

"It looks like there's some kind of party going on in there," Imogen said.

"That'll be the delegates' banquet. This is good," I said, trying to keep an encouraging tone. "At least with all the people coming in, the gates are open. We'll just ride in behind the carriages and hope nobody gives us a second glance."

"Hope nobody gives us a second...?" Imogen's expression was dumbfounded. "Katie, we'll be riding into the Garrison on Lieutenant Lovegood's horse which, in case you forgot, you stole. You're wanted in there."

I let out a long, frustrated sigh, resenting that Imogen was right. "Well what other option do we have? ... Wait a second. There *is* another way in. Last time I sneaked out by a corral door behind the stables."

Imogen considered this option and finally nodded. "A stable is probably the best place to sneak in a horse without getting unwanted attention."

"The question is, what do we do once we get in?"

"More like *if* we get in." She stood up and brushed the leaves from her skirt. "We'll figure that out when we come to it."

Several horses turned curious eyes towards us as we approached the corral, but there was no sign of any other person. With as much stealth as we could manage, I led

Robin Hood through the gate, and Imogen closed it behind us. We crept along the fence and up against the Garrison's outer wall towards the corral door. Imogen poked her head around the open upper half of the door to peek inside the stables.

Pulling her head back after a moment, she whispered, "There are a ton of horses in there. We might just be able to get away with sneaking in one more."

I nodded. "On your signal."

She craned her head through the stable door again, waiting. Then, with an excited nod, she waved her hand for me to come forward and, unlatching the corral door, pulled it quietly open while Robin Hood and I crept through.

My heart jumped into my throat when I heard voices close by. One of the grooms was bragging to his companions about a game of cards he'd won against a soldier. I exhaled and kept moving away from the voices, leading Robin Hood past the row of stalls right down to the end. The last stall was empty, making the perfect hiding spot for our next stage of plan-making.

"all right," Imogen began. "Now the real question. How do we cross the courtyard? I don't see any way of getting to the prison without parading right in front of the Governor's mansion."

Once again recalling my escape from the Garrison just a couple of days earlier, I suggested, "We can go *behind* the Governor's mansion. There's a narrow passageway, and nobody's likely to be there at this time."

"What, you mean with Robin Hood?" She looked doubtful.

"If we leave him here, we might not be able to get back to him once we've freed Wattie."

She blew out a gust of air. "Let's do it then."

We inched along between the house and the outer wall, retracing my steps from my earlier escape from the Governor's mansion. Only this time, we were walking right into danger's way … and we had a horse. An enormous, stolen horse. *One day*, I tried to reassure myself as we tiptoed along, *we are going to look back and laugh about this.*

I tried to keep my eyes straight ahead, focused on the shortening distance between us and the prison, but the lights and sounds coming from the mansion windows drew my attention.

"There are people dancing up there," Imogen whispered, her eyes glued on a tall row of windows in the upper storey.

I looked up and winced. It hadn't occurred to me that the ballroom where the Governor would be hosting the delegates might face the back of the house. "Let's hope they keep dancing and don't look out," I answered, dropping my eyes down to the lower floor windows where they connected with the stunned gaze of a woman holding a silver tray. I smiled innocently while pushing Imogen forward. "Hurry up, hurry up. We've been spotted."

Throwing caution aside now that our cover was blown, we picked up the pace to the end of the house and turned the corner. The relief of being in the dark side of the house, safe from window-gazers, lasted only a second. The prison was in sight now. The real danger was just beginning.

"There's just one guard, a young one," Imogen said as we crept to the edge of the shadows to scout the area.

"Katie, do you think you could shoot him from here with that venom stuff?"

I shook my head. "What if I miss? Hitting Black Fox was just a lucky shot. I'll keep a dart ready, just in case, but can't we think of a less violent way of distracting him?"

"Like what?" Imogen demanded.

I bit my lip. "You remember how you persuaded the guards to let us into the Garrison?"

"That's not gonna work *again*."

"Why not? You were amazing!"

"Because I've been riding through the forest on the back of a sweaty horse and I have dirt on my face."

I stared through the darkness at her slightly frazzled appearance. "We can tidy you up. And as to the smell, well, I don't think anyone's wearing body splash around here anyway."

Imogen grimaced as I spat on my sleeve and wiped her face, then smoothed back the flyaway bits of hair around her face. "There. He won't be able to resist you now." I bit my lip again, trying not to smile.

She rolled her eyes. After straightening up and taking a few deep breaths, as if getting into character, she strolled confidently out into the clearing, her hips swishing slightly more than normal.

I led Robin Hood as close as we could get while remaining hidden in the shadows and cupped my hand to my ear.

"Oh!" She squealed, followed by a girly giggle. "I do beg your pardon. I was just coming out for a bit of fresh, American air. But what are you doing out here in the dark? All the other officers are inside, dancing."

The guard's voice was high, as if it hadn't broken yet. "Well you see, Miss, somebody has to guard the prisoners."

"Oh, I see." Imogen sounded convincingly dimwitted. "It's so brave of you. Must be some terrible ruffians locked up in there. But still… it does seem awfully unfair. I don't see why you should have to do the job while all the others get to enjoy themselves."

"I'm just a junior cavalry officer," the boy replied modestly. "The others leave all the bad jobs to me."

"How horrid!" Imogen sounded scandalised. "You have as much right to enjoy the banquet as any of them. And I've been longing to have a dance with a *handsome* American officer like you."

The boy's voice was even higher when he answered. "But what about the prisoners?"

"Oh, don't worry about that. I'm sure they're all locked up. What could possibly happen during one dance?"

"Well, I'd hate to disappoint a…a lady…"

They were walking towards the mansion. I couldn't believe it! Imogen's expertise in flirting had saved the day again. If she could just manage to get the keys and then lose the guard, we might actually pull this off.

"Well, if it isn't the little horse thief."

My smile fell as my blood turned to ice at the sound of Lovegood's callous, haughty voice. I turned slowly around to face him. His cold smile glinted as he made his way towards me through the dark passage.

I stood frozen until he was no more than an arm's length away and glaring down at me smugly. "You know, you shouldn't get mixed up with those Cherokee. You'll end up just like them."

With gritted teeth, I looked him in the eye. "I *am* Cherokee," I growled, and without a moment's hesitation, I launched myself up onto Robin Hood's back. Together we shot out into the clearing, but before we'd passed the prison, I pulled back on the reins and turned to face Lieutenant Lovegood as he stepped out into the moonlight, the frosty smile still making his face a menace.

"You really think I'm going to let you take my horse again?"

He raised his right hand gripping a pistol and squinted one eye, pointing the weapon right at me. "I don't normally hurt little girls, but I *will* shoot horse thieves. This is your last chance to give me back my horse."

I looked from the horse to the weapon. "I'll give him back," I said, and the pistol lowered ever so slightly as he opened his shut eye. "When you give back everything you stole from Nickajack." Robin Hood and I charged forward.

"How dare you?" he said, his face turning furious. He raised his gun hand again, but as he did, Robin Hood gave a mighty roar. Next thing I knew, I was holding on for dear life as the horse reared up on his hind legs. Before Lovegood knew what had hit him, one of the horse's hooves pawed out and struck him on the side of the head, sending his cap with the golden sabres spinning like a Frisbee disc and the pistol flying from his hand.

Lovegood stayed on his back only for a moment before he sat up, clutching the side of his head with a look of dazed pain. I glared down at him as he squinted, trying to focus on me. "You shouldn't run around with criminals, Lieutenant. You'll end up just like them."

With an enraged growl, he stumbled to his feet, staggering back and forth. I jumped down and sprinted for the pistol just as he made a clumsy lunge for it. I got there first. He raised his hands up beside his head, and at the same time, someone ran up behind me. I spared a quick glance over my shoulder to see Imogen approaching, her eyes wide and mouth open.

"Well, looks like you found something to do while I was away," she said with what was almost a disbelieving laugh in her voice.

"Did you get the keys?" I asked.

She held up a ring of keys and gave them a shake. "My new little friend has just been enjoying his first few glasses of rum punch." She practically skipped past Lovegood towards the prison door. "I even got him to tell me which keys to use."

Within a minute, Imogen swung the door open.

I motioned towards the open door with my head. "You first, Lieutenant."

He didn't move. His eyes were becoming more focused, his hands lowering. "Do you even know how to shoot that?"

"You wouldn't want to find out, would you?" I tried to sound fearless, but I felt unnerved by the slight smile that was returning to the corners of Lovegood's mouth. With a sudden swoop, he reached back and grabbed Imogen around the shoulders, pulling her in front of him like a shield.

"Now give me the gun," he demanded through

clenched teeth. All his arrogant dignity had vanished. He looked like a wild man.

I stood frozen, but glanced at Imogen, who looked terrified at Lovegood's menacing face so close to hers.

"Ok," I breathed at last.

"Don't, Katie!" Imogen screamed and started flailing her legs around wildly, trying to stomp on Lovegood's feet. The struggle bought me the time I needed to pull the blowgun out of my quiver. The dart was already prepared. I pulled it out by the thistly end – I couldn't afford to miss – and hurtled towards the struggling pair. Moving behind them, I raised my fist and jabbed the dart into the back of Lovegood's neck.

With a howl, he let go immediately and reached his hand back to feel what had hit him. Imogen and I scurried back as he yanked out the dart and blinked at it a few times before slumping over in a heap.

"Quick. Someone will have heard all that," I said, grabbing hold of Lovegood's limp arms.

Imogen took hold of his legs and together we dragged him into the prison.

"What the devil?" came a familiar voice from the corner.

"More like your guardian angels," Imogen grunted back as we heaved the Lieutenant against the wall and let him flop over into a pile of straw.

"Dilli? Katie Fire-Hair? How in heaven's name—"

"No time," I whispered hoarsely. "Immy, can you unlock him? I'll get Robin Hood ready."

The next few minutes felt like hours as I stood in front of the wide-open prison with the reins clutched in my fist.

My eyes darted from the Governor's mansion to the main gates to the stables, expecting to see troops at any second. But no one stirred in the clearing. They seemed not to have heard a thing or to have noticed that the Lieutenant had gone missing from the party.

At last, Wattie came out blinking in the moonlight and rubbing his wrists. With a huge smile on his face, he shook his head in disbelief. Imogen quickly shut the prison door and locked it. Then the three of us climbed up on the horse.

"What's your plan?" Wattie whispered from behind me.

I turned to speak over my shoulder. "We don't have one."

Just then, the double doors of the Governor's mansion burst open. Two cavalry officers swayed out onto the porch, their arms over one another's shoulders. They were singing at the top of their lungs, but sounded more like a couple of sick hound dogs.

"Let's go!" Wattie said, giving Robin Hood a slap on the rump that sent him shooting like an arrow for the open gate. I shot one look back as we passed through, but saw no sign of pursuers. Still, I didn't let Robin Hood slow down until we were safe under the cover of dense, dark forest.

FACING THE SNAKE

*W*e bedded down in a dense patch of ferns to wait for help. Wattie listened with amazement as we told him all that had happened since his arrest.

"That villain Blunt," he said after a moment. "To think he had the stone all the time. I knew Old Grizzly had to be innocent, but I must admit, I did sometimes suspect he might've taken the stone for Ramona. She was... an unusual woman. Kind, but there certainly was something strange about her."

As he trailed away, Imogen and I shot each other a glance. We had both carefully left out the discovery of Ka-Ti's magic painting from our retelling of the day's events. We could tell Wattie the truth about where we'd come from another time. The important thing now was to wait and watch.

But as the night hours wore on, a sinking feeling started to take over, and from the worried expressions on the others' faces, they were feeling the same. What if no one was coming? After all, any number of things might get in the way. What if something had happened to Ka-Ti on her journey to Nickajack? Or what if she'd reached Nickajack only to find it in shambles? There was no telling what mischief Lovegood and his posse might already have played in the past two days. He might've left guards to keep watch in case I came back for help. With rising horror, I wondered if we'd sent Ka-Ti straight into a trap.

"You two should get some sleep," Wattie said, breaking into my nightmarish thoughts. "I've had plenty of rest chained up in that prison, and you'll need your strength when Nickajack gets here." He smiled faintly, but I could hear the doubt in his voice. Still, he was right. Whatever happened, we would need all the strength we could muster to face it.

I lay down and closed my eyes, but worries continued to stab at my mind. Here we were, on the verge of enemy territory, and possibly no one coming to our aid. Soon the sun would rise, Governor Blunt's treaty would be signed, and Lieutenant Lovegood would wake up and call for help. Then the whole cavalry would be on the hunt for three fugitives on a big grey horse. What chance would we have of escape then? And—perhaps the most terrifying thought of all—what chance would Imogen and I ever have of getting back through the painting if we were locked up in a jail cell?

After what felt like only a few minutes, I was shaken out of my restless sleep by Wattie.

"Have they come?" I asked, springing upright.

Imogen bolted up beside me, looking around expectantly.

But Wattie shook his head, his expression hard as stone. "It's nearly sunrise. No one's coming."

Imogen and I looked at each other, and in that look, we both knew that all our worst fears had come true. All we'd fought for had come to nothing. We'd lost our chance of getting home, and it was unlikely that another one would ever come.

But there was something else in that look... something that shone through the fear. We both saw it and nodded. And then I spoke. "Well, we're not just going to lie here and wait for the Governor's men. Let's go make as much trouble for him as we can."

Wattie looked surprised, then shook his head. "No. I can't let you give yourselves up. I'll go back. I can buy you some time to run at least."

Imogen got up on her knees and looked Wattie straight in the eye. "Look, we didn't come here just so we could run away from danger. If standing up for Nickajack... for your family... for Little Beaver is the reason we're here"— she gave me a meaningful sideways look— "then we're going to make the most of it."

Wattie looked between the two of us uncertainly, no doubt confused by what Imogen had said. But whether or not he understood what she meant, he realised there was no point arguing. At last, a defeated smile broke out on his hardened face. He held his hand out. *"Wado."* Then shaking Imogen's hand as well, he added, "you are brave to take a last stand for Nickajack, and you are true friends to face capture with me. There's no telling what Blunt may do with—"

He was interrupted by a swift soaring sound and loud

ping! We all craned our heads back to look at the arrow stuck in the pine tree just an arm's length above our heads.

Imogen and I immediately ducked down low, but Wattie stayed standing, his sharp eyes sweeping the forest. Then a haunting, low bird call sounded out of the gloom.

I looked at Wattie. A smile spread across his face and I understood. "Is it—?"

Before I could ask, Grasshopper dropped out of a tree right in front of us. Imogen screamed, but after the initial shock, she was beaming and hugging Grasshopper with the rest of us.

"Have any others come with you?" Wattie asked after we'd all embraced.

Grasshopper threw back his head and hooted. "Come and see for yourself. They are waiting for you on the road. Waiting to follow Katie Fire-Hair into battle against the Governor."

I felt my stomach plummet. "Follow me?"

"Yes, *you*, Katie," Imogen said in an exasperated tone. "This is all happening thanks to *you*."

I shook my head. "You know I wouldn't even be here if you hadn't saved my life from Lovegood on the first day."

She smiled with a modest shrug.

"Come," Grasshopper urged. "There's no time to lose. The sun already rises."

IT WAS a glorious sight that met our eyes when we reached the road at the edge of the forest. There must've been twenty men as well as a few fearsome-looking war women on horses. Leading the group were Mr. McKay, Terrapin Jo and—my jaw dropped when I saw him—Jim with his leg bound up, and beside him, Ka-Ti.

As Wattie rushed forward to greet his father, Imogen nudged me in the ribs. Her eyes were glued on a handsome, proud-looking man with a long black ponytail beside Terrapin Jo. "Is that...?" she whispered.

"Crow Feather!" I said more loudly than I'd meant to, and all eyes turned to me. I blushed, but Crow Feather's stern face softened into a smile and he nodded. "Yes. I am well, and I have you both to thank."

A strange little giggle came from beside me where Imogen stood, and I was relieved when Jim spoke up and drowned it out.

"Now ain't no time for a powwow. We got business to take care of. Now I reckon if we're to beat Blunt at his own game, we're gonna have to outfox Black Fox."

Some of the warriors looked confused.

"You mean play a trick on Blunt?" I asked.

Jim nodded once. "That's what I said, ain't it?"

BIRDS WERE ALREADY BEGINNING to announce that dawn was on its way as Imogen and I led the party on horseback across the plain towards the enormous, spiky silhouette of Hiwassee Garrison. We dismounted a good way off.

"This is where we wait," Jim said, holding up his hand the way I'd seen him do dozens of times before.

On his cue, Crow Feather and Grasshopper leaped from their horses, threw reels of rope over their shoulders, and crouched low, slipping silently into the murky shadows.

I held my breath for what felt like ages. Imogen was shaking her foot nervously. "Immy, you're making Robin Hood jittery," I said over my shoulder.

"Sorry. Can't help it," she whispered hoarsely. "The suspense is driving me batty."

Thankfully, before I suffocated or Imogen turned completely batty, the signal came. Off in the darkness, two lanterns were swinging back and forth in a ghostly dance.

"They've done it!" I said, finally letting out my breath.

Jim looked around at the warriors who were awaiting their orders and nodded. "Time to pay our respects to the Governor."

WHEN WE REACHED THE GATE, it was already wide open. Crow Feather and Grasshopper were standing just outside over two guards who had been expertly bound and gagged, their rifles propped neatly against a post. A long rope hung from an arrow sticking out from one of the wall's tree posts.

"You climbed that?" Imogen asked with an impressed tone as she dismounted after me.

"Grasshopper did," Crow Feather said, putting a muscular arm around his brother's scrawny shoulders. "Instead of Grasshopper, we should call him Skinny Squirrel."

With the gate wide open and guards out of the way, the plan was in full swing. A few of the warriors were placed at the gate to keep watch for Black Fox in case he came looking for Blunt. The rest mounted their horses and stayed out of sight just beyond the gates. Only the four of us – Jim, Wattie, Imogen and I – ventured into the Garrison yard, Jim with his arm around Wattie's shoulder for support as he hobbled on his injured leg. Together, we hid in the shadows of the Governor's mansion and waited.

My ears were alert to every sound. Somewhere near the stables, a rooster crowed, then a horse whinnied, then, faintly but surely, a door creaked slowly open. I craned my neck around the box hedge and saw him there. The round-bellied Governor, his fluffy hair ruffled as if he'd just got out of bed, stepped out onto his porch and closed the door with extra care. He checked his pocket watch. I could just make out the words that he grumbled under his breath: "Lovegood is late." His eyes darted around nervously, as if he was worried someone might be watching.

Jim threw a cloak over his head and stepped out of the shadows. Though he limped, his stride was bold. If anything, the dragging of his bad leg only made him appear more frightening. Blunt's head turned and I could swear he jumped at the sight of the cloaked figure. With his fat hand on his heart, he leaned over and squinted, as if he were trying to make out who it was in the dim light, but Jim let the cloak hang low over his face.

"Who's there?" Blunt tried to sound impressive, but the words came out in a croak instead. "Is that you, Black Fox?"

Jim gave no answer, only took a few slow, dragging steps forward.

The Governor's eyes were darting around again, no doubt hoping his bodyguard Lovegood would turn up any minute. Again the Governor tried to sound in command, but his voice came out breathless; he swayed on the spot as if dizzy. "You're early, you know. This is not the time we'd agreed. If you can't keep your side of the deal, then I'm afraid I can't guarantee mine."

I had been waiting for this moment. With the Uktena stone clasped in one hand, I strode out to stand beside Jim. Then holding out my palm for the Governor to see, I asked, "You mean this?"

Governor Blunt blinked stupidly. "You again? Black Fox sent you before, didn't he? You were spying. Who are you, the devil's child?"

I slipped the stone in my pocket. "I'm Katie Watson. Or as my Cherokee friends like to call me, Katie Fire-Hair."

Clinging to the iron railing, Blunt took a step down and reached out his open hand. "I don't care what they call you. I insist that you give me that stone at once. I don't know how you came by it, but it doesn't belong to you."

"As far as I recall, it don't belong to you neither, Cyrus." Jim let his cloak drop to the ground. There was enough light now to see every hard line of his face, his heavy, furrowed brow and the grizzly scar. He looked every bit Old Grizzly.

Blunt's legs seemed to give out beneath him. He caught the rail with both hands. "Jim! What are you...?" He looked like he was fighting to get a grip on himself. Standing up straight again, he puffed up his chest and tugged down on his waistcoat. "You shouldn't be here. You've been arrested for stealing that stone once. Don't think I won't have you put in prison for the same crime again. You and this little urchin."

"I don't think yer gonna do that, Cyrus," Jim said with a sly smile.

"And why wouldn't I?"

"Because then you'd have to return the stone to the people of Nickajack. I think you've got other plans for it. We know what yer up to. How you've been terrorising the village just to try and scare folk into selling their land to you. And when that didn't work, what'd you do? You made a deal with that bloodthirsty Black Fox. The stone for his signature on your treaty. But as I see it, you got a couple of holes in your plan."

"Like what?" Blunt snarled.

"For starters, all land treaties have to go through Washington. You'd have to get the President's signature to make it legal, and somethin' tells me he ain't heard nothin' about this treaty that names all the land of Nickajack your own personal property." Jim gave a dry laugh. "Blunts Town."

All the gusto deflated out of Blunt, as if he'd just been punched. "How could you know that? You've got no proof of …"

This was Imogen's moment. She too stepped into the growing daylight with a scroll of paper. She let the map with Blunt's seal unfurl before his eyes. "Actually, we do."

Blunt's chins quivered. He took a backwards step up the stairs. "How did you… What is this charade?"

Now Wattie stepped out to take his stand with the rest of us. "You know all about charades, don't you, Governor? You really thought you could hoodwink the Cherokee Nation *and* the President of the United States?" He tutted in an imitation of Blunt.

The Governor's eyes narrowed, and his face contorted

into a hideously vicious expression. "The President will never believe the word of three children and a convicted criminal against mine," he spat. "Anyway, once I've cleared Nickajack of its inhabitants, the President will thank me for ridding the land of these quarrelsome, uncivilised—"

"The only quarrelsome, uncivilised one of them is the one you're making a bargain with, Blunt. Black Fox ain't got no right to sign a treaty sellin' their property. He ain't their chief."

Blunt threw back his head. "Ha! He will be Chief if I say he will. I'm the Cherokee Agent. Who's to stop me?" He stepped back up onto the porch.

I watched, wondering how long it would be until the Governor darted back into his house and bolted the door. The warriors were ready to beat it down if necessary, but I hoped it wouldn't come to that.

Jim took a step closer. "You really believe Black Fox is gonna lie down and let you take that land once you've run the rest of 'em off it?"

The Governor looked at Jim and, to my disgust, actually smiled, the same simpering smile he'd worn when I first met him. He crossed his hands over his fat belly. "Jim, Jim. This is why I'm in command and you're an outcast. You never understood how to manage these people. Black Fox may be as lawless as the rest, but dangle the bait in front of him, and he becomes as docile as a kitten. The trick is to make them dependant, desperate even." He shook his head and gave a pitying sigh. "And you. You actually believed you could win the Cherokees' hearts by befriending them. You are a fool, and you've lost yet again."

I expected Blunt to make a run for it, but instead he smiled a ghastly smile, reached out and pulled a rope. I hadn't even noticed the giant copper bell hanging over his front door. Blunt kept pulling with all his might, making it gong so loudly Imogen and I covered our ears.

There were shouts from behind. I spun around to see four, five, six cavalry officers spill out of a barracks, rifles on the ready. When they appeared, the Governor stopped gonging and shouted "Guards, arrest this man! ... And these children!"

The officers advanced, but as they did, Wattie threw back his head and let out a war cry that sent prickles up my spine. Everyone froze. The officers stopped dead in their tracks and looked at one another uncertainly. Then, from outside the gates, Wattie's cry was returned, louder, stronger, more piercing for the many voices joined into one.

We all turned to face the gate. Backed by the golden light of the sun's first rays, the warriors of Nickajack galloped into the Garrison with the rushing might of a waterfall. They rode up behind us and stopped, making an arc around us. Not a one of them raised a weapon. They didn't have to. The look on all of their faces was enough. First one guard dropped his weapon and raised his hands in surrender, then another, then one turned and ran toward the stables. His five companions followed after him, none of them paying any mind to the Governor's shouts of "Cowards! Come back at once! Where is Lovegood when I need him? Where is that disgrace of a Lieutenant?"

"I think he's still asleep," Imogen called out. "In there." She pointed to the prison.

Blunt glanced at the prison with a dazed, lost look in his eyes. They widened when he noticed Mr. McKay ride forward. "McKay!" He called out, gulping like a bullfrog. "Tell them not to hurt me! Tell them, McKay. When have I been anything but a loyal servant to these Cherokees? I… I've been like a ffffather to you all. Only doing what I thought was best... Yyyou surely wouldn't hurt your own father?"

Mr. McKay dismounted and nodded to Wattie. The two of them approached the bottom of the stairs. "Of course, we haven't come to hurt you. The Cherokee are a civilised people. Not like you, Governor." He advanced up the stairs with Wattie behind him. "But to show our appreciation for all your service, we're staying right here and keeping an eye on you and your lackey Lovegood until the President arrives."

Blunt didn't even put up a fight as they tied his hands behind him and led him down the stairs. He was looking at Mr. McKay with terror in his eyes. "The President? Coming? But how? When?"

"Soon, Governor. Soon. We sent an express message to Washington last night, so I expect he'll know all about your little plot soon enough."

"The President will never believe the testimony of a gang of savages. He relies upon me!" Blunt bellowed.

Jim stepped forward so he was towering over the man who had destroyed his life. The Governor cowered as if expecting Old Grizzly to take a swing at him. "Looks like you lost, Blunt." Then Ka-Ti appeared by his side and took his arm to help him walk away.

"You'll pay for this! You'll be sorry!" Blunt's threats grew fainter as Wattie and I pushed the prison door shut behind him, and Imogen did the honour of locking it.

35

BEHIND THE WATERFALL

*T*he long night was over. Morning had come, but there was still work to be done. Not long after the sun came up, a messenger came flying on horseback into the Garrison with a letter for Mr. McKay. We all watched him open it and all held our breath until a smile spread across his face.

"The President is in Nashville! Blunt and Lovegood are to be tried in the Tennessee Supreme Court."

Cheers and hoots went up at the news, but at the same time, many curtains covering the windows of the Governor's mansion shifted. Since daybreak, his household had been peering out at the frightful sight of the Cherokee warriors, probably expecting a raid at any moment. Jim and Mr. McKay formed a delegation to reassure the frightened people they were not under attack. The rest of us went outside the Garrison walls to let the horses graze in the grassy meadow by the river.

Some of the warriors built fires and started preparing

breakfast. A hum of low voices surrounded the five of us. Wattie and Grasshopper were roasting fish on sticks over a little fire, chatting in Cherokee and laughing as if they were two boys on a campout. Wattie had practically swung Ka-Ti off her feet when he first heard her speak; but just now, she was silent, watching the flames with a faint smile and a faraway look in her eyes. Imogen's head was getting heavier by the minute on my shoulder.

But as much as I wanted to join in, I couldn't rest, couldn't laugh. I rubbed my thumb across the smooth surface of the Uktena Stone still clasped in my hand, thinking.

"Dilli sleeps like the bear in winter, but Katie Fire-Hair is too troubled to sleep." Grasshopper was smiling in his usual mischievous way, but Wattie and Ka-Ti were watching me curiously now.

Ka-Ti rose up and sat down close beside me. Her eyes looked into mine as if searching for something. Then she said in her whispering, windy way, "Katie Fire-Hair. It is time."

I didn't have to ask what she meant. I knew it was time to go home. Our job here was done. But I still had a bit of unfinished business which I had just tucked into my pocket. "I just need to speak with Terrapin Jo. Then I'll be ready."

I wriggled out from under Imogen's head and helped her gently slump over onto Ka-Ti's lap where she carried on sleeping peacefully. Terrapin Jo was sitting beside another fire with Crow Feather and one of the war women, telling a story in the singsong way I'd become used to hearing the Cherokee speak. When he'd finished, he turned and, seeing me standing there, got up to speak to me.

"Katie Fire-Hair, what troubles you?"

I reached my hand into the little pocket and pulled out the stone, holding it out in my palm. "It's this. I've come to give it back to you, only …"

Terrapin Jo didn't immediately take the stone. His eyes moved to my hand and back again. "Only you fear what its power may do to the Cherokee. To Jim Weaver."

I was shocked. He knew exactly what I had been worrying about. I nodded. "It's just that it's caused so many people to get hurt. And Black Fox. He still wants the stone more than anything. What if he never stops hunting it? What if he finally gets his hands on it and destroys Nickajack?"

Terrapin Jo's deep, dark eyes narrowed in thought. "I have learned something, Katie Fire-Hair. The power of greed is strong. It causes many to suffer. But there are stronger powers."

I looked at him, confused. "You mean the stone?"

He smiled and shook his head. "I mean the power of family. Of friendship. Of forgiveness."

Then he reached out, I thought to take the stone. But instead, he cupped my hands in his own big, worn ones, curling my fingers around the smooth object. "You keep it," he said.

"But I couldn't take it," I protested.

Terrapin Joe's face became very serious. "You do not take. You have given us much. May this remind you always of your friends here."

He was so earnest, almost stern, that I didn't dare try to argue anymore. With a gulp, I pulled my hands close to my heart and whispered, "Thank you. I will always remember."

BACK AT THE fire with the others, Ka-Ti caught my eye and I nodded. "I'm ready."

"Ready for what, Katie Fire-Hair?" Grasshopper asked with a grin.

"We're going home," I said, and at the same time Imogen sat up scratching her head. "Did I just dream that, or are we actually going home now?"

Wattie's eyebrows were furrowed under his black curls. "Do you mean you have found your uncle?"

"Not exactly," I began, shooting a glance at Ka-Ti. "But we think we've found a way home all the same."

"Then I will help you get to wherever it is you need to go," Wattie announced with an air of chivalry. "It's the least I can do after all you've done for my family."

I smiled. "We wouldn't have any other guide."

WHEN WORD GOT AROUND that we were travelling back to the cave where the stone had been hidden, it was decided among the Cherokee that a group of warriors would travel with us for our protection in case Black Fox was still lurking around waiting for Blunt.

Wattie insisted that we rest a little and have a good breakfast before the journey. All the time I waited, I hoped Jim Weaver would come … that I'd have a chance to thank him. But business in the Garrison kept him away, and when the time came for us to mount our horses and take the road, it looked like we'd have to go without saying goodbye.

One foot was already in the stirrup when I felt a heavy hand on my shoulder. I looked up into Jim's scarred face and could hardly believe it: his eyes, the very eyes that had frightened the living daylights out of me the first time I'd looked into them, were misted with tears.

"Well I don't reckon we'll be seein' each other again this side of Beulah Land, Miss Fire-Hair."

I gulped down the lump in my throat. "Thank you for everything," I said, feeling suddenly at a loss for words.

His voice was quiet but steady. "You'll never know just what you've done for my Kingfisher and me. You'll always be part o' the family."

I looked into his eyes and felt no words would be enough. I threw my arms around Jim's middle. He hesitated just a moment before wrapping one of his big arms around my shoulders and patting my head with the other hand. "You get on now, and you have a good ol' life, you hear?" he mumbled.

I looked up and grinned through my tears. "I will if you promise to."

He winked and ruffled my hair, then his face turned grave again, like he was struggling with the thoughts inside him. "If you see her," he said at last, "if you see my Ramona, tell her we can't never forget her. We just want her back."

"I will," I promised.

. . .

WE RODE AWAY from Hiwassee Garrison, from Jim, in silence. I tried to take in every moment of the ride, knowing that if Ka-Ti's song worked, it would be the last time I'd see 1828, the enormous ancient trees, the untamed forest, the great grey horse whose steady, strong gait was taking me closer to home with every step. I could swear Robin Hood wore a smile in the way he walked since we'd locked his former master behind bars.

When we reached the ravine near the cave, I started to dismount, then realised the warriors were staying on their horses' backs.

"It looks safe, so they will travel around the base of the mountain," Wattie explained. "They want to find the other passage Jim led you in through. Maybe not all of Nicka-jack's stolen possessions were destroyed when the cave collapsed."

As the warriors rode on, I tethered Robin Hood's reins to a maple tree and stroked his neck. "You'll look after him, won't you?" I asked Wattie. "He deserves a better life from now on."

"Of course, we will," Wattie promised. "Now can you tell me why coming to this cave is going to help you get home?"

Imogen gave an exasperated sigh. "We've already told you, Wattie. You'll just have to wait and see."

At that moment, we were silenced by a shrill cry like the call an eagle makes before swooping down on its prey. It seemed to come from the ravine. Then an echoing cry came from our left. We all turned and saw them coming, five or six bare-chested, fierce-eyed Cherokee men running out of the trees with rifles, knives and tomahawks raised.

Wattie threw himself in front of us and spread out his arms, and Imogen and I clutched each other, not wanting to watch, but not able to look away. When they were close enough for us to hear their heavy breathing, a thundering storm rose up behind us. The warriors who had ridden with us! They had heard the enemy's cry and come back! But now we were in the crossfire.

"Come on!" Wattie was shouting. He ducked down low and we followed him, running into the trees just as the two groups of warriors collided in combat.

"Will they be all right?" I said through heaving breaths once we'd reached the waterfall and slipped behind it into the safety of the cave.

Wattie nodded, panting. "Those were Black Fox's men. They were outnumbered two to one. They will surrender."

We all leaned against the wet cave walls, catching our breath when, without warning and before I could so much as scream, something hooked me around the neck, strong as a python's death grip, and I felt cold, sharp metal touch my chin. Even as terror blinded me, I knew we had walked right into Black Fox's trap.

I was only vaguely aware of the others watching, speechless, as Black Fox hustled me across the cave floor, coming to stand with his back to the waterfall. The stone was slippery, and it was only his anaconda arm around my neck that held me upright. I was seeing spots, gasping for each breath. I heard Black Fox say something in Cherokee. It sounded muffled, far away.

"We don't have your stone, Black Fox!" Wattie was shouting.

The stone. Of course, he wants the stone. The thoughts flitted across my mind like moths around a fire. *He doesn't even realise it's right here, in my pocket.*

I would surely pass out if I didn't get a breath soon. Was I imagining things? "Sophia?" I gasped, but no sound came out. I looked again. No, it wasn't Sophia. It was Imogen standing there with a face as fierce as any warrior's. She had something in her hand, and she was shouting as she pulled back her arm. Then she hurled the thing, and I saw what it was. Imogen's mobile phone whistled through the air. I felt its impact when it made contact with Black Fox's skull.

The second the phone struck, I was jerked backwards. Three sets of hands grabbed hold of mine and pulled, even while Black Fox still kept his grip on me, pulling me back. I thought I'd tear in two, but the hands holding mine held tighter, and at last I swung forward, gasping for air.

I saw Wattie, Imogen and Ka-Ti panting with relief, then swung around just in time to see Black Fox stumble backward over the ledge. Even he was no match for the waterfall. It swept him down with a mighty roar.

We watched in disbelief. Imogen put her arm around my shoulder, and I realised I was shaking and she was crying.

"Katie Fire-Hair, it is time," Ka-Ti leaned over and said in my ear.

I took a deep breath and nodded. Then finding my voice again, I said, "We're ready."

Wattie helped me and Imogen stand up. He looked shaken.

"Thank you for everything," I said, giving Wattie a hug. He hugged me back but still looked too bewildered to speak. "And please tell your parents and Grasshopper and … and all the others, that we will never forget them."

I stepped aside to give Imogen her chance to say good-bye. Sniffling, she held out her hand to Wattie. "Sorry for being so difficult sometimes. You're a great leader, really." And to the surprise of all of us, but especially Wattie, she stood up on her toes and planted a kiss on his cheek.

Wattie tugged on his collar and stumbled back a step into the wall. I turned back to Ka-Ti, whose cheeks had also turned slightly pink. I remembered what I had to say. Taking the quiver from my back, I pulled out the leather folder of paintings she'd given me, all snapshots of Ramona's travels through time.

"These are yours," I said.

She shook her head. "They are yours."

I threw my other arm around Ka-Ti's neck. "I hope your mother finds her way home one day too," I whispered. We released each other, and with a heavy sigh, I turned back to face the wall with the painted horses.

Imogen and I locked arms and slowly approached until we were close enough to reach out and touch them. I slipped my hand into my pocket and squeezed the Uktena Stone. Then, as quiet as a gentle breeze, Ka-Ti began to sing. Her voice grew into the pure notes of a pan flute and spoke words I didn't understand. And yet each word sounded just right. And as I listened, I felt a wriggling in my hand. I looked down. The serpent etched into the stone seemed to glow and wriggle like a living snake.

When I raised my eyes back to the horses, they had begun to trot. Soon they quickened into a canter. At last, as the song reached a triumphant note, the horses broke into a mighty gallop, and Imogen and I fell forward into a swirling whirlpool of wind and autumn colours.

36

THE JOURNEY JUST BEGINNING

A whirlpool of autumn leaves settled to the forest floor all around us. Imogen and I, arms still linked, sat in a pool of freshly fallen leaves and afternoon sunlight. We looked at each other, but no words came. Wiping our eyes dry, we helped one another up, brushing off the leaves that clung to our clothes.

Imogen straightened up, frowning. "We're still in the same clothes ... Do you think it worked?"

Before I could answer, a familiar voice calling our names turned our eyes downriver. My dad appeared on the trail with the bucket and water filter. "I came down to see if you girls needed help, but it seems you've been off exploring." He rustled my hair, then stood back to look at me, frowning. "Were you wearing deerskin leggings and moccasins earlier?"

Again, I was prevented from answering by another call; this time it was my mum. "Peter! Girls! Hurry up with that water if you expect to have any dinner tonight. I'm aching for a cup of tea!" She too appeared just uphill and immediately stopped in her tracks, taking in the strange sight of Imogen and me in our muddy, old-timey dress. "Where on *earth* did you girls get those clothes?" she asked.

Imogen thought faster than I could. "Oh, we bought them, Auntie Jemima, at that gift shop we stopped at on the way." She gave me a sideways look.

Mum was still eyeing us both as if we were mad. "Ok? I ... didn't realise you two were such enthusiasts for Native American dress."

"Oh, didn't you?" Imogen answered, a little *too* enthusiastically, "I just can't get enough of it. Nothing I love better than Cherokee history."

Mum laughed nervously and scratched her head. Dad, on the other hand, lit up at the words "Cherokee history."

"Well, why didn't you say so before, Imogen? If you're that interested in Cherokee history, there's a brief history of all the local villages in my archives."

Imogen and I exchanged another look, then took off running up the hill towards camp, leaving my mum and dad behind and no doubt bewildered.

I FOUND the archive tucked safely away in Dad's duffel bag. We carried it back to our own tent, zipping up the door for privacy, and eagerly dove in, flipping through the pages until we found the one with "A Brief History of the Cherokee of Lower Tennessee" typed at the top.

I tried to read it, but I found that my heart was in my throat. I was terrified to find out what had become of our friends ... of finding out things we might wish we never knew. "You read it," I said, passing the scrapbook into Imogen's lap.

She took a deep breath and scrolled her finger down the page, stopping suddenly about halfway down. "Oh, Nickajack. Here we go. Oh my gosh!"

"What? What is it?" I asked, dreading the answer.

"It says here Jim Weaver became the Indian Agent in 1828! Oh, and here's Wattie! William McKay (also "Oowattie"), son of a Scottish trader Joseph McKay and Ulma McKay (daughter of the prominent Cherokee chief Grey Wolf) served as a respected member of the Council and delegate on behalf of his people to Washington, D.C. He was a strong voice of opposition against President Jackson's *Removal Act of 1830* which resulted in the Trail of Tears in which thousands of Cherokees were forcibly removed from their homes and relocated in Oklahoma."

All the excitement drained out of Imogen's voice. Her eyes flickered up for moment, but she carried on reading. "No records show William or his family having made the journey to Oklahoma, and it is believed that they settled in the Appalachian Mountains where the Eastern Band of the Cherokee still survives today." Imogen stopped reading. "It says 'see page three for family records'."

I barely heard her. My heart had dropped from my throat into the pit of my stomach.

"You were right," I mumbled, not able to look Imogen in the eye.

"Right about what?" she asked.

"I was childish to think I could change history." I pointed to the page, wishing I could scratch out what was written on it. "President Jackson's *Removal Act*. He was no better than the Governor. Blunt or no Blunt, they *still* had to leave their homes just a few years after we left." I took a deep breath. "After all we did or tried to do, none of it made any real difference."

After a silent moment, I dared to look at Imogen. I expected her to look as miserable as I felt, but instead, she was giving me one of her classic "that's the dumbest thing I ever heard" stares.

"Katie, you're not serious. *Of course* it made a difference! Do you think it didn't make a difference to Crow Feather to live another day? Do you think Wattie would ever have become a delegate if we'd left him in prison and let his town be stolen by crooks?" She paused, then, in a softer voice added, "Anyway, it made a difference to me. I'll never forget what we've been through together, Katie. Seriously, it's been the best holiday of my life. Snakes and all."

A smile forced its way onto my face and we both laughed. Then I remembered how Imogen had just saved my life. "But Im, your phone! It went over the waterfall ..."

She shrugged. "To be honest, I'd kind of gone off it. Not that I wouldn't have sacrificed it to rescue you from Black Fox anyway."

I reached out and squeezed her hand. "Thanks for rescuing me."

In her most Imogen-like know-it-all way, she answered, "Really, Katie. That's what cousins are for ... obviously."

"Hey, speaking of cousins, what was that it said about family records?"

"Oh yea." Imogen scanned the page again. "On page three it says." She licked her fingers and turned the pages back. The spread of pages two and three together made one big family tree. We both scanned the page, but I found Wattie's name first.

"No way," escaped my mouth. Imogen's mouth fell open at the same time.

"He and Ka-Ti got married!" she squealed, clasping her hands over her heart. "That is *so* adorable. Did they have kids?"

"Yes. But ... that's weird. Wattie's name was McKay, but the kids all have the surname 'Wolf'."

"That's *your* surname," she said. "Even if you did tell everyone it was Watson for some strange reason of your own."

I didn't respond. I had that prickling feeling in my skin again, like something important was about to happen. "Look. It says in the footnote here that Oowattie McKay, following the Cherokee tradition of taking the mother's name, passed down the Cherokee name Wolf to his children and all future generations." I placed my finger on the line connecting Wattie's and Ka-Ti's names and traced it down, right to the bottom where the names *Peter* and *Jemima* were joined. Beneath them, in my dad's handwriting, the names *Charles* and *Katherine* had been scribbled in.

"Do you know what this means?" I whispered.

Imogen nodded slowly. "It means ... I kissed your great, great grandfather!" Imogen cupped her hands over her mouth.

"Well, yea, but not *just* that," I said, giving her a gentle shove. "It means that Ka-Ti is my great-great-grandmother, and Ramona is my great-great-*great*-grandmother!"

A look of revelation came over Imogen's face. "So there *is* a reason you're a time traveller. It's in your blood."

As fast as I could, I took my quiver off my back, took out the folder of dream paintings once again and opened to the first page, the painting of the fire-haired girl on the horse. "I think Ramona meant for us to have these. That's what Ka-Ti was saying. These aren't keepsakes; they're clues of the places she's been."

She glared at me. "Wait, are you thinking what I think you're thinking, Katie?"

I bit my lip, but didn't answer.

Imogen raised her eyebrows and pointed her finger like a scolding teacher. "Because if you're thinking of travelling through time again, you had better not dare leave me behind!"

I smiled and flipped to the next picture of me and Imogen side by side. "I couldn't if I wanted to. You're part of the story."

IMOGEN and I could hardly stay awake through supper that evening. We barely made it through s'mores. When Dad took out his pack of playing cards, we begged him to let us go to bed, promising we'd play tomorrow.

"I hope you girls aren't coming down with some kinda Cherokee fever," he said as we crawled into our tent.

"Nothing a little bear fat wouldn't fix," Imogen said just before zipping the door shut.

Although our discoveries from the archives left us with a billion things to talk about, it didn't take long for Imogen to start snoring. I felt I'd been awake for years, yet I still couldn't fall asleep. I slipped my hand under my pillow and stroked the smooth stone I'd hidden there. Then I closed my eyes and let the images of our adventures take shape in my mind. Wattie and Ka-Ti ... Old Grizzly with his sad but hopeful eyes. Those images would stay with me forever. I would never, ever forget them. But something Jim had said was beginning to make sense to me for the first time: *Don't use up too much of today on yesterday.*

He was right, I thought. Well, partly right anyway. The past would always be part of my story, but – my fingers brushed the soft leather of Ka-Ti's notebook where it lay beside my pillow – I had the mysterious feeling my adventures were only just beginning.

37

DEAR IMOGEN

Dear Imogen (Dilli),

Good news! Mum says I can come and spend Christmas with you! She's actually talking to your mum on the phone about it right now, so you'll probably already know by the time you get this. But we agreed to write each other snail mail, so I had to share the exciting news anyway.

Speaking of phones, how is your mobile phone ban going? I bet your friends at school think you've lost it. Don't worry about it. My friends at school think I'm a little odd too. I think it's just because we've been through a lot of things they can't understand … and we can't explain it to them. But it's way better for me than it used to be … because I have you to talk to!

I can't wait 'til we're together in London. This is going to be the best Christmas ever!

Write back soon!
 Lots of love,
 Your cousin and TTB (time-travel-buddy), Katie

ACKNOWLEDGMENTS

Books have personalities all of their own. The writer only discovers what her book is like as she undertakes to write it. Some books cooperate beautifully and seem almost to write themselves. Others kick and bite and make themselves as difficult to write as they possibly can. This book was the second sort.

Were it not for my wonderful team of Advance Readers, I believe Katie Watson and the Serpent Stone would've got the better of me. Thank you, each and every one of you, for your golden patience as you waited through many a revision. Your enthusiasm for Katie and eagerness to share this adventure with her kept me going through the hard bits.

You all deserve medals:

Mark & Ruth (the wordsmith) Smith, Marion & Tamsyn Alston, Jo Wallis, Linda Gore, Layla Everitt, Fiona & Izzy

Kennedy, Susan & Aurelia Beattie, Ella Thomas, Alice & Florence Bolton, Jemima Haynes, Millie Lamb, Jenifer Dunn, Aiden Cameron, Lexy Oesterwind, Natasha & Jasmine Fenner, Kelly Brockett, Paydee Pruitt, Ruth Nelson, Nellie Viernes, Rachael, Amelia & Anna Grant, Phillip, Eileen & Jasmine Blume, Michael Dormandy, Shirley Tivey, Alex Thaxton, Joanna, Sophie, Annabelle & Katie Etherington. Thank you all!

I also owe a whopping load of thanks to the people who helped to make this book presentable: to my editor, Anna Bowles, without whom I would still be stuck in a messy tangle of plot problems; to my proofreader, Dr. Sarah Bell, whose eagle eye for English grammar saved this book from the taint of many a typo; and to my cover designer Patrick Knowles who has managed once again to set the stage beautifully for Katie's American adventure. And, of course, to my faithful writing buddy, Bri Stox, who is my number one Beta Reader and Cheerleader, and to Gordon for your daily pep-talks and prayers that have kept me going. I hope this book does you all proud – it would not exist without you!

Finally, I'd like to shout a resounding "Wado!" to the The Museum of the Cherokee Indian in Cherokee, North Carolina for bringing the world of the Cherokee to life for me. Special thanks to Mike Crowe of the Cherokee Friends who told his people's story so personally and took the time to answer my countless questions. Any authenticity this book can claim owes itself to you and the museum gang. It is my hope that this book will inspire many young adventurers to visit Cherokee and dig a little deeper into the roots of the Cherokees' epic story and fascinating culture.

Unlock your

BONUS FEATURES

behind-the-scenes clips & interviews

cherokee words & recipes

downloadables

activity ideas

contests

more!

JUST SCAN THE QR CODE

OR VISIT

MEZBLUME.COM/SERPENT-STONE/

ABOUT THE AUTHOR

Mez Blume grew up in Georgia, USA, spending every moment she could in the forest. At age 21, she followed her nose to England for an MA in Gothic Cathedrals at the Courtauld Institute of Art. Mez lives in Berkshire with her husband Gordon and Jack Russell Terrier Hugo. She still spends every spare moment in the forest. Visit Mez at:

www.mezblume.com

facebook.com/mezblume

twitter.com/mez_blume

instagram.com/mez_blume